I was leaving, I was saving my life. I was keeping my son safe, too, not because his father had ever hit him—he never ever had—but because the secret inside our house, the secret about what happened at night, when Daddy was drunk and disgusted with himself and everything around him, was eating the life out of our son....

HIGH PRAISE FOR ANNA QUINDLEN'S
SPECTACULAR *NEW YORK TIMES* BESTSELLER

BLACK AND BLUE

"A COMPELLING AND SUSPENSEFUL STORY THAT GOES STRAIGHT TO THE GUT."
—*St. Louis Post-Dispatch*

"The novel is good enough to become to domestic violence what *Uncle Tom's Cabin* was to slavery"
—*Time*

"A SAD AND IMPORTANT STORY, CONVINCINGLY TOLD . . . *Black and Blue* is enormously readable . . . Quindlen depicts Fran's predicament with terrifying clarity. Like her columns, Quindlen's novels are written with intelligence, clarity and heartrending directness."
—*Newsday*

"QUINDLEN WRITES WITH . . . POWER AND GRACE. [A] smoothly written, nicely structured, engaging work . . . There is not a badly written sentence in 300 pages. The scenes are deftly drawn."
—*The Boston Globe*

"In her third novel, Pulitzer prize–winning journalist Anna Quindlen demonstrates the same winning qualities that inform her journalism: close observation, well-reasoned argument and appealing economy of language. This portrait of a battered woman is intimate and illuminating and, as is true of most anything Quindlen writes, well worth the read."
—*People*

"QUINDLEN'S PROSE IS PRECISE AND UNRELENTING."
—*Booklist*

Please turn the page for more extraordinary acclaim. . . .

"QUINDLEN HAS WRITTEN HER BEST NOVEL YET in this unerringly constructed and paced, emotionally accurate tale of domestic abuse. [She] establishes suspense from the first sentence and never falters. Quindlen is wise and humane. Her understanding of the complex anatomy of marital relationships, of the often painful bond of maternal love and of the capacity to survive tragedy and carry on invest this moving novel with the clarion ring of truth."

—*Publishers Weekly*

"A REFRESHING, WISE AND TRUTH-TELLING NOVEL ABOUT LIFE AND MARRIAGE . . . Quindlen writes about women as they really are—neither helpless victims nor angry polemicists, but intelligent human beings struggling to do what's right for those they love and for themselves. A book to read and savor."

—*Kirkus Reviews*

"SKILLFULLY TOLD, SUSPENSEFUL . . . FILLED WITH STRONG CHARACTERS."

—*BookPage*

"[A] TALE OF PASSION AND VIOLENCE . . . With *Black and Blue*, Quindlen unravels the mysteries of loyalty and lies, faith and fear, rage and regret."

—*Home News Tribune* (New Brunswick, N.J.)

"EMINENTLY READABLE . . . QUINDLEN KNOWS HOW TO BUILD A STORY."

—*The Philadelphia Inquirer*

"QUINDLEN SHEDS LIGHT ON A TOUGH ISSUE . . . *Black and Blue* builds its power slowly, through Fran's particular strength and clear-eyed analysis of her life and decisions."

—*Dayton Daily News*

BY THE SAME AUTHOR

One True Thing
Thinking Out Loud
Object Lessons
Living Out Loud

BOOKS FOR CHILDREN

The Tree That Came to Stay
Happily Ever After

BLACK AND BLUE

A NOVEL

ANNA QUINDLEN

A DELL BOOK

Published by
Dell Publishing
a division of
Random House, Inc.
1540 Broadway
New York, New York 10036

ISBN: 0-440-22610-4

Reprinted by arrangement with Random House, Inc.

Printed in the United States of America

Published simultaneously in Canada

February 1999

10 9 8 7 6 5 4 3 2 1

OPM

For Quin Krovatin
From one writer to another,
with admiration and enormous love.

BLACK
AND
BLUE

The first time my husband hit me I was nineteen years old. One sentence and I'm lost. One sentence and I can hear his voice in my head, that butterscotch-syrup voice that made goose bumps rise on my arms when I was young, that turned all of my skin warm and alive with a sibilant *S*, the drawling vowels, its shocking fricatives. It always sounded like a whisper, the way he talked, the intimacy of it, the way the words seemed to go into your guts, your head, your heart. "Geez, Bob," one of the guys would say, "you should have been a radio announcer. You should have done those voice-over things for commercials." It was like a genie, wafting purple and smoky from the lamp, Bobby's voice, or perfume when you took the glass stopper out of the bottle.

I remember going to court once when Bobby was a

witness in a case. It was eleven, maybe twelve years ago, before Robert was born, before my collarbone was broken, and my nose, which hasn't healed quite right because I set it myself, looking in the bathroom mirror in the middle of the night, petals of adhesive tape fringing the frame. Bobby wanted me to come to court when he was testifying because it was a famous case at the time, although one famous case succeeds another in New York City the way one pinky-gold sunset over the sludge of the Hudson River fades and blooms, brand-new each night. A fifteen-year-old boy from Brooklyn was accused of raping a Dominican nun at knife-point and then asking her to pray for him. His attorney said it was a lie, that the kid had had no idea that the woman in the aqua double-knit pants and the striped blouse was a nun, that the sex was consensual, though the nun was sixty-two and paste-waxing a floor in a shelter at the time. They took paste wax from the knees of the kid's pants, brought in the paste-wax manufacturer to do a chemical comparison.

The lawyer was an old guy with a storefront in a bad neighborhood, I remember, and the kid's mother had scraped together the money to hire him because Legal Aid had sent a black court-appointed and she was convinced that her son needed a white lawyer to win his case. Half-blind, hungover, dandruff on the shoulders of his gray suit like a dusting of snow, the kid's attorney was stupid enough to call the kid as a witness and to ask why he had confessed to a crime he hadn't committed.

"There was this cop in the room," the boy said, real low, his broad forehead tipped toward the microphone, his fingers playing idly with his bottom lip, so that his words were a little muffled. "He don't ask none of the questions. He just kept hassling me, man. Like he just keeps saying, 'Tell us what you did, Tyrone. Tell us what you did.' It was like he hypnotized me, man. He just kept saying it over and over. I couldn't get away from him."

The jury believed that Tyrone Biggs had done the rape, and so did everybody else in New York who read the tabloids, watched the news. So did the judge, who gave him the maximum, eight to fifteen years, and called him "a boil on the body of humanity." But I knew that while Tyrone was lying about the rape he was telling the truth about that police officer, because I lived with that voice every day, had been hypnotized by it myself. I knew what it could do, how it could sound. It went down into your soul, like a confessor, like a seducer, saying, "Tell me. Tell me." Frannie, Frannie, Fran, he'd croon, whisper, sing. Sometimes Bobby even made me believe that I was guilty of something, that I was sleeping with every doctor at the hospital, that I made him slip and bang his bad knee. That I made him beat me up, that it was me who made the fist, angled the foot, brought down a hand hard. Hard.

The first time he hit me I was nineteen.

I can hear his voice now, so persuasive, so low and yet somehow so strong, making me understand once again that I'm all wrong. Frannie, Frannie, Fran, he says. That's how he begins. Frannie, Frannie, Fran. The first time I wasn't your husband yet. You were already twenty, because it was the weekend after we went to City Island for your birthday. And I didn't hit you. You know I didn't hit you. You see, Fran, this is what you do. You twist things. You always twist things.

I can hear him in my head. And I know he's right. He didn't hit me, that first time. He just held onto my upper arm so tight that the mark of his fingertips was like a tattoo, a black sun with four small moons revolving around it.

It was summer, and I couldn't wear a sundress for a week, or take off my clothes when my sister, Grace, was in the room we shared, the one that looked out over the air shaft to the Tarnowski's apartment on the other side. He had done it because I danced with Dee Stemple's brother and then laughed when he challenged me on it. He held me there, he said, so that I couldn't get away, because if I got away it would be the end of him, he loved me that much. The next night he pushed back the sleeve of my blouse and kissed each mark, and his tears wet the spots as though to wash the black white again, as white as the rest of my white, white skin, as though his tears would do what absolution did for venial sins, wash them clean. "Oh, Jesus," he whispered, "I am so goddamned sorry," And I cried, too. When I cried in those days it was always for his pain, not for mine.

As rich and persuasive as Bobby Benedetto's voice, that was how full and palpable was his sorrow and regret. And how huge was his rage. It was like a twister cloud; it rose suddenly from nothing into a moving thing that blew the roof off, black and strong. I smell beer, I smell bourbon, I smell sweat, I smell my own fear, ranker and stronger than all three.

I smell it now in the vast waiting room of Thirtieth Street Station in Philadelphia. There are long wooden benches and my son, Robert, and I have huddled together into the corner of one of them. Across from us slumps a man in the moth-eaten motley of the homeless, who smells of beer and vomit like so many I've seen in the waiting room at the hospital, cooking up symptoms from bad feet to blindness to get a bed for the night, an institutional breakfast on a tray. The benches in Thirtieth Street Station are solid, plain, utilitarian, like the pews in St. Stanislaus. The Church of the Holy Pollack, Bobby called St. Stannie's, but he still wanted us to be married there, where he'd been baptized, where his father had been eulogized as a cop's cop. I had never lived in one place long enough to have a real home parish, and I'd agreed. Together we'd placed a rose from my bouquet at the side altar, in front of the statue of St. Joseph, in memory of Bobby's father. It was the only memory of his father that Bobby ever shared with me.

The great vaulted ceiling of the train station arched four stories over us, Robert and I and our one small carry-all bag, inside only toothbrushes, a change of clothes, some video-game cartridges and a book, a romance novel, stupid, shallow, but I had enough of real life every day to last me forever. Gilded, majestic, the station was what I'd believed the courtroom would be like, that day I went to court, when my husband took the stand.

State your name.

Robert Anthony Benedetto.

And your occupation?

I'm a police officer for the City of New York.

The courtroom in the state supreme court had been nothing at all like Thirtieth Street Station. It was low-ceilinged, dingy, paneled in dark wood that sucked up all the light from low windows that looked out on Police Plaza. It seemed more like a rec room than a courtroom. The train station in Philadelphia looked the way I'd always imagined a courtroom would look, or maybe the way one would look in a dream, if you were dreaming you were the judge, or the accused. Robert was staring up at the ceiling, so high above that those of us scattered around the floor so far below were diminished, almost negated by it. At one end of the huge vaulted room was a black statue of an angel holding a dead or dying man. I thought it was a war memorial, and under normal circumstances I would have walked across to read the inscription on the block beneath the angel's naked toes. But whatever the opposite of normal circumstances was, this was it. I shivered in the air-conditioning, dressed for July in a room whose temperature was lowered to April, my mind as cold as January.

The statue was taller than our little house down the block from the bay in Brooklyn, taller than my in-law's house or the last building where I'd lived with my parents, the one in Bensonhurst, where, in the crowded little bedroom, I'd dressed in my wedding gown, snagging the hem of my train on a popped nail in the scuffed floorboards. The sheer heroic thrust of the station made me feel tiny, almost invisible, almost safe, except that my eyes wandered constantly from the double glass doors to the street at one end to the double glass doors to the street at the other. Waiting, watching, waiting for Bobby to come through the doors, his hands clenched in his pants pockets, his face the dusky color that flooded it whenever he was angry about anything, which was lots of the time. I'd been waiting for Bobby to come through doors most of my life, waiting and watching to gauge his mood and so my own.

A finger of sweat traced my spine and slid into the cleft where my underpants began. The cotton at my crotch was wet, summer sweat and fear. I'd been afraid so many times that I thought I knew exactly what it felt like, but this was something different altogether, like the difference between water and ice. Ice in my belly, in my chest, beneath my breasts, between my eyes, as though I'd gulped down a lemonade too quickly in the heat. "Brain freeze," Robert and his friends called it when it happened to them, and they'd reel around the kitchen, holding their heads.

"Wait on the bench by the coffee kiosk," the man had said. He had driven us from New York to Philadelphia in total silence, like a well-trained chauffeur. As we got out of the old Plymouth Volare in front of the train station, he had leaned across the front seat, looking up at me through the open passenger door. He had smelled like English Leather, which Bobby had worn when we were both young, before we were married. Bobby had worn it that time when I was nineteen, the first time. Or twenty. I guess it was right, Bobby's voice in my head; I guess I'd just turned twenty, that first time. Maybe he was testing me then, to see how much I could take. Maybe he did that every time, until finally he had decided that I would take anything. Anything at all.

"What?" Robert had said, looking up at me as the man in the Volare drove away from wherever he came from, whoever he was. "What did he say? Where are we going now? Where are we going?"

And there was the coffee kiosk, and here was the bench, and here we were, my ten-year-old son and I, waiting for—what? Waiting to escape, to get gone, to disappear so that Bobby could never find us. I think Robert knew everything when he saw me that morning, cutting my hair in the medicine-cabinet mirror, whispering on the phone, taking off the bandages and throwing them in the trash, putting all the recent photographs in an envelope and addressing it to my sister, Grace, so that Bobby wouldn't have good pictures to show people when he started to search for us. "Where are we going?" Robert had asked. "On a trip," I'd replied. If Robert had been an ordinary ten-year-old he would have cajoled and whined, asked and asked and asked until I snapped at him to keep quiet. But he'd never been ordinary. For as long as either of us could remember, he'd been a boy with a secret, and he'd kept it well. He had to have heard the sound of the slaps, the thump of the punches, the birdcall of my sobs as I taped myself up, swabbed myself off, put my pieces back together again. He'd seen my bruises after the fact; he'd heard the sharp intakes of breath when he hugged too hard in places I was hurt. But he looked away, the way he knew we both wanted him to, my husband for his reasons, me for mine.

It was just that last time, when he came in from school and I turned at the kitchen counter, his apple slices on a plate, his mine in a glass, my face swollen, misshapen, the colors of a spectacular sunset just before nightfall, my smile a clownish wiggle of a thing because of my split lip, that he couldn't manage to look away, disappear upstairs, pretend he didn't see. "Mom, oh, Mom," he'd said, his eyes enormous. "Don't worry," I'd replied before he could say more. "I'll take care of everything."

"Mom," he'd said again. And then maybe he remembered, remembered the secret, remembered all those mornings after the horrible sounds and screams, how his father would sit at the table drinking coffee from his PBA mug, how I'd come in from running and go up to shower, how everyone acted as though everything was just as it should be. So the wild light in his eyes flared, flickered, died, and he added, "Was it an accident?"

Because that's what I'd said, year after year. An accident. I had an accident. The accident was that I met Bobby Benedetto in a car, and I fell crazy in love with him. And after that I fell further and further every year. Not so you'd notice, if you knew me, although no one really did. On the outside I looked fine: the job, the house, the kid, the husband, the smile. Nobody got to see the hitting, which was really the humiliation, which turned into the hatred. Not just hating Bobby, but hating myself, too, the cringing self that was afraid to pick up the remote control from the coffee table in case it was just that thing that set him off. I remember a story in the *Daily News* a couple of years ago about a guy who kept a woman chained in the basement of the building where he was a custodian. Whenever he felt like it, he went down the concrete steps and did what he wanted to her. Part of me had been in a cellar, too, waiting for the sound of footfalls on the stairs. And I wasn't even chained. I stayed because I thought things would get better, or at least not worse. I stayed because I wanted my son to have a father and I wanted a home. For a long time I stayed because I loved Bobby Benedetto, because no one had ever gotten to me the way he did. I think he knew that. He made me his accomplice in what he did, and I made Robert mine. Until that last time, when I knew I had to go, when I knew that if I told my son I'd broken my nose, blacked my eyes, split my lip, by walking into the dining-room door in the dark, that I would have gone past some point of no return. The secret was killing the kid in him and the woman in me, what was left of her. I had to save him, and myself.

"Where are we going, Mom?" he wined in the station, but he did it like any kid would, on any long trip, and it almost made me laugh and smile and cry, too, to hear him sound so ordinary instead of so dead and closed up. Besides, he knew. He knew we were running away from his father, as far and as fast as we could. I wanted to say, Robert, baby, hon, I'm taking you out of the cellar. I'm taking you to where there won't be secrets anymore. But that wasn't exactly true. They'd just be different secrets now.

There are people who will do almost anything in America, who will paint your house, paint your toenails, choose your clothes, mind your kids. In Manhattan, at the best private schools, you can even hire a nitpicker if your kid gets head lice. And there are people who will help you get away from your husband, who will find you a new house, a new job, a new life, even a new name. They are mysterious about it because they say it's what they need to do to keep you safe; when she goes on television, their leader, a woman named Patty Bancroft, likes to say, "We do not even have a name for ourselves." Maybe that's why I'd felt I had to whisper when I talked to her on the phone, even though Bobby was long gone from the house: to keep their secret, my secret. There are people, Patty Bancroft had said, who will help you; it is better if you know no more than that.

I looked down at Robert, hunched over on the bench, bent almost double over a little electronic game he carried with him everywhere. Ninjas in glowing green lunged forward and kicked men in black masks; the black masks fell back, fell over like felled trees. The ninjas bowed. The number at one corner of the screen grew larger. Robert was breathing as though he had been running. I ran my hand over his dark hair, cut like a long tonsure over his narrow, pointed skull. My touch was an annoyance; he leaned slightly to one side and rocked forward to meet the ninjas, take them on, knock them down. He was good at these games, at losing himself in the tinny electronic sounds and glowing pictures. My sister, Grace, said all the kids were, these days. But I wondered. I looked across the station at a small girl in overalls who was toddling from stranger to stranger, smiling and waving while her mother followed six paces behind. Even when he was small Robert had never, ever been like that. Grace said kids were born with personalities, and Robert's was as dignified and adult as his name. But I wondered. When Robert was three he sometimes sat and stared and rocked slightly back and forth, and I worried that he was autistic. He wasn't, of course; the doctor said so. "Jesus, talk about making a mountain out of a whatever," Bobby had said, reaching to lift the child and never even noticing the way in which the small bony shoulders finched, like the wings of a bird preparing to fly, to flee.

"We're going on a trip," I'd told Robert that morning.

"Where?" he'd said.

"It's kind of a surprise."

"Is Daddy coming?"

Not if we're lucky, a voice in my head had said, but out loud I'd replied, "He has to work."

Robert's face had gone dead, that way it does sometimes, particularly the morning after a bad night, a night when Bobby and I have gotten loud. "Is that why you're wearing glasses?" he said.

"Sort of, yeah."

"They look funny."

In the station he looked up from his video game and stared at me as though he was trying to figure out who I was, with the strange hair, the glasses, the long floaty dress. The ninjas were all dead. He had won. His eyes were bright. "Tell me where we're going," he said again.

"I will," I said, as though I knew. "In a little while."

"Can I get gum?"

"Not now."

Around the perimeter of the station were small shops and kiosks: cheap jewelry, fast food, newspapers, books: the money changers in the temple. The voice of the train announcer was vaguely English; there was a stately air to the enterprise, unlike the shabby overlit corridors of the airports. No planes, Patty Bancroft told me when we first talked on the phone two weeks before. Plane trips are too easy to trace. The women she helped never flew away; they were not birds but crawling creatures, supplicants, beaten down. Trains, buses, cars. And secrecy.

When I'd first met Patty Bancroft, when she'd come to the hospital where I worked, she'd said that she had hundreds of volunteers all over the country. She said her people knew one another only as voices over the telephone and had in common only that for reasons of their own they had wanted to help women escape the men who hurt them, to give those women new lives in new places, to help them lose themselves, start over in the great expansive anonymous sameness of America.

"What about men who are beaten by their wives?" one of the young doctors at the hospital had asked that day.

"Don't make me laugh," Patty Bancroft had said wearily, dismissively.

She'd given me her card that day, in case I ever treated a woman in the emergency room who needed more than sutures and ice packs, needed to escape, to disappear, to save her life by getting gone for good. "Nurses are one of my greatest sources of referral," she'd said, clasping my hand, looking seriously into my eyes. It was the most chaste business card I'd ever seen, her name and a telephone number. No title, no address, just a handful of lonely black characters. I put the card in my locker at the hospital. I must have picked it up a hundred times until, six months later, I called the number. She remembered me right away. "Tell me about this patient," Patty Bancroft had said. "It's me," I said, and my voice had faltered, fell into a hiss, a whisper of shame. "It's me."

"Where are we going?" I had asked her when we spoke on the phone two days before the man in the Volare had picked us up at a subway stop in upper Manhattan, two weeks after Bobby had beaten me for the last time. My voice was strange and stiff; my nose and jaw had begun to heal, so that if I didn't move my mouth too much the pain was no more than a soft throb at the center of my face.

"You'll know when you get there," Patty Bancroft said.

"I'm not going away without knowing where I'm going," I said.

"Then you'll have to stay where you are," she replied. "This is the way it works." My hand had crept to my nose, pressed on the bridge as though testing my resolve. I felt the pain in my molars, the back of my head, the length of my spine. I felt the blood still seeping from between my legs, like a memory of something I'd already made myself forget. "The bleeding will stop in a week or so," they'd said at the clinic. Pack plenty of clean underpants, I thought to myself. That's what it comes down to, finally, no matter how terrifying your life has become. A toothbrush. Batteries. Clean underpants. The small things keep you from thinking about the big ones. Concealer stick. Tylenol. My face had faded to a faint yellow-green in the time it had taken me to plan my getaway. Bobby had been working a lot of nights. We'd scarcely seen one another.

"What will happen if you leave and then your husband finds you?" Patty Bancroft had said.

"He'll kill me," I answered.

"He won't find you if you do what we say." And she'd hung up the phone.

The station public-address system bleated and blared. "Mom, can I have a Coke?" Robert said, in that idle way in which children make requests, as though it's expected of them. The video game and his hands lay in his lap, and he'd tilted his head back to look up at the ceiling.

"Not now," I said.

A line of people in business suits had formed at the head of one of the stairways leading to the tracks. Two of them talked on cellular phones. A woman with a handsome leather suitcase on a wheeled stand left the line and walked toward the coffee kiosk. Her heels made a percussive noise on the stone floor. "Café au lait, please," the woman said to the girl behind the counter.

She looked at her watch, then turned and smiled at me, looked down at the floor, looked up again. "You dropped your tickets," she said. She handed me an envelope she stooped to pick up from the floor.

"Oh, no, I—"

"You dropped your tickets," she said again, smiling, her voice firm, and I could feel the corner of the envelope, a sharp point against my wet palm.

"Metroliner!" called a uniformed man at the head of the stairs, and the woman picked up her coffee and wheeled her suitcase to the stairway without looking back. I sat down heavily on the bench and opened the envelope.

"God!" groaned Robert, hunched back over his game.

"What?"

"Nothing," he said.

Inside the envelope were two tickets to Baltimore on the 4:00 PM Metroliner. I looked at the big digital clock and the wall timetable. 3:12, and the next Metroliner was ON TIME. There were other things in the envelope, too: bus tickets, a driver's license, Social Security cards. For a moment I was blind with confusion, and then I found the names: Crenshaw, Elizabeth. Crenshaw, Robert.

I had not liked it when Patty Bancroft gave me orders on the phone, but now I felt a powerful sense of gratitude. She had let me have my way in at least one thing: Robert had gotten to keep his own first name.

And I was to be Elizabeth. Liz. Beth. Libby. Elizabeth Crenshaw. Seeing myself reflected in the glass of the coffee kiosk, I could almost believe it. There she was, Elizabeth Crenshaw. She had short blond hair, a pixie crop that I'd created with kitchen scissors and hair dye in the bathroom just before sun-up, just after I heard the door shut behind Bobby as he left for work. She wore a pair of gold-rimmed glasses bought from a rack at the pharmacy, clear glass with the kind of cheap sheen to the lenses that turned the eyes behind them into twin slicks of impenetrable glare. Elizabeth Crenshaw was thin, all long bones and taut muscles, because Fran Benedetto had been running for more than a decade and because terror had made it hard for her, these last few years, to eat without feeling the food rise back up into her gorge at a word, a sound, a look. "Skin and bones," Bobby said sometimes when I was naked, reaching for me.

It had taken me a while, that morning, to decide what to wear, but I was accustomed to being concerned with my own clothes, even though I didn't care about them much, not like Bobby's mother, who was forever seeking discount silk and cashmere, trousers cut perfectly to her tiny frame, jackets and skirts with good linings and labels. Much of the time I wore my nurse's uniform, the white washing out my thin freckled skin and making a garish orange of my hair. But let me change into anything snug, or short, or low, and I would see Bobby's eyes go narrow and bright. Although it was always hard to tell exactly what would offend until the moment when he put his head to one side and looked me up and down until my pale skin flushed. "Jesus Christ," he'd say in that voice. "You wearing that?" And I would feel like a whore, me, plain Frannie Benedetto, who had been up half the night with her little boy who had a stomach bug, who had been on her feet all day carrying syringes and gauze pads and clipboards and pills, calming down the drunks and hysterics, stopping to talk to the children, placating the doctors. Fran Benedetto, who had never been with a man other than her husband. But let her wear a blouse whose fabric suggested the faintest hint of slip strap, and all of a sudden she was a slut. Slip strap over bra strap, of course, for if I wore a skirt and didn't wear a full slip, the way Bobby's mother always had, there was no telling what Bobby might do. It was funny, after a while: I could tell you what Bobby liked and didn't like, what might set him off and how much. But I couldn't have told you as much about myself. I was mostly reaction to Bobby's actions, at least by the end. My clothes, my makeup: they were more or less his choice. I bought them, of course, but bought them with one eye always on Bobby's face. And his hands.

But Beth Crenshaw I would create myself, without reference to Bobby. I started to create her even before I found out her name in the waiting room at Thirtieth Street Station. Beth Crenshaw wore a loose, long flowered dress I'd found in the back of my closet from two summers before, the sort of dress that Bobby always said made women look like grandmothers. Bobby's own grandmother, his father's mother, always wore black, even to picnics and street fairs. "C'mere, Fran," she'd yell across her daughter-in-law's white-on-white living room, where she sat like a big blot of ink on the couch. She'd fold herself around me and cover me in black, make me feel small and safe. "Aw, God bless you, you're too thin," she'd say. "She's too thin, Bob. You need to make her eat." She'd died just before Robert was born, Bobby's Nana. I missed her. Maybe it would have happened anyhow, but I think Bobby got harder after that. Harsher, too.

"The reason you hooked up with me," I said to Bobby once, when we were young, "is because my red hair and white skin look good next to your black hair and your tan."

"That was part of it," he said. That was a good day, that day. We played miniature golf at a course owned by a retired narcotics guy in Westchester, had dinner at that Italian place in Pelham, made out in the car at a rest stop on the Saw Mill River Parkway. Both of us living with our parents, he in the Police Academy, me in nursing school: we had no place else to go. The first time we had sex it was in a cabana at that skanky beach club his mother liked; a friend of his from high school who vacuumed the pool let us stay after closing. It didn't hurt, I didn't bleed. I loved it. I loved how helpless it made him, big bad tanned muscled Bobby Benedetto, his mouth open, the whites of his eyes showing. It made me want to sit on his lap the rest of my life.

He talked about getting a tattoo on his shoulder, a rose and the word *Frances*. I said I'd get *Yosemite Sam* on my upper thigh. "The hell you will," he said. It turned out I didn't need it; Bobby tattooed me himself, with his hands.

"Red hair is too conspicuous," Patty Bancroft had said on the phone. It had been the only conspicuous thing about me, all these years. Smart, but not too. Enterprising, but not too. Friendly, but not too. The kind of girl who becomes a nurse, not a doctor. The kind of nurse who becomes assistant head, but not head nurse. The kind of wife—well, no one knew about that.

"There's still some good years left on her." Bobby would say when his friends came over, and they'd laugh. It was the way they all talked about their wives, and I wondered, looking at their flushed and friendly faces, if they were thinking of bones that had not yet been broken, areas that had not yet blossomed with bruises.

And they looked at me and saw a happy wife and mother like so many others, a working woman like so many others. Fran Flynn—you know, the skinny redhead who works in the ER at South Bay. Frannie Benedetto, the cop's wife on Beach Twelfth Street, the one with the little boy with the bowlegs. Gone down the drain that morning. Transformed, perhaps forever, by Loving Care No. 27, California Blonde. Hidden behind the glasses. Disguised by the flapping folds of the long dress. California blonde Elizabeth Crenshaw, with nothing but thin milky skin and faint constellations of freckles on chest and cheeks to connect her to Frances Ann Flynn Benedetto. A bruise on my right cheek, faded to yellow, and a bump on the bridge of my nose. And Robert, of course, the only thing I'd had worth taking with me from that tidy house, where Bobby liked to walk on the carpeting barefoot and I cleaned up the blood with club soda and Clorox before the stain set. Beth. I liked Beth. I was leaving, I was starting over again, I was saving my life, I was sick of the fear and the fists. And I was keeping my son safe, too, not because his father had ever hit him—he never ever had—but because the secret inside our house, the secret about what happened at night, when Daddy was drunk and disgusted with himself and everything around him, was eating the life out of Robert. When he was little he would touch a bruise softly, say, "You boo-boo, Mama?" When he got a little older he sometimes said, narrowing his big black eyes, "Mommy, how did you hurt yourself?"

But now he only looked, as though he knew to be quiet, as though he thought this was the way life was.

My little boy, who had always had something of the little old man about him, was becoming a dead man, too, with a dead man's eyes. There are ways and ways of dying, and some of them leave you walking around. I'd learned that from watching my father, and my husband, too. I wasn't going to let it happen to my son.

Frances couldn't. Beth wouldn't. That's who I was now. Frances Ann Flynn Benedetto was always watching and waiting, scared of her husband, scared he would turn on her, hit her, finally knock her out for good. Scared to leave her son with no mother to raise him, only a father whose idea of love was bringing you soup after he'd broken your collarbone. Frannie Flynn was gone. I'd killed her myself. I was Beth Crenshaw now.

Beneath the rippling skirt I could feel my legs trembling as an announcer with a sonorous voice called out the trains. But I could feel my legs, too, feel them free. No slip. I'd left that goddamn slip behind.

Frannie Flynn—that's how I'd thought of myself again, even though my last name was legally Benedetto. The name on my checks, on my license, on the embossed plastic name tag I wore on the breast of my nurse's uniform. Frances F. Benedetto. But in my mind I'd gone back to being Frannie Flynn. Maybe Bobby knew that. Maybe he could read my mind. Maybe that was part of the problem, that he could read my mind and I never had a clue what was going on in his.

Frannie, Frannie, Fran. I heard his voice saying my name, like the ringing in my ears, when he brought his open hand hard against the side of my head in a dark corner of the club foyer, that time I argued with him in front of his friends about whether we were staying for another round of beers at a retirement party. Fran. I can hear his voice in the sound of the train moving south down the tracks. I'm coming, Frannie. You can't get away. You're mine, Fran. Both of you.

I still can't figure out why everyone in New York talks about Florida as if it's a cross between Paris and Lourdes. The pilgrimages to Disney World, the fabled retirement condos in Lauderdale. "Moria Doherty, now she's got a life," one of the cop wives said at a barbecue. "Kevin put in his time and now there they are, not even fifty yet, in Boca, both of them working part-time. She gave me her rabbit jacket. I won't be needing it, hon, she said. Nice and warm down here, even in January. What a racket."

Maybe Moria's lying on a lounge chair watching the sun on the water, but Robert and I wound up in a garden apartment court in a dusty town called Lake Plata, almost an hour's drive to the ocean. Or that's what I'm told; I don't have a car, so I wouldn't know. There's an irony for you: I went from Brooklyn to Florida and wound up trading down, exchanging a house with the Atlantic at the end of the block, shimmering between two rows of attached imitation brickfronts like a mirage, for a square of gravel studded with gnarled bushes, no water in sight except for the pools that sit outside the motels on the highway. There's a flatness to Florida, or at least this part of it. It makes me feel like I'm in one of those rooms in a horror film, where the ceiling lowers and lowers and the floor rises, trapping you, squishing you flat. Although, come to think of it, that's the way I'd felt in my own living room for a long time, whenever I heard the sound of Bobby's Trans Am pulling into the garage beneath the couch and the carpeted floor.

When we got to Florida and Robert and I stepped inside the apartment Patty Bancroft's people had arranged for us, I'd realized it reminded me of the apartments I'd lived in when I was a kid. I could almost smell the bland steam that was the smell of cooking in my parents' house. I could almost hear the soft *woosh* of my father sucking oxygen hungrily through the heavy black rubber mask. And I could almost see the notes my mother left for me next to the stove in her angular handwriting and then in Gregg shorthand once she'd made me take the secretarial course at Queen of Peace: white wash, ham butt, drugstore. Frannie's "To Do" list. My mother had needed to work for as long as I could remember. And so, as a result, had I.

Robert had known the worst as soon as we stepped inside the place, as soon as he looked around at the dim *L*-shaped living room with a wood-grain dinette in the short arm of the *L*, seen the nubby tweed couch, the kind that's supposed to be stain-resistant but couldn't possibly look any worse with a stain or two. He tried to pull up the blinds and I told him sharply to get away from the window. "Are we going to Disney World?" he'd asked, back when we were taking the IRT from Brooklyn to Manhattan and then again as we drove from Manhattan south to Philadelphia in the old Volare, its driver wordless behind the wheel. Now he knew the answer.

On the train from Philadelphia to Baltimore he'd fallen asleep open-mouthed, his face mirrored in the window, and he'd slept on the bus we took from Baltimore to Atlanta. The bus tickets had been tucked into the envelope behind the Metroliner tickets.

"Mom, where are we?" Robert had said when we got off the bus in Atlanta, his eyes dim with sleep and fatigue.

"You must be the Crenshaws," said a short woman whose car was parked at the curb, a minivan full of children's car seats. "Yes," I said, and Robert had looked at me as if I'd lost my mind. "Where are we going?" he'd said again, more insistently. The woman ignored him, glided over his words with her own as though she was used to doing it. "I've got a nice snack for you in the back," she said cheerily.

She was kind, that woman, although she talked for three hours straight about her show dogs, corgis, just like the ones the queen of England had. She was nervous, but she'd brought some juice, some crackers, and an apple for Robert, and a blessed thermos of coffee for me. Robert got carsick twice, throwing up on the shoulder of the highway while I rubbed the sweet spot between his shoulder blades and the dog breeder called, "Hurry up, hurry up!"

"How did you get into this work?" I'd asked after Robert had fallen asleep again, after the woman had finished feeding me on the false biography to go with my new name, finished filling me in on the made-up life in Wilmington, Delaware, and Robert Crenshaw, Sr., the estranged husband who was an accountant. "How do you know Mrs. Bancroft?"

She'd turned on the radio. "Didn't they tell you not to talk about any of that?" she said.

"They didn't tell me much of anything."

"That's for the best," the woman said. "There's a box of doughnuts in the back. Here's your house key."

I don't know what I'd expected when I opened the door of No. 7 Poinsettia Way, its aluminum painted dark brown, its peephole glowing like a glass eye. I was just glad to stand still, to stop moving, to stop running. "Where are we, Mom?" Robert had said for what seemed like the hundredth time, and what could I say to him? We're home? His home was on the bay in Brooklyn, his room carpeted in a blue so thick and vivid that it was like walking through the sky, his shelves and drawers filled with everything he'd ever wanted: stuffed bears, battery-powered robots, plastic Supermen, electronic games, so that he could sit in his room for hours and not go out where things were scary. Out on the streets, his father said. Out in the kitchen, I thought, where there were loud voices and sharp noises and sometimes crying, too.

Numbers were singing in my head. 153 49 5151. That was Elizabeth M. Crenshaw's Social Security number. $1,256. That was how much had been in our joint checking account, and half of it was in a wad at the bottom of my purse. And Gracie's phone number. If only I could talk to my sister, the way I had in the half-light of our bedroom when we were girls, the streetlamps shining in a divot of yellow across our twin beds, the car wheels a hiss outside on the city streets. I'd never hidden anything from Gracie, at least until after I was married. She was six years younger than I was, my baby as much as my mother's, probably more, me pushing her around the neighborhood in my old stroller when she was a toddler, telling her the names of things, singing "Old McDonald," always interrupted by people making comments about her burning bush of curly hair, like mine but brighter, wilder. If only I could talk to Grace the way I did when we were older, lying in the darkness, listening to her questions, answering them as best I could. How come the nuns can't get married? How old were you when you got your period? How many feet in a yard, yards in a mine? What's our address now? Eight apartments I'd lived in with my parents before I'd married Bobby when I was twenty-one, in six of them I'd shared a room with Gracie. There was never any discernible reason for why we moved; we never moved up, or even down, just from one shabby two-bedroom in Brooklyn to another. As suddenly as the weather changing, we'd get dressed one Saturday, the first week of the month, and load the couch and the easy chair and my father's oxygen into a U-Haul and lie down to sleep that night a dozen blocks away. What's the point of hanging pictures, my mother always said, the sound of my father's wheezing a counterpoint from in front of the television. The mirror was always sitting atop her bureau, propped against the wall.

They'd given me low expectations, all those places. All I wanted was a house that felt like home, where the furniture matched, where the carpet was clean and a color I liked. I wanted to sit in a big chair in a den somewhere, with my feet up on an ottoman, and look around and think: this is my home. I wanted to be able to picture myself in that same room thirty years in the future, with my kids grown and my grandchildren babies and the smell of my cooking so familiar that no one even noticed it anymore. It didn't seem like too much to ask, and there was a while there, with Bobby, when I thought I had it nailed. I'd had a neighbor who kept the key to my house in case I locked myself out, a butcher who knew that I wanted loin of pork with the bone out, a school at the end of the street, a climbing rose working its way up the supporters of the deck out back. I'd had roots. I knew how deep they'd gone.

Knew it so powerfully when we stepped into that fugitive apartment, my boy and I, my eyes burning as we stood on the threshold. It was not an anonymous apartment, this narrow duplex somewhere in central Florida, miles and miles from the coast. That would have been bad enough. It was, like those others where I'd spent the years before I married Bobby, redolent of the lives of dozens upon dozens of strangers who'd smoked cigarettes, fried chicken, taken showers, slept late, risen early. It was a transient place, right down to the ubiquitous sound of the tap dripping into the scarred stainless-steel sink. When I entered that apartment I hated Bobby Benedetto with a ferocity I had never allowed myself to feel while I was living with him. I hated him on behalf of my lost life, on behalf of my bedspread and dust ruffle, my landscape over the couch and my guest towels in the powder room. Forced back into the rootless life I thought I'd left behind when I married him, I hated him so that, in that moment, I thought if we ever met again, I'd be just as likely to murder him as he me.

But after two weeks the feeling dulled, and I kept thinking I should count my blessings. Isn't that what Daddy always said, coughing in his recliner, when I complained about not being able to go away to college or take a job at the beach with my girlfriends in the summers because then Grace would have no one to look out for her? Count your blessings. My nose no longer hurts. The bleeding has stopped. And four doors down in the horseshoe of our little apartment court is a family named Castro, and among their five children is a ten-year-old boy who has mastered the sixth level of Double Dragon, whatever that is. "You know the finishing move?" Bennie Castro asked Robert the third horribly bright morning we had been there. The games kept them grounded, so that Robert with either upstairs or on the front steps, he and Bennie shoulder to shoulder bent together over the flickering screen. Bennie has two sisters, twelve and four, and brothers who are seven and five, and it is a great luxury for him to be almost alone, with no siblings demanding his attention or his toys. So every day now he comes to our apartment and he and Robert sit upstairs, the ninjas punching one another incessantly. Mrs. Castro just smiles and nods and says in pidgin English that this is very nice of me and acts as though there is nothing noteworthy about the fading bruises on my face. With her round cheeks, her hair scraped back into a ponytail, her Tasmanian Devil T-shirt and dimpled knees, she seems younger than any of her children. "Good-boy," she said, nodding at my son.

Occasionally the two boys go outside to ricochet around the quadrangle of stunted grass and cement, and I stand guard and watch their every move, flushed and sweating in the Florida heat. Sandy, the youngest Castro, shadows them as Gracie once did me, running back and forth on the ragged pavement that makes a broad *U* around the perimeter of the garden apartment complex. Occasionally she stumbles and falls on a piece of concrete heaved up by a tree root, sees narrow red pinstripes begin to form on the yellow-brown skin of her knee. She wails, shrieks, forces enormous tears from beneath her spiky lashes, and calls Mama as though she is drowning and her mother is on the boat. A moment later there is the thin sound of chimes in the muggy air: "Ice cream," the little girl shrieks, tears still glittering on her cheeks as she dances and claps. The definition of redemption.

My son scarcely ever cries. And his smiles comes so seldom that it's like bright sunshine on winter snow, blinding and strange. It's been this way for as long as I can remember. "Robert's an old soul," Grace used to say, maybe because she knew I needed to hear it, to think Robert's silence, his preternatural self-possession, were inherent, not acquired, not the equivalent of covering your ears, hiding your eyes. But when Bennie's little sister hugs Robert's legs, he always smiles down at her. I had a kid in a coma once, when I was working med-surg instead of ER, and I remember the look on the face of his mother when he blinked his eyes and muttered "water" after he'd been close to death for a month. That must be the look I have as I watch Robert smile down upon the shiny ebony head of Sandy Castro, the look of a woman whose child has come back to life.

"This isn't a vacation," Robert had said in a low shaky voice when we'd first entered the apartment, and he must have seen the look on my face, because he went up the narrow stairs and didn't come down again. I lay on the couch, exhausted, the cheap fabric scratchy against my face, and all at once I was asleep, a sleep as deep as unconsciousness. When I woke most of a day had gone. The place was as quiet as if it was still empty, and I took the stairs two at a time to the bedrooms, calling Robert's name, and found him asleep yet again. I stood over him and looked down at his splayed legs, the hands let loose from their habitual half fists, the big bottom lip like his father's, the light coffee skin. I'd breast-fed him for almost a year, an excuse to hold his warm body close. "Who'd have thought, and you as small as you are," my mother-in-law had said, eyeing the exposed breast disapprovingly. On the beach on summer Sundays I'd taken my time rubbing on his sunscreen, feeling the stalk of his spine beneath my fingers, vertebra after vertebra, loved by me. At night in his room I'd read him *One Fish, Two Fish* as he curled into the semicircle of welcoming torso. "You baby that kid," Bobby said, sometimes with a sweet smile and a hand on my arm, sometimes with a sneer, a snort.

"Hey, big guy," Bobby always said to Robert, and he'd cuff the boy lightly, playfully, as though to prove that Robert had nothing to fear from his father's fists. Once one of the cop wives asked me why Bobby didn't wear a wedding ring, asked me in a way that suggested that maybe my husband spent time in the bars and clubs of Manhattan passing himself off as a single guy. And maybe he did. But the reason he'd stopped wearing his ring was because it had once split the skin when he punched me in the shoulder. I guess you could consider it considerate, that he didn't want that to happen again.

But of course it implied that there would be an again. And there always was.

The second day after we'd arrived in Florida, when Robert still hadn't spoken, I sat down on the edge of his bed as evening deepened into night and talked to his back as I rubbed it.

"We're going to stay here for a while. Maybe for a long time."

He was curled up on his side, his hands, with their long fingers, pressed together between his knees. "This isn't a vacation," he had said again, but this time with the dull flatness of fact.

"We're kind of hiding, Ba," I said. "No one knows we're here. No one knows who we are."

"Who from?" he said, even though I knew he knew. "Why?"

"What?"

"Who are we hiding from? Why are we hiding?"

I took a breath and looked at my nails. They'd grown long, too long for a nurse's nails. But I hadn't been able to go to work in almost two weeks, not with my face every color, blue and yellow and green, like the faces we'd worked on in the emergency room, shrugging our shoulders and scrawling comments on the chart. Poss DA. Possible domestic abuse. It had always come over me, a weakness in my legs, when I wrote that on some other woman's records. I should know.

"From Daddy. We're hiding from Daddy. You know that. You know he hurt me. You saw my face. I know that's hard for you, but Daddy hit me, Ba. He really hurt me. More than once. A lot more than once. You know that. You saw me. You saw what I looked like. Lots of times. This last time was bad. Really, really bad."

And suddenly he was up and at me. His black eyes were big and his face flushed, and I reared back and then tried to reach for him as I saw the ghostly curlicues where tears had dried on his cheeks.

"No he didn't. You said he didn't. I heard you tell the people at work that you fell. And Aunt Grace. And Grandmom. You said you fell down, or got sick. Stuff like that. I heard you on the phone."

"Ba," I said, his baby name, Ba Ba Black Sheep shortened to Ba Ba and then to a single syllable, explosive with love. I reached out my hand and he pulled back, curled up, and turned away, his raised shoulder like a fin, a blade, a wall. How many times had he lain in bed at night just like this and heard the sound of hand against flesh, shoulder against wall, the sound of the arguments, about dinner, disrespect, adultery, a trip to Dorney Park, washer fluid for the car, no garbage bags, no rye bread, the wrong kind of mustard.

"I lied," I said. "I lied so people wouldn't know. I was ashamed. And I was afraid. I was afraid of Daddy." I took a deep breath. "I'm still afraid of him."

His sobs shook him and me and the flimsy bed, no more than a cot, not like his loft bed at home, with the desk and the computer beneath, the Yankees season calendar on the bulletin board. Would it be so dangerous if I found another Yankees calendar and put it on the wall? Was there someone out there looking for us already, looking for a woman buying a Yankees calendar in July, more than half the months of the year already gone? More than half her life gone, too, thirty-eight years of it, much of it devoted to tending her wounds, hiding but never healing them. All I'd ever wanted was to be an ordinary woman, an ordinary wife and mother. Now all I wanted was an ordinary divorce, one of those sad, shamefaced affairs in which the children carried duffle bags from one parent's house to another amid the sounds of bickering about the support check. Even that was denied me. "You're not going anywhere Fran," Bobby had said more than once. And he meant it.

"Mommy, why can't we go home?" Robert had cried, turning and reaching for me. And I didn't know whether he was mourning his familiar room, and his Little League team, and his friend Anthony from kindergarten and his and his grandmother's gravy on Sunday afternoon and his old familiar school and block and park and car and his beloved father. Or whether he was wishing for something more, all those things overlaid with the sense of safety and security I'd never managed to give him and had run away to try to find for him. For me, too.

"I know, baby," I said, holding him warm and sticky against me, smoothing his hair and crying myself. "I love you, Ba. I love you so much. You are the best boy."

The next morning he'd met Bennie, and that was that. We hadn't spoken about it since. I had to let him get used to things by inches: new town, new school, new friends. No more accidents. No more pretending that that was what they'd been in the first place. How do you tell your son his father did things you can't always believe yourself? Sometimes I think of Bobby pushing me into the wall, or backhanding me in the car. And for just a minute I think I've got to be exaggerating, which is just what Bobby wanted me to think. But then I can taste blood in my mouth again, and I know its all just as I remember it. I even started using a soft toothbrush so I wouldn't have to taste blood in my mouth more often than I already did. How do you tell that to a kid who loves his dad?

One evening two weeks after we'd gotten to Florida I was kissing Robert goodnight and he reached up and touched my cheek. The old cotton spread was pulled up to his chin, the air conditioning laying a light chill and the smell of mildew over the thick, humid air. His hair was getting long, flopping over one dark eye. In the dim light from a small window he looked more like Bobby than ever, but the Bobby I'd always loved, the sweet soft boyish Bobby. I kissed his forehead and smoothed back his hair, and instead of stiffening or pulling away he smiled.

"Your face looks better now," he said. "Can we go to the movies sometime?"

I went into the bathroom, the only place in the house where there was a mirror, which I figured was no accident. The tenants of this particular place wouldn't want to look at their own reflections, see the bruises and the scars and the grief and humiliation looking back from their own eyes. When I was a little kid I'd stood on a shoe box in front of my mother's bureau when Gracie was taking a nap in our room, and stared into my own eyes in the mahogany-framed mirror. I don't know why I did this; maybe just to really see myself, to try to figure out who was looking back at me out of those hazel eyes. I seemed more real to myself if I could see my own face, not walk behind it. Maybe that was why I'd avoided mirrors the past couple of years, because it was so strange to me to see the look on my face, alert and oddly empty all at the same time, like the face of a blind person moving around a dangerous corridor, her arms outstretched.

I didn't look that way all the time. Not at the hospital, where I was never afraid, even with the blood and the screams and the crazies. Not when I was with Robert alone, when I walked him home from school or took him to the movies, when it was just the two of us. But the rest of the time I was afraid. In my own home. With my own husband. It made me ashamed, to live behind that face, to think of myself as a person who looked that way. I left to be that person all the time, every day, every night. Twenty-four seven, as the kids say.

But it was almost as bad going as it had been staying. Everyone I loved was lost to me. There was country music on the radio downstairs. It had already been tuned to the station when we'd come to this godawful place, with its scrubby trees and its strangers. The good thing about country music is that you can cry when you listen to it, pretend it's the music you're crying about.

I checked the locks on the windows after I came down from Robert's room. I checked the windows every day. They were still locked. In the closet I had found two boxes of clothes, women's size eights and boy's size twelve, T-shirts and jeans mostly. There were some half-used bags of sugar and flour in the cabinets, some tea bags and a jar of peanut butter, and I wondered who Patty Bancroft's people had last sheltered here, where that woman had gone, whether her husband had found her and talked her into coming back, back home where her own clothes hung in the closet. Maybe he was like Bobby, that shadowy husband, devoted to the notion of the happy family even as he shattered it with his own hands and his words and his dark, dark eyes. "I'm leaving you, Bobby," I'd said once after he'd grabbed me by the hair, and another time after he'd pushed me down, and another time, and another, and another. "No you're not, Fran," he'd said. Real flat, just the way Robert sounded sometimes. His father's son. Once when I wouldn't let Robert buy a game at the mall he'd pushed me away, hard, and I'd felt the echo of his father's big hands in his small ones. Robert had said he was sorry in the car on the way home. But Bobby always said he was sorry, too.

The venetian blinds were closed. The neighbors must think we're vampires. Or perhaps they're used to it. Perhaps all the women who lived for a time in this apartment kept their blinds down.

From a mailbox on a corner in Manhattan I had sent Grace an envelope of family photographs. Inside was a scribbled note: "Don't worry. We'll be fine." She must have gotten it by now. Her phone number sang in my skull as I stood in the small kitchen. And it was like I was still chained in a basement somewhere, only this time I'd just stay here forever, alone. I felt so alone that if I'd looked out the windows and seen nothing but black all around me, I wouldn't have been surprised. But upstairs my son was sleeping with a soft look on his face, a gentle curve to his mouth, that I hoped could someday be the legacy from me to him. And I was going to get through every day so he could have that. I ate stale cereal from the box with one hand and felt my face with the other. Bruise or no bruise, it still hurt deep in the bone, where only my fingers could find the damage. And all I could think was that if I hadn't gone to one particular Brooklyn bar on one particular night when I was just a kid myself, knew next to nothing about men or marriage or shame or pain, I wouldn't be where I was. But then I wouldn't have had Robert. And Robert was all I had that mattered.

I didn't begin a new life; it began me. A letter came informing me that Robert was enrolled at the local elementary school, that he would be in class 5-C and that he needed No. 2 pencils and a three-ring binder on the first day.

Together we walked through the flat, stifling streets of Lake Plata to stand and look at the school building. His school, I called it when Robert and I talked, but it seemed so strange to us both. The architecture was strange, and the plants and shrubs, too, so that there was nothing to remind us of our former life except each other. Robert even took my hand as we stood across the street from the school, a low stuccoed building ten minutes from our apartment, beige plaster, red tile roof, stunted palms at all four corners. P.S. Hacienda, I called it to myself. P.S. Taco Bell, grades K through 6. When I called the principal's office the secretary said they'd already received Robert's documents from his old school. It was all I could do not to ask them where that might have been, and whether he'd been a good student there. All Patty Bancroft had told us, at the hospital, was that she had people working for her who were able to create paper trails. Work histories, school transcripts, passports. "I won't be more specific than that," she'd said.

A few days before school started Robert had taken out his black-and-white marbled composition book and sat down at the dinette table angled between the kitchen and the living room. I stood behind him as he wrote "Robert Crenshaw" in the little box that said "This book belongs to." I made him do a page of "Robert Crenshaw"s until I realized that it was like a punishment, like writing "I will not talk in class" 100 times, the way the nuns made Grace and I do when we were young. And he'd been so good, Robert—too good, I thought sometimes, going to bed as soon as I asked, although I'd been letting him stay up later than usual to keep me company, to keep the walls from bearing down on me and the sound of the moths batting against the screens from sounding too loud. I could tell that he thought if he was good enough I'd take him home. Maybe that's why he'd always been so quiet and clean as a kid. Maybe he figured if he was good enough his father wouldn't hit me anymore.

"This is kind of hard, isn't it, hon?" I'd said, looking over his shoulder. "A new school, new friends. Plus the name, and the story about where you're from and everything. I wish I'd come up with some other way to do it. But I couldn't. I'm sorry."

Robert silently put his composition book in his new backpack. School supplies, a backpack, a new polo shirt: the little wad of bills in the bottom of my bag was melting away. It was like my boy and I were playing a role in some phony TV show. Everything felt artificial. I went into the kitchen for a glass of water and stayed there for a minute, trying to figure out whether I could go through with it. The phone was on the wall. Grace would have plane tickets waiting in Tampa before dinner. I don't know what I might have done at that moment, if I hadn't stumbled and brought the glass up against one of my front teeth with a sound, a feeling, I never wanted to hear or feel again. I couldn't go back to Bobby now without Robert thinking that that was all right, that what would come afterward was the natural order of things. He'd traded one set of secrets for another. But this second set was nothing compared to the other.

"It's phonetic, Crenshaw," I said, handing him a cookie. "You can just sound it out. And you remember about Daddy not being a police officer, and not talking about New York or Grandmom or anything when you talk about family stuff. We're from Delaware. Are you sure you can remember that? It's that real teeny state on the map, the one just down from New Jersey."

"Mom," Robert said, "kids don't talk about that stuff that much. They don't talk about their last names or where they moved from that much. Only grown-ups talk about that stuff."

At times like that, I did count my blessings. We'd arrived only three weeks before school began, only three weeks of aimless summer emptiness for my son in this still-strange place, and those weeks filled by Bennie, who was to be in the same class with Robert. Once in a while I felt the presence of someone behind all this, moving us artfully around the chessboard of this strange expatriate life. For that I was grateful.

Children need structure. That had always been my motto, had been from the time I set up story time and park visits and bath before bed for Grace, when I was little more than a kid myself, my mother secretary to the head of the municipal worker's union, my father signing over his disability check the third of every month. Gracie and I left home at the same time every day, the redheaded Flynn girls, one carroty as a cartoon character, the bigger girl more auburn. "Knowledge," I'd say. "Unpleasant . . . mythic." Spelling words on Friday mornings before the test. Times tables on Tuesdays. And every afternoon, as we met on the corner, I'd say before anything else, "What'd you get?"

"A hundred," Grace almost always said, student outstripping teacher. Structure. With structure there was no room for doubt, mistakes, sadness, loneliness. Except occasionally, for me, at night, when I could tell by her breathing that Gracie had drifted off to sleep. Ah, Bobby. I was so ripe for you when I first saw you, saw you glowing in the darkness of that Brooklyn bar like a fire on a cold night.

Now Robert would have structure every day, the hours in school, the hour of homework, not too much time left over to think, to brood. He had Bennie to go with him on the bus every day and a poster of Don Mattingly in pinstripes over his flimsy bed upstairs. There would be sports teams to join and practices to fill the hours. Now only my own day would lie before me, less like a life than like the interruption of one, the part on an old record when it skipped, one chord over and over. When Bennie and Robert were playing upstairs I allowed myself one soap opera on television, an hour of family feuds, impossibly grand weddings, suggested sex. I took the boys on long trips to the Home Depot, a twenty-minute walk for a can opener and a pot holder. I counted my money at least twice a day. I was so worried about going broke that one day I picked up a job application from Kmart, then put it in a drawer in the kitchen, baffled by how to fill in the section on previous job experience. I bought a pack of index cards, intending to tack them up on the bulletin boards at the supermarkets: Will clean your house. But out on walks with Bennie and Robert, looking at the flat, cinder-block ranch houses and dolled-up aluminum-sided trailers planted on concrete slabs on the side streets, I wondered if anyone in Lake Plata could afford a house cleaner. And when I looked at the phone in our living room I saw that there was no number on the dial, and realized I knew no phone number to put on the index card, no number at which I could be reached. I would be reduced to asking for my own telephone number the next time I talked to Patty Bancroft.

My one luxury was a fat collected edition of some of Agatha Christie's mysteries that I picked up off a remainder table at the Job Lot store. I read while I listened to the spoken song of an afternoon radio talk-show host, who appeared to hate Hispanics, Democrats, and homosexuals in equal measure, but who enjoyed his hatred so much that it was almost a pleasure to hear. He always said the word *influx* as though it was gum and he was popping that *X* between his molars. Big John Feeney, his name was. I always turned him off when the boys came downstairs.

I still had $402 of the money I'd brought from home. From home. Would I ever learn to stop thinking that way?

"What if the principal at your new school is a giraffe . . ." I said the Friday before school began as Robert and Bennie were eating Blimpies, a special lunch I'd arranged as a treat, along with an hour at an arcade in a strip mall on the highway.

". . . and she keeps banging her head going into the classrooms . . ." Robert replied.

". . . so she wears a football helmet all the time . . ."

". . . and plays quarterback on the team, which has a winning season . . ."

Bennie was looking at us big-eyed, open-mouthed. "It's a game we play," Robert said. "My mom made it up. It's called 'What If?' "

"What if," I'd say to Grace Ann when she was on the swings, "we had a house in the country . . ."

". . . and I had a horse and you had a horse and Daddy had a big car with no roof . . ."

"A convertible, they call that. And what if we had a governess instead of school . . ."

". . . and she made us eat worms!"

Or, when we were older, walking to the bus stop, she on her way to Queen of Peace, I to nursing school: "What if you fell in love at the hospital with a doctor with blond hair and blue eyes . . ."

"And you fell in love with a writer with an apartment in the Village . . ."

"And you and your husband got the apartment next door to us and you both worked at St. Vincent's Hospital . . ."

"And you became a full professor at NYU . . ."

"What if," I said to Robert as he was eating his breakfast on the first day of school, "you went to school today . . ."

"And got the desk next to Bennie's . . ." he replied.

"And had a really really nice teacher who liked you a lot . . ."

"And got picked for the soccer team . . ."

"What if it turned out you really liked it here . . ."

"I have to go get Bennie or we'll miss the bus," Robert said, picking up his backpack.

Every first day of school he'd ever had I'd gone with him: carrying him whimpering into nursery school, walking hand-in-hand to first grade. Don't let anyone tell you New York is a big city. "I know you," said the cop outside P.S. 135 in Sheepshead Bay as we passed him on our way to St. Stannie's. "You look just like your dad."

"I know," Robert had said, so faintly you could scarcely hear him. The school at St. Stannie's was red brick, an unadorned box in the shadow of the Gothic church, all the flourishes and frills used up in the service of the tabernacle, the stained glass, and the carved limestone apse. The only thing distinguished about the school was a long brick pathway to its door. Robert had trudged up it on his way to Mrs. Civello's first-grade class, with that strange defenseless look a dress shirt gives a little boy, wheeled and run to me, holding tight to my legs, pressing his face into my belly. Then he'd turned and run inside, his navy uniform tie whipping around behind his skinny neck. Some of the other kids hadn't lost their baby fat yet, round thighs emerging from the plaid parochial-school skirts, bulbous cheeks above gap-toothed grins. But Robert was always a wraith, narrow and bony, a chest like a fledgling, his eyes taking up half his face.

By third grade I'd been ordered to stay half a block behind him, while he walked with Anthony and Sean and Paul and his other friends. But I'd never wanted to be with him so much as that first day of fifth grade in Lake Plata, and instead there was the yellow bus at the corner, on which no parents were allowed. Robert shoved Bennie into the seat by the window, so that he was even further away from me than the thin yellow skin of metal and glass. "It's vacation time for Mom," the bus driver shouted over the raucous sound of the engine and the kids.

" 'Bye, Mrs. Crenshaw," Bennie called, then turned away to talk to Robert.

I made it to the school building almost ten minutes before the bus did, and checked to see that no one was watching the school from the parking lot. I peered into the lobby, even looked around the corner down the hallways and saw nothing but the occasional teacher whisking by. I went back outside and stood behind a minivan across the street and waited for Robert's bus. The driver was a heavy woman in a Dolphins hat, who counted heads aloud as children spilled down the steps. Robert was the nineteenth, disappearing into a river of dark and light heads moving toward the doors. "And that's twenty-seven and I'm outta here," I heard the bus driver say. When she'd pulled out I could see the door of the school, could see a little girl in a pink dress being wrestled away from her mother and led wailing into the building by a man in khaki shorts and a polo shirt with a whistle around his neck. "She'll be fine," he called back to the mother, who was wiping her eyes. Another little boy had turned in the doorway to look back at his father, who was standing on the sidewalk with a video camera. The kid was squinting, one eye shut so tight that it pulled the rest of his face up into the kind of grimace I'd seen on stroke patients. People kept bumping into him, hurrying into the building.

"What do you want me to do now?" he said to his father.

"Wave and say 'good-bye,' " his father said.

"Good-bye," the kid said, without waving. He carried a lunch box shaped like a Mickey Mouse head, even though they served lunch at school. I knew because I'd asked Bennie a dozen times, finally satisfied when I saw the menu in the local paper. Today they were having chicken nuggets, green beans, and tapioca pudding.

"Jason is now officially in third grade," said the dad with the video camera in a phony weathercaster's voice. Next to him a knot of mothers were talking about overcrowding in the kindergarten.

"Poor Jason," said a woman who'd been standing next to me, shading her eyes with her hand.

"Dad goes a little overboard?" I said.

"They had to ban that sucker from the school with that camera of his," the woman said. She was wearing pink linen shorts and a matching blouse, white sunglasses, and pink nail polish. She sounded like an actress playing Blanche DuBois in summer stock, looked and smelled as though she'd groomed herself as painstakingly for this morning as I had the morning I got married. A drawl and Diorissimo, or something that smelled a whole lot like it.

"First grade, he filmed Jason on his first field trip, Jason giving his report on alligators to the class, Jason trying out for peewee soccer, which, by the by, he's not real good at. Last year he tried to film Jason taking some standard reading test they were giving. I figure that was the last straw. He's not allowed inside the school with the camera anymore. Came close to suing, too, I heard, 'cause of infringement on his constitutional rights. Does the Constitution guarantee you the right to be a weenie?"

Both of us looked toward the school. The sun made such a glare on the windows that they looked like one-way mirrors; we couldn't see a thing. But I could feel Robert inside, feel him sitting at his new desk looking furtively around the room, trying to get used to this, trying to scope out who mattered and who didn't, who it was safe to approach and who would backhand him with a word, a look. I could feel him watching the teacher, trying to pay attention to what Mrs. Bernsen was saying while every hair on his body was vibrating to the atmosphere in the classroom the way the new kids' did. Or at least the way mine had when I'd been the new kid. And, along with it all, he'd have to remember his last name as though it was fractions, or division, something difficult he'd barely been introduced to. I could see Robert taking a test, writing in his crabbed script a capital *B* to begin his last name. I could see him erasing the *B*, his tongue snagged between his front teeth, writing a capital *C* instead.

Or maybe not. Maybe when you were a kid you were so unsure of yourself that every school year was a time of reinvention; maybe only adults were stupid enough to think they knew exactly who they were. "Hi," I said over and over in my head sometimes in the morning as I was making coffee, or in the evenings as I fixed toast and eggs for dinner. "I'm Beth Crenshaw." I practiced writing it the way I'd once written "Mrs. Robert Benedetto" in the margin of my notebooks in nursing school.

"If a man who says he is Robert's father comes to the school, you have to call me immediately," I had said on the phone to the school secretary.

"We already know that, Mrs. Crenshaw," she said wearily, as though her entire life was made up of custody disputes and parents' paranoia. And again I felt an invisible hand at work. It was a hand that made it impossible for me to ask questions, for surely there would be something peculiar about a mother who didn't know who had given the school fair warning, about a mother who asked where her son's school records had come from and who had sent them, about a mother who asked the office, "By the way, do you know our phone number?" "Guardian angels" Patty Bancroft always called the members of her invisible nameless network, and I was grateful. But at times it felt less celestial than intrusive, almost suffocating, for other people to know more about me than I knew about myself. It was as though I existed in someone else's imagination. I glanced at the narrow-hipped, narrow-shouldered woman next to me in the parking lot, and wondered whether our conversation was accidental or whether the clothes I wore every day, those charity size eights, had once belonged to her.

"Beth Crenshaw," I said a little irritably, sticking out my hand, watching for a reaction.

"Oh," she said, "sorry. Cindy Roerbacker. You new?"

I nodded.

"What grade is your kid in?"

"Fifth."

"Which class?"

"Mrs. Bernsen."

"Good. Mrs. Jackson is an idiot. The sweetest woman in the world, but my two-year-old could teach her social studies."

"What about yours?"

"Fourth." She sighed. "Her name's Chelsea. My little one's Chad."

"Your husband Charlie?"

"Craig," she said. "Isn't it awful? I got carried away, and now I'm stuck with it. If we have another girl we'll have to name her Caitlyn, I guess." The man who'd led the screaming child into the school emerged from the double doors in front and walked halfway down the walk, looking from one end of the road to another. He was still wearing the whistle and carrying a clipboard, and his face was as flushed as my own.

"Vice principal," Cindy said, her arms folded on her

chest. "Mr. Riordan. Nice man, but a little—" she whiffled a slender hand through the air like a bird. "Maybe not. I can't tell."

"You never can," I said, grinning. I remembered the day at the hospital I pulled an aide into the supply closet and gave her hell for telling one of her friends as they were unloading lunch trays that Dr. Silverstein smelled like a fairy. "Jesus," I said to my friend Winnie afterward, "if a man dresses nicely and has the littlest bit of drama about him, everyone has him written off as gay."

Winnie had patted my hand with her own, with its square nails and short fingers. "Fran, I love you dearly," she said, "but Dr. Silverstein's been living with an architect named Bill since he was in medical school. You need to pick your fights."

I missed Winnie, the head nurse in the emergency room at South Bay Hospital, who could calm a rape victim just by rubbing the back of the woman's hand as I combed her pubic hair for evidence, Winnie who made me feel afterward, as I cried in the bathroom, that I'd done good instead of harm. I missed Mrs. Pinto, our neighbor, who left Baggies full of ripe tomatoes on my steps during August and September and called Robert "handsome man," making his olive skin darken to a dull red-brown. And God, how I missed Grace, missed talking to her on the phone every blessed day, about her students, about my patients, about nothing at all, where to buy cheap sneakers, what mascara didn't irritate your eyes. "Where were you?" she'd say if she couldn't reach me in the morning. God, how she must miss me.

I wished I missed my mother more, but after my sister had gone away to college and my father had died, she's moved in with her sister Faye and out of our lives into a life of day trips to factory outlets and Atlantic City, of communion breakfasts and bingo games. It was as though her marriage and children had been only a brief interlude in her real life, Marge and Faye, two sisters watching the Weather Channel and bickering about the verisimilitude of their girlhood memories. I had talked to my mother once a week, said less than I'd just said to Cindy Whatever-her-name-was, a complete stranger squinting at her watch in the merciless sun.

"You going to work?" she said.

I shook my head. "What about you?"

"Not until this afternoon," she said. "I sell Avon part-time. In this weather the lipsticks melt half the time. Sometimes I keep everything in the fridge—they don't like it if you do that, but darned if I can sell cream blush that's as soupy as paint." She sniffed down the front of her blouse. "Lord, I wish I could get inside into the AC. The first year with Chelsea I had to sit in the kindergarten for half the day and then sneak out when she was at music. That's how I wound up doing PTA. First grade we tried to make her go cold turkey, but she cried so hard I had to stay out in the hall where she could see me at least until circle time. Second and third grade I stayed around for the first hour until January. Volunteered in the library and all that. This year, I said, Chelse, honey, it's time to cut the cord. But she asked me to stay outside where she could see me out the window for just half an hour the first day. Craig said, first it's half an hour, next thing you know it'll be until lunch. I don't know." She shrugged. "Do you think I'm crazy?"

"Nah," I said. "It's hard being a kid, never mind a mother. I can't ever figure out whether I'm doing things because they're good for him or because they make me feel better."

"That's it in a nutshell," she said, fanning herself with her hand. "Although I'm still wondering where she got all this fear stuff from. Like she'll ask whether you can get your shoelaces caught in the escalator at the mall. They'll be earthquakes or tornadoes on television and she wants to know where you could stand or how you could hide to get away." She shielded her eyes and looked toward the school. "Our house got struck by lightning once, when Chelsea was three. All it did was char the side of the chimney, but who knows with kids what sticks in their minds? You have one of those real fearless boys?"

I shrugged. "He's a boy. He keeps his fears inside."

She nodded. "Boys," she said, and I looked at her, at her glossy dark hair and painted nails, and wondered what she'd say if I replied, Yeah, that and the fact that his father used to beat the shit out of me and he figures he'd better be quiet and nice or the whole world will blow up. What would she say if I replied, Your kid wants to see a natural disaster, she should have seen my face after the last fight?

What if, I thought to myself, I'm talking to myself the rest of my life? What if I can never say what I'm thinking to anyone ever again? I looked back at the school building, and then grabbed Cindy by the arm. "What?" she said, and turned to see the two patrol cars, white and red and blue, pull up outside the school. Men in uniforms were stepping out of the cars, loping up the path and into the building, stopping just inside the door to talk with the man in the khaki shorts. Telling him, telling him. Next, one of the cops would pull a photograph from his breast pocket, the picture of Robert taken last year at St. Stannie's, sitting on the steps beneath the statue of the Blessed Mother, wearing the same polo shirt he'd worn as we traveled from New York to Lake Plata. I'd given a copy of it to my mother-in-law; she kept it in a gilt frame on her bedside table, with the tissues and the Sominex. I could see her handing it to Bobby, see him taking it into the photo shop to have copies made, see him finger his big lower lip as he tried to figure how best to deal with me when he found us.

The men were moving inside; I could almost see the three of them bent over a sheaf of manila folders in the office. I imagined them looking through the files for new students, walking to the fifth grade classroom, seeing Robert, whispering to the teacher, taking him out of class. It all came to me, like one of those flip books Robert had gotten for Christmas, all the little pictures moving fast, making a story, the story of the beginning of the end of my life.

"What are those two cops doing going into the school?" I said. The only woman in America terrified at the sight.

"They always come here the first day," Cindy said. "They talk to the kids about not talking to strangers, not taking a ride from anyone, only going with someone you know, the usual." She squinted across the lot. "That one's Officer Bryant, I think. I don't know about you, but I hate knowing the police are younger than I am."

"You're sure?"

"Positive," she said. "He's a good ten, twelve years younger than I am. The other one, I can never remember his name, but he's even younger than that." She looked at me. "Are you okay? You want to have a cup of coffee?"

It sounds stupid, saying how I felt at that moment.

Maybe it was the sheer chemical relief, the balloon deflating in my stomach, the buzz subsiding in my head. Maybe it was knowing that the police officer would see my boy as nothing more than another face in a crowd of children and that this woman saw me as nothing more remarkable than one of the moms. Maybe it was the way Cindy talked about her daughter, that combination of fear, ego, and love that oozes out of a good mother like perspiration when the kids are small, the fuel that had stoked my fires for a decade. Or just the way she stuck one pinkie under the white sunglasses to wipe away a raccoon circle of mascara from beneath one blue eye. Maybe it was that cornpone accent, so different from my own. Or the sense of relief I felt knowing that the police were there to tell the kids to be careful, although the attentions of a stranger toward my boy took a distant second place to my fear of a rental car parked at the corner and his father with his arm right-angled out the driver's side window, saying "Hey, buddy," in that rich, persuasive voice.

Or maybe it was me remembering female friendship, what I had with Winnie and with Gracie, too, as much friend as sister. What I had with Bridget Foley in elementary school, until her parents moved to the Island, and with Dee Stemple in high school. I hadn't had too much of it; I'd never been the kind of girl who traveled with a big boisterous pack. Maybe that's why I'd been pulled so powerfully toward Bobby, because there was always a circle around him, faces turned toward his, listening, looking, laughing. I'd had too much to do always, filling jelly doughnuts at the bakery to earn money for nursing school, helping Grace with her papers, taking my father in a taxi to the doctor's office, waiting for a plumber when the heat cut out on a January day. But I'd always had one good girlfriend, and looking at Cindy Roerbacker, hearing her easy confidences, I remembered how much that friendship had meant to me, that way you could just open your mouth, sitting on a bench in the park, lying across your twin bed, standing over a sink in the girls' room, pulling the phone into the closet—just open your mouth and let your whole self out, all those small mosaic pieces of self that felt barely held together with plaster of personality half the time. And then it had been wrecked for me by Bobby, who didn't like my girlfriends, called Dee a tramp, Winnie a dyke, Grace a bleeding heart, and who gave me a secret so big that it might as well have sat in the middle of the friendship like a wild animal, ready to tear it apart.

"So how's Bobby?" someone would say.

"Good. Good. Fine. Busy, you know?"

"Everything okay?"

"Sure. Everything's fine."

So much of my life was stuck in my throat like a

bone, and I could never, ever let it out. But I had gotten used to that. Bobby had given me one secret about who I really was, and now I had another. Or Fran Benedetto had a thing she couldn't tell, not over a beer, a burger, a cup of coffee. But Beth Crenshaw could talk about her life all she liked. Lies were so much easier than the truth. Maybe I'd be good at this.

It was clear to me in only a few minutes that our meeting was chance, that Cindy wasn't a Patty Bancroft construct. In the minivan she said her best friend had moved to California over the summer, commiserated with me over the difficulty of divorce, apologized for the juice box and the cracker wrapper beneath my seat. In her kitchen she made decaf and put out a plate of mini-muffins, and something about the way she talked and laughed and sometimes stared out the sliding doors to the deck and the pool told me that she needed company as much as I did. Her life sounded more like an itinerary than an existence, Gymboree with Chad two mornings a week, lunch every Wednesday for the seniors at the Baptist Church, Chelsea's ballet and gymnastics, Sunday school, selling Avon. But it seemed like the patches stretched a little long once she got back here to her own kitchen table.

"I got a bunch of stuff I cleaned out of Craig's mom's house when they moved to a condo," she said. "It's just sitting in the basement, if you're short anything. Curtains or chairs or whatever. I had a girlfriend from high school, she was so busy holding onto the big pieces, the armoire and the entertainment center, that she didn't even notice till after her husband was gone that she hadn't saved one single chair. She was standing around in her own place for the better part of a week."

"It's all right," I said.

"Sure, now?" Cindy said. "There's a mess of stuff down there. Go look if you want. Some of it's real nice. Well, not *real* nice, but presentable. And clean. Craig's mother's a real clean person."

Our kids give us courage, I think. The only way I'd gotten through Robert's first day of first grade had been to remember the stalwart set of those little shoulders, and the thing that kept me in my seat during soccer games when the coach yelled at him was the dignified way he'd lift his bony pointed chin. And I thought of how he'd refused to let me unearth his fears about a new school, a new name, a new life, of how he'd decided to swim in alone in the stream of children I'd seen that morning, with only Bennie and his backpack as life preservers. He was beginning a life, a life as Robert Crenshaw, making a place for himself. And so would I. Goddamn Bobby Benedetto, so would I. Maybe I was supposed to hide behind my blinds, to make myself invisible. Maybe that was what Patty Bancroft thought would be safest. Maybe that was what most of the women did. Not me. I'd changed my hair and my clothes, my name and my address, so that I could live, really live. I needed a job, and a friend, and a shot at changing that closed-up little apartment, with its thin carpeting and colorless couch, into someplace that seemed like people lived there, lived ordinary uneventful lives.

"Actually," I said, "I could use some curtains."

"Couldn't we all?" said Cindy Roerbacker, laying on the drawl plenty thick, her eyes bright, smile big, a smudge of lipstick on her teeth. "Girl, let's decorate."

Robert started his second week of school, liked the kids, liked his teachers, slept less, spoke more, although not as much as another kid would have done. And I splurged on a gallon of butter-yellow paint, to mark a month in Lake Plata, living through it, learning to let some of the fear out of the tight muscles in my shoulders. That's how small the living room of the apartment was: one gallon of paint was enough. I'd hung a sampler in the kitchen that I'd found in Cindy's basement: in cross-stitch it said, "May you be in heaven an hour before the devil knows you're dead." Mrs. Roerbacker's old multicolored afghan hung over the back of the couch, and some throw pillows were plumped up at either end. From Cindy's basement I'd taken an old oak rocker, a seascape in a maple frame, a chenille spread with blue and yellow pompons, a set of café curtains with cherries printed on them, and some drapes with stripes so bright they made you dizzy. "You sure about those?" Cindy said when we put them in the back of the minivan. She didn't try to patronize me when she helped me carry all the stuff into the apartment on Poinsettia Way. She just looked around and nodded as though it was what you could expect from a divorce, a dislocation. That's how she was, realistic but never grim. "You can work with this," she said. It didn't take long to paint the place, it was so tiny. But when I was done with the downstairs it looked like a feature in a woman's magazine on decorating on a budget. Except that the venetian blinds were still closed tight. The overhead light stayed on all day.

"It looks different in here," Robert said when he came home from school and dropped his backpack on the table.

"You don't like it?"

"It looks different." At dinner he slumped over his buttered spaghetti, mumbling. School was fine. Bennie was fine. Mrs. Bernsen was fine. The spaghetti was fine. *Fine* is a kid's way of telling you he doesn't want to talk. I'd watched parents ignore that in the emergency room; fine, fine, fine, the kid would say, and Mom and Dad would probe deeper, like dentists with those little sharp silver instruments. Kids used *fine* as the Novocain.

"It smells like paint in here," Robert said.

"The smell'll be gone in a day or two."

"I guess if you painted we're going to stay," he finally mumbled. His voice was hollow, deep, with grace notes of tears.

"It'll get better, Ba. You'll see. You'll make more friends, play sports, figure out the fun things to do around here. Maybe once I get a job we'll find a bigger place."

"Can I write to Anthony?"

"No," I said. I rubbed my hand along his arms. There was yellow paint around my cuticles, faint autumn moons. "This is really hard, I know. You're being so good about everything. And maybe someday things will be different. I don't know yet."

"I have homework," he said.

"I know, Ba, but I want to talk for a while."

"I want to do my homework first."

We sat together on the couch after dinner, watching situation comedies, families fighting and making up in the span of a single half-hour, while an unseen audience laughed at everything they said or did. Direct conversation had never been the way to engage Robert; I had always had to wait through the silences for his words to swim up at me. It was like the time Bobby and I had spent a week in the Bahamas and gone snorkeling off a steep reef, how the bright fish would appear from the dark navy shadows of the sea, dart past, disappear. That's how Robert's words were, small pretty fish swimming up at me and then disappearing into the depths. After we put our dishes in the sink, two cheap china plates, two forks, a saucepan, Robert sat next to me, my arm around him. From the time he was a little boy he had rubbed a strand of my hair idly against his cheek when we sat side by side. It was an automatic tic, a habit like thumb-sucking or nail-biting; it had driven Bobby nuts. "It's fucking weird, Fran," he said. Now that my hair was short Robert couldn't do it anymore, but I dipped my head down close to him, so that at least my hair was near, so he could smell it, sense it. I was letting it grow a little bit, as much as was safe.

"Bennie's parents came from Cuba," he said, his eyes bright in the glow of the TV.

"A lot of people came here because the government was bad for them. A lot of them came to Florida. It's the farthest south you can go in the United States before you get to Cuba."

"His mother can't speak English that much. Like Mrs. Pinto, the way she mainly spoke Italian."

"It's really hard to learn a new language if you're older."

"Jonathan in our class says people in America should only speak English. That's stupid. Everybody in Brooklyn speaks another language. Or lots of people."

"I wish Bennie would teach me some Spanish."

"How come you don't know Italian?"

I shrugged. "I know how to say 'What a beautiful face' because every lady in the neighborhood used to say that about you when you were a baby." He wasn't looking at me but I could see that he was smiling slightly.

"Jonathan says he has a pool in his backyard."

"The lady I had coffee with the other day, the one I told you has a girl in fourth grade? They have a pool, too."

"Above ground or in ground?"

"What?"

"Jonathan said his pool is in ground. He said above ground pools were cheap."

"The lady I met, Mrs. Roerbacker, her pool is sort of both. Because it's built into the deck in back of their house but it's sort of above the yard. You'll see. She wants you to come swimming."

"Jonathan is kind of a jerk," Robert said, leaning into my shoulder, his hooded eyes at half-mast, black onyx glinting from beneath the lids and the heavy fringe of lashes.

I could hear his breathing deepen, could hear the second hand of the old kitchen clock jerking around, hear the faint sound of a car out on Poinsettia. Both of us started to nod off. Sleep had become a refuge in which, for at least a few hours, the world seemed less uncertain.

Both of us, I think, could imagine that we were still where we belonged. Or had once belonged. Maybe Robert dreamed of everyday life, dreamed of those mornings when he'd come downstairs to the sunshine splashed across the linoleum in the blue-and-white kitchen in Brooklyn, on one of those mornings when Daddy was eating bacon and eggs, pushing his food around the plate with a half piece of toast, and Mommy was standing at the stove with not a mark on her.

"No offense, Mom," Robert has said several times, trying to make things the way they used to be, "but you look better without glasses."

Both of us flinched when the phone rang. The sound seemed so loud, so strange in the quiet room, and we stopped as though we were playing "Red Light, Green Light," and whoever was It had wheeled around to catch us moving. But I was paralyzed, not so much by the sound, but by the look on Robert's face. It was transfigured by a combination of hope and fear so strange and strong that it made me want to look away, the way you look away when someone's weeping. I did not know who was on the phone, but I knew who Robert imagined it was.

"Answer it, Mommy," he finally said.

There was the sound of background noise: the screech and honk of a public address system, the sharp *bing* as coins hit the insides of a pay phone, the insect clicks as the phone recognized and accepted the payment. *Clang, clang, click:* I knew who was on the other end. Patty Bancroft always says she fears any attempt to trace her women. That's what she calls them, her women, as though she oversees a harem, or is a madam in a bordello. My body must have relaxed at the noises, for when I looked up at Robert I could see by his face, blank again, that he knew it was not his father on the phone. "Christ, does that kid know how to read you," Bobby had said sometimes. Sometimes I thought he was jealous, when he said that.

"We've arranged a job for you, Elizabeth," Patty Bancroft said, as someone called a flight in the background.

"Beth," I replied.

"Pardon?" said Patty Bancroft.

"Beth. Beth Crenshaw."

A silence. "All right, then," she said. "We've arranged a job for you, Beth. As a home health-care aide. Unfortunately you can't work as a nurse without a nursing license, and that was difficult to arrange. This was as close as we could get. The wages aren't bad. No benefits, sorry to say, but it's the best we could do. They'll call tomorrow."

"Thank you," I said. "I wondered. I'm going a little crazy here, with nothing to do."

"You must be patient," she said. "We know how to do this."

"I don't even know my own phone number," I added.

"Well, that was an oversight." She read the numbers to me slowly. "Don't give it to more people than you must," she added.

Secrecy, Patty Bancroft had said when she came to speak at the hospital, was the hallmark of her organization. No stray piece of paper, no phone number, no newspaper clipping, could give her volunteers away as they spirited women out of their own homes and into the anonymous America where Robert and I were now living. Along the main stretch of highway in Lake Plata, or what I've seen of it without a car, is a Burger King, a storage place, a drive-through bank, a Taco Bell, a House of Pancakes, an enormous supermarket with a salad bar just inside the automatic doors, a Toys 'R' Us, a Kmart, and a Home Depot. The only way I'm certain we're in Florida is the license plates on the cars; otherwise it might be September in Colorado or California or either of the Carolinas. Generic America, 97° and sunny. "Thank you for stopping at Burger King," says an older man with a Spanish accent when I take Robert out for lunch every Saturday, hoping that the sameness of the bun, the burger, the decor, the logo, the greeting, will make this strange and unfamiliar life feel less strange, more familiar.

"Is there anybody who lives in Florida who's really from Florida?" I said to Cindy as we sipped at decaf.

"Well, me, actually," she said apologetically, as though it was a character defect.

Secrecy, Patty Bancroft had told us at the hospital, is the secret of her success. I know all about keeping secrets. There is no one in the world who knows the topography of my injuries, who knows all the secrets of my body. There is no one in the world who knows that my husband twisted my wrists, pushed me down the stairs, broke my collarbone, and, finally, my nose. Not my mother, who seemed to lose interest in me after I married, as though I was her responsibility only until I could be handed on to someone else. Not my sister, who saw me only when I could arrange it, which is to say when I could lift a sandwich without wincing. Not my friend Winnie, although she had treated more women like me than either of us could count. Only Bobby knows it all, but he always said I exaggerated. Mountain out of a molehill. That's one of his favorite expressions.

My son knows some of it, but he knows it in his own peculiar way, in some closed-up closed-down corner of his mind. I'm afraid over the years he's developed a strange kind of color blindness. At some point he stopped being able to see black and blue.

Secrecy, secrecy. As I listen to the sound of her voice on the phone I can picture Patty Bancroft adjusting the triple strand of pearls she wears on TV, wore that day at the hospital, that hide the lines around her neck and complement her pretty pink-and-white skin. Winnie had invited her to South Bay in February to talk to the senior staff. We'd had three women die in our emergency room in a single year. One had fallen out of a window when her boyfriend came at her with a box cutter, another had had a bottle broken over her head by her husband, and a third had been shot with a Saturday night special by a man she'd divorced the year before. All three women had had restraining orders against the men who finally killed them, legal papers saying that the men had to keep away. Maybe they were the last three women in New York to know what all emergency-room nurses know, and cops' wives know, too: that restraining orders are a joke, made, as they say, to be broken. One of the tabloids did a big story about the three women, about the hospital and what it had done for them, and what it had failed to do.

"Here's a story about the hospital," Bobby had said, shoveling in his eggs before going out on an undercover narcotics assignment. He'd sipped at his coffee, glanced up and seen the look on my face, thrown the paper down and then his fork, too, so that it skipped across the surface of the china and landed tines down on the tablecloth. "You take yourself too fucking seriously, Frannie," he'd said, putting on the army camouflage jacket he wore when he was supposed to be a druggie. "You didn't used to be like that."

God, how many conversations I had with Bobby Benedetto inside my own head, so many words bouncing around, fighting, dying to get out and instead dying on the vine like one of the squash he planted in our little backyard after the black bugs got to them. I didn't used to be like that because you didn't used to hit me quite so hard, Bob, I'd say silently. I didn't used to be like that because I didn't have to call in sick or stay away from my own sister, with her sharp eyes and sharp mind. Or see my son look at a welt on my arm, a welt like the shadow of a hand, and see the question form in his mind and watch as he shoved it back into the closet where he keeps his fear of his father and his fears for his mother. And for himself.

Talking to myself, always talking to myself. I didn't used to be like that when I was younger, Bob, twenty and twenty-one and full of dreams and plans and love, because the good times overwhelmed the bad and your hands were gentle more often than they pushed and jabbed. You'd take me out to that restaurant on City Island and you'd talk to me, not about anything important, just like you thought I was your friend. You'd tell me about the lady you met who'd been standing naked, all 320 pounds of her, in her kitchen on a hot, hot New

York City afternoon when some young guy with burglary tools tried to climb in her window. When you told her to cover up she said, "Well, I figured I shouldn't be touching nothing at the scene of the crime." And we'd laugh until the tears ran down our cheeks into our shrimp fra diavolo. Or you'd tell me how you shoved some punk up against the wall, a kid who'd grabbed a television set from the old Jewish man who'd said he'd never move his appliance store from the old neighborhood, and how you'd discovered the punk had enough warrants to really put him away, not like the other times, the times when you finished your paperwork and then cruised by the projects and saw the guy you'd busted just sitting out by the hydrant with a big smile on his face. And I'd look at you, with your dark skin and eyes and heavy brows and big bottom lip, the inside the color of a red grape, and think what I'd thought when Tommy Dolan introduced us at that bar down by the water my first year in nursing school, when I was nineteen, when Tommy said, "You got to meet Frannie Flynn. Everybody likes her." I'd think that you were the best-looking man I'd ever seen.

And, maybe seeing that thought in my eyes, seeing yourself in my eyes, so big and strong and sure of himself, that Bobby Benedetto, always a crowd around him at the bar, listening to his stories, buying him drinks—

seeing yourself like that in my eyes, you'd take my hand across the table. And you'd even listen to a few of my stories, too. Although that stopped after a while; you gradually stopped listening and I stopped talking the last couple of years, when you were so angry all the time instead of just occasionally. When you'd been passed over for a couple of promotions and there hadn't been another baby, when you'd wrecked one car and talked your way out of a DWI, given a free ride by the two young cops at the scene after they saw your badge. A thousand small disappointments, a half dozen big ones, and you'd stopped talking about the people trying to keep their sons out of trouble in the projects, the teenage girls taking good care of their babies, and started talking all the time about the spics and the jigs, the people you busted and I patched up. They live like animals, you'd say, and you'd look around our house, with the flowered couches and the flowered drapes and the flowered canisters lined up on the kitchen counter, flour, sugar, coffee, tea. You always liked things to be so neat, just like at your mother's. "The baby's got fingerprints all over this coffee table," you yelled upstairs one Sunday morning before your friends were coming over for football and lasagna. "You know where to find the Windex," I yelled back.

What possessed me? What possessed me, after the

guys were gone, to say, "When Jackie Ferrin chews, you can hear him in the next room."

"Jackie's a good man," you said.

"He still eats like a pig."

"Yeah, God forbid anyone should offend your ears, huh, Fran? Plus he scratches himself sometimes, right? That's it, let's take him off the guest list. Jackie Ferrin's got God knows how many goddamn decorations for bravery, but he scratches his balls and chews with his mouth open."

"I'm going to bed," I'd said. "I'll do the dishes in the morning."

"We'll have roaches all over the goddamn kitchen. And with the new carpeting we got no money left over for an exterminator."

And on, and on, and on, about nothing, until finally he shoved me into the kitchen table so hard I fell and cracked my collarbone. "Jesus Christ, Fran, I was just a little lit," he said the next day, but it was past the time when he would take me in his arms to say it. The Bobby he saw in my eyes now was no hero. My eyes had become a funhouse mirror that reflected back a grotesque. For two weeks he laid off the beer and came home early from work. He even took Robert out a couple of times by himself. "The boys'll go to the park and give Mom a rest," he said. Things were good there for almost a year. It was my first broken bone; I think maybe that scared him. But I knew he'd try again, and again, and yet again to wipe that look off my face, that reflection of himself in my eyes.

"Women who have had this happen need to understand that domestic violence has nothing to do with them, with what they did or didn't do," Patty Bancroft had told the hospital auditorium full of doctors and nurses, advising them on how to treat their patients, how to get them help. It was like listening to an oncologist give a case history when you were rotten with cancer. I spent so many nights listening to the sound of Bobby's breathing in the dark and trying to figure out what had happened, whether it was his mother or his father, Robert's birth or envy over the big collar some other guy had made. Or the booze. Or the raise I got that meant I was making $900 more than he was every year, 900 lousy dollars they could have back at the hospital for all I cared.

"Hey, Frances Ann," he said, doing our taxes at the desk in the little den overlooking the alley behind the house, "you make more money than I do." And a shiver went all through me. I could read his voice as well as I could read an X ray.

I think that was the night I realized I could never merely divorce or leave him the way other women could leave their husbands, knew he would never let me go. I was packing Robert's school lunch, making a peanut-butter sandwich with no jelly, quartering an apple, and he was sitting at the kitchen table, drinking a beer.

"What, the kid can't eat an apple like everyone else?" he said, watching me.

"He likes it cut up."

"You baby him." That's what Bobby always said about Robert. "You baby him."

The phone rang, I remember, and he sighed because he thought it was someone from work, and it was, but mine, not his. "Hey, nurse," Ben Samuels had said. That's how he always greeted me, at the hospital. Hey, nurse. Hey, doctor. He was a good doctor. He always touched the patients when he talked to them. He always looked into their eyes.

"Hi," I said, looking at Bobby.

"Remember that book on spiritual healing we talked about a couple of weeks ago?" Ben Samuels said. "There's a documentary about it on PBS tonight. In about a half an hour. I thought you'd like to take a look at it."

"Thanks," I said. "See you tomorrow." I could tell by the silence that he was puzzle by my brusqueness. I had my back to Bobby as I hung the phone up. Every phone call was like espionage by that time.

"That was Winnie," I said. "About some documentary on spiritual healing on TV at ten."

"What the hell is spiritual healing?"

"The idea that the power of the mind can overcome illness as effectively as medical treatment. We've been talking about it at the hospital."

"Sounds like bullshit to me," Bobby said. He went to the refrigerator, opened another beer, rubbed against me as he went back to the table and sat back down, lifted his beer in the Bobby Benedetto patented lift, drank deep. His sweat smelled like beer at night, his sweat and his breath. He looked up at me. "Who did you say that was?" he said.

"Winnie."

"It didn't sound like Winnie from where I was sitting."

At ten I turned on the television and sat down on the couch. Bobby dropped into his lounge chair. "Give me the remote, Fran," he said. He had another beer in his hand. Two minutes of narration and he shook his head. "Can the human mind control the human body?" said a voice, and Bobby switched to the Sports Channel. Ah, what a rare pair we were.

"I'm going to bed," I said.

"You didn't really want to watch that shit, did you?" he called after me.

"Actually, I did."

"Bring me another beer, all right, Frances?"

I carried another bottle of Bud into the living room, leaving fingerprints on the icy bottle.

"You couldn't open it?"

"For God's sakes, Bobby, it's a twist-off cap. Even if it wasn't, you could probably get it off without an opener."

"What the hell is that supposed to mean?" I'd carried the empty back into the kitchen and didn't answer. When I turned from the trash he was standing in the doorway. He looked good when he was drunk. I'd noticed it when he was younger. His eyes glittered and his mouth went slack in a way that had once made me warm and willing and now made me very, very careful. Most of the time.

"Who'd you say that was on the phone?" he asked.

"Oh, for Christ's sake, Bob," I began.

"Oh, for Christ's sake what, Fran?" he said in that low, slow voice, his eyelids at half-mast. He put down the bottle and moved in on me, and I didn't know which was worse, my first thought—that he was going to make me do it in the kitchen, pressed back against the edge of the white Formica countertop—or my second, that he wasn't going to be able to do it himself. I could feel that he couldn't, could feel him feeling it.

"You need to put a little weight on, Fran," he'd said, pushing against me. "You're nothing but skin and bones." He kissed me hard, more holding my mouth down with his face than a kiss. I couldn't breathe, and I tried to slide my face away from his but he had a hand at the back of my neck, and finally I had to push him, had to, I was suffocated, smothered, fighting for air. He tried to push his mouth back down on mine, although I was gasping, and I slid sideways and he fell forward, bumping his chin into the cabinet door. It was like one motion, the fingers lifted to his own face, the backhand to mine, so that I fell and cut my head on the pointed corner of the cabinet by the window, felt the blood warm in my hair and on my neck.

When I'd imagined marriage, when I was standing at the altar of St. Stannie's the week after I'd turned twenty-one, I'd never imagined staring at the ceiling, the back of my hair matted with blood, willing my husband to get done and get off.

We'd written our own vows: "I will follow you," Bobby said, his voice making it sound as though it was in bold italics, "to the ends of the earth." And he would. I knew it as he snored beside me that night, he smelling of Budweiser, me of blood.

That night I got pregnant again, but I lost the baby after four months, and for a week he gave me a massage every night, working the muscles in my shoulders with his strong hands, straddling my body. Maybe it's hard to understand, for a woman who has never had it happen to her, never watched her husband sob in contrition with those choking sobs that sound like he's swallowing glass. He made me feel cared for, Bobby did, at times like that, cared for the way no one had ever cared for me. Babied the way I'd never been babied, even by my own parents. He reached me somehow, reeled me back in, rolled me over and said, "I love you so much, sweetheart," and touched me so softly all over that I reached for him, although the doctor said to wait, and got pregnant again. And lost that one, too. For the best. For the best.

When we were dating, I thought it would stop when we were married. When we were married, I thought a baby would help. After the baby, I thought if we had another child he'd feel better. And when Robert was two I couldn't leave because those were the formative years, although maybe I didn't think enough about what we were forming, Bobby and I. And when Robert was starting school I couldn't leave because school was a big adjustment. And I couldn't leave in May because I'd screw up our family summer vacation, and I couldn't leave in November because it would screw up the holidays. So I stayed, and stayed, and stayed.

And then those three women were killed, and when I read their stories I realized that all of them had left, the way everyone expects you to when he hits you, beats you up. They filed the papers, got the restraining orders, said, "No more." But two had been enticed back, over and over again, and one had never managed to get away even after the divorce. Her husband had kicked in the apartment door, showed up at her office, grabbed her at the bus stop in front of a dozen witnesses who watched him lay into her. Then finally killed her. All dead, all three of them, even though they left, even though they tried to break away. They were the ones who wound up broken. And I could hear Bobby's voice, begging, begging, breaking me down. And I could see him following me on my morning run, sitting three seats away on the bus to the hospital, talking Robert into letting him into the house. That's when I realized that I wasn't going to be able to leave the way other women left their husbands. I wasn't going to be able to leave at all. I was going to have to disappear.

I looked around the apartment as Patty Bancroft talked. Maybe, then, this was the ends of the earth. But at least it had curtains.

"They'll give you uniforms," Patty Bancroft said about my new job after she'd fed more quarters into the phone.

"Do they know?" I said.

"What?"

"Do they know who I am?"

"They know you're Elizabeth Crenshaw," said Patty

Bancroft. "You have excellent references. There's no licensing requirement in Florida. It's one reason you're there. They'll send you out on a case or two next week."

"Beth," I said. "I've decided on Beth."

"Everything will be fine, Beth," she said, "if you do what we say."

"You sound like my husband."

"Excuse me?"

"You sound like my husband. Everything will be fine if you do what I say."

There was a silence in which I could hear people talking and laughing, walking through what must have been an airport on their way to somewhere else, traveling, not fleeing. "Make no mistake about it," Patty Bancroft said. "He is looking for you right now."

Scut work was what the agency gave me, work for an orderly, not a nurse. Cooking, cleaning, shopping. But it was fine. It was wonderful. Places to go, people to see. My first visit was to a thirty-year-old woman with cerebral palsy in a blank-faced apartment complex for the handicapped. Her name was Jennifer, and she told me what she needed by tapping on the keyboard of a computer with a long straight stick harnessed to her quivering hand. She looked like a bird, her head rising and falling as though she was eating instead of just telling me what she wanted to eat, her eyes rolling above a slack mouth that appeared to smile. "Instant oatmeal," she wrote my first day. "Quart skim milk. Jello-O pudding cups, chocolate. TY." TY for thank you.

She said it, too, although it sounded more like a growl or a throat clearing than a word. When I came back with the groceries I could hear the printer attached to her computer humming. After I'd changed the sheets on the single bed in the tiny back room, she used the stick to point to a stack of papers in the printer tray. Eleven pages of painstaking notes, including dates of all her hospitalizations. The first sentence was "My name is Jennifer Ann March, and I was born in Atlanta, Georgia, at 6:14 AM on Tuesday, November 7, 1967. The attending obstetrician was not available and an obstetrical resident, Dr. Gregory Littel, performed the delivery with high forceps."

"The forceps," I said aloud, not really meaning to, and she made the growling noise again and bobbed her head, as if to say, yes, yes, that's why I am the way you see me today, because of damage done by the forceps and the resident. If not for those high forceps I would be a thirty-year-old woman playing tennis at the public courts and working evenings as a waitress at Daisy's on the highway. Or maybe, given the intelligence and diligence of the medical history I held in my hands, a thirty-year-old woman finishing her doctoral dissertation on single-celled organisms or nineteenth-century chamber music. Everyone needs a way of making sense of their deformities, and a difficult birth was as good a way as any of explaining CP, of explaining to herself why she was slumped sideways, imprisoned in her own body, proffering these single-spaced pages as a way to make me see her as human.

"Is this for me?" I asked, and her head bobbed again. On her computer screen words appeared like magic, messages from people jousting with one another verbally in a chat room. "The meteor showers this weekend were stupendous," said the last line on the screen. "From Manitoba they looked like silver fireworks."

"I'm going now," I said. "I'll be back Tuesday. Can I bring anything with me?"

Her wobbly head swayed from side to side. Her hair was cut short, perhaps an inch long all over; I knew a nurse dressed her in the mornings. Count your blessings, my father always said. It shames you, to count yours by the hardships of other people. That noise again, deep in her throat.

"You're welcome," I said, closing the door behind me, stepping outside into the heat.

Maybe Patty Bancroft was right; maybe Bobby was looking for me even as I put pudding and milk into Jennifer's refrigerator. But I was looking for him right back. I walked to my jobs by a different route each time, peering into parked cars, turning around if someone came up slowly behind me. Cindy and I volunteered in the school library for the first hour of every day; she could tell Chelsea she was in the building and I could keep an eye on Robert and on the door to the school, just opposite the library double doors. We traded in sweating in the parking lot for reshelving and covering books under the querulous direction of old Mrs. Patrinian, who called each of us "Mommy." The school secretary got to know me, to expect to see me around. "If Robert has any problems, you'll call?" I asked one day when I brought her an iced tea from the cafeteria. "Absolutely," she said, tapping an envelope of Sweet 'n Low into her cup with a long nail painted pink and white.

Most days Cindy and I had coffee after, unless Chad had Gymboree. "All first-time moms, who talk about the baby falling off the bed like it's the *Titanic*," she said dismissively. "If I hear one more debate about putting tubes in for ear infections, I will spit." Then we went to work. Cindy loaded her black imitation leather display cases into the minivan and I went to see my patients. There was Jennifer twice a week, and a dialysis patient from the local hospital named Melvin, whose skin was as yellow as margarine. He never even looked away from the television as I took his blood pressure and listened to his heart. He watched the stock ticker on the financial network and made notes on a legal pad. "He's not taking this well," said his wife. He was a long-distance trucker waiting for a kidney transplant. In the meantime he played the stock market on paper, buying and selling in his head, GM, Textron, IBM, The Gap. Every morning he sent his wife to the 7-Eleven for lottery tickets. "You think it's wrong to pray for a transplant?" said his wife, whose name was Ada.

"Why would you think it was wrong to pray for a transplant?"

"I offered to give him one myself, but the doctor said it was no good. Otherwise someone has to die. I mean someone has to die for him to get a kidney. It seems like a hard thing, to pray for someone to die."

"Don't worry about that, Ada," I said.

I saw Melvin twice a week, too. I couldn't warm to him, although I felt sorry for Ada, who washed his sheets every day in Clorox to get out the sweat stains. But my main job, and my favorite one, was taking care of the Levitts, in a building called the Lakeview on the other side of the highway from our house. It was a good long walk, about twenty minutes, the twin towers of the senior citizens' complex rising before me like a mirage amid a sea of small white stucco houses with red tile roofs, vibrating with window air conditioners. Some days I would sit down on the steps of one small house or another, scraggly flowered bushes shielding me from view, and wipe my forehead with a Kleenex. Sometimes

I stopped at the 7-Eleven myself for a Big Gulp. "Hot out there," the Asian man behind the counter always said, making it sound like one big polysyllabic word, an idiomatic expression he proferred, along with a big grin, as the price of doing business in this crazy, crazy country. It seemed possible that I was the only person in Lake Plata who didn't travel in an air-conditioned car. Since we'd arrived in Florida my face had been crimson most of the time, all the blood visible through my thin skin, my hair in spikes every which way.

The first day I went to the Levitts had been a school holiday, Faculty Development Day, and I'd reluctantly entrusted Robert to the Castro family, slowly, loudly asking Milagro Castro if she could look out for him while I was gone.

"Let me tell her," Bennie had said, turning to his mother. A birdsong of Spanish from the boy, then a series of manic nods from his mother, then more Spanish and another emphatic nod.

"She says she will take care of him the same way she takes care of the rest of us. She says he is a good boy."

Mrs. Castro poured forth a torrent of words, her head and hands dancing.

"She says Robert will have lunch with us and it will be a pleasure to have him. She says he is a good boy and she will not let him out of her sight. All right, Ma, that's enough." Bennie had turned back to me. "She's saying a lot of praying stuff. Well, not praying exactly, but God stuff. That's okay, Mommy, she understands." And the two boys had trudged into the Castro apartment, arguing about which comic superhero was more indestructible, as Bennie's mother and I bowed and grinned like dolls on the back of a car dash. Women's work, they seemed to say with their retreating backs. The screen slammed. Then Robert came back out, pulled me aside as Mrs. Castro smiled upon us both and whispered, "When are you coming back?"

"Around four," I said.

"Four in the afternoon?"

"Are you sure you don't want to come with me? I said you could come with me and sit in the lobby."

He shook his head. "I just want to know." He turned back to Bennie, and I turned toward the Lakeview and the Levitts.

"Look, Irving," Mrs. Levitt said the first time she opened her apartment door to me, as I stood outside in a hallway that smelled like Lysol and old people. "Look," she said, after standing on tiptoe and peering through the peek hole. "They sent a new one."

The Levitts lived in a one-bedroom apartment with a kitchen so small that Mrs. Levitt and I could not make iced tea and sandwiches in it at the same time. It had one of those balconies so many apartment buildings in New York had, just big enough to stand on, small, ugly, and useless, the appendix of modern architecture. Mrs. Levitt used it only to check for a storm coming when she heard the warning on the Weather Channel, and to hang her hand washables. Sometimes, as I got close to the building, I could tell which apartment was the Levitts' by the assortment of corsetry baking in the still air.

The apartment was as plain and simple as the inside of a box, but it was full of rococo furniture, sideboard next to highboy, a big sectional with old brocade pillows worn soft as baby skin, an assortment of sepia photographs displayed in Lucite frames on a bureau pushed into one corner. There were dining-room chairs but no dining table, end tables with geometric inlay and flimsy plastic tray tables. The Oriental rug was tucked under at one end, six inches too long for its surroundings. One corner of the living room was crammed with a hospital bed, a card table with medications and spray cleaners and adult diapers, and a large oil painting of a dark forest in an elaborate gilt frame. When I was a student nurse I'd done home visits to a seventy-year-old cancer patient, a retired furrier whose small efficiency had been much the same. "Their lives shrink as they get older, but their furniture stays the same size," my clinical supervisor had said.

"That color washes you out," Mrs. Levitt said the first day I went there, as she opened the door and looked at the blue polyester zip-front shift that I wore on the job, which fomented and held perspiration like the plastic weight-loss wraps I'd seen in women's magazines.

"And hello to you, too," I said.

"Uh-oh, Irving," Mrs. Levitt said. "This one's got a funny bone."

There wasn't much for me to do at the Levitts, really. Mrs. Levitt and I turned Irving over; he had had a stroke that left him incontinent, mute, and largely paralyzed except for the occasional wild spasm. Together we changed Irving's sheets and his pajamas. Mostly we drank tea after feeding Irving pureed peas and broth through a straw and changing his diapers.

"Can I use the phone to call my son?" I said that first day. "It's a local call."

"Mom, I'm fine," Robert said, impatient. "We were in the middle of something."

"I'll be home soon," I said, hearing in his voice, in his breathing, impatient little snorts, that he didn't care, that part of his great slow sinking into normalcy was to go about the business of being a boy with everything that was in him.

"I'll be honest, sweetheart," Mrs. Levitt said in her accented English. "I can sure use the help with Irving here. But it's also a pleasure to have someone to talk to. Not that Irving's not someone. But you were never a wonderful conversationalist, even before, were you, Irving?" She winked at me, lifted a hand to her woolly hair, stippled white and gray, which looked as though it had been permed and then left to get by as best it could for the duration. "Florida, Florida, he says as soon as he starts thinking about retiring. Everybody's going to Florida. What am I going to do in Florida, Irving, I say, but next day we woke up and there was a foot of snow. Oh, boy, I said to myself, that's that. Next thing I know, he's got the house on the market. Look at this." She heaved herself out of a mahogany chair, using the beautifully carved and curving arms for leverage, and motioned me over to a broom closet in the hallway between living room and bedroom. Inside there was a vacuum cleaner, a quilted gold garment bag that smelled of mothballs, and a set of golf clubs.

"You golf?" Mrs. Levitt said. I shook my head. Lots of cops golf, a slightly more athletic variation on the theme of sitting together out on the patio talking about how the transit cops are morons and the patrol cars all need new shocks. Bobby lifted weights instead. His forearms felt like a boneless rib roast before defrosting. God, he had a beautiful body. "You got nothing to complain about, Fran," one of the cop wives had said to me once at a PBA clambake in Hampton Bays, looking from Bobby to her husband. "Baby likes beer," her husband used to say, patting his belly.

Mrs. Levitt gave the golf clubs a kick with her bedroom scuff. "He says he's going to take up golf. Seventy-one years old and he thinks he's, what was his name, Arthur Somebody, big golfer. Weren't you, Irving? All that handicap nonsense you picked up from Bernie Meerson and his gang at the swim club. Do you think I should put an ad in the paper, try and sell them?"

"The golf clubs?"

Mrs. Levitt nodded, went back to her chair, the tea and cookies. She leaned toward me and lowered her voice. "What would happen is this," she said, squinting at me. "Somebody'd buy the clubs, Irving would wake up or come out of this"—she waved her hand toward the corner as though to indicate the whole mess, the adjustable back of the bed, the box of diapers, the catheter bags—"and he would say, Selma, where the hell are my clubs? You sold them? What, Selma, you thought I was going to die?" She shrugged, her pillowy torso rising and falling with certainty and resignation. I looked over at Irving, a yellow mummy with rheumy dark eyes, his fingers twitching, his breathing the closest he came to conversation. The bed was angled so he had a panoramic view of the cluttered random landscape of Lake Plata, one small roof after another broken only by the skeleton supports of the water tower and the boxy sprawl of the Wal-Mart and Kmart, but he seemed to see nothing, hear nothing. Perhaps he could still feel the drumbeat of his heart beating in his body; who could tell? It was hard to imagine him demanding his nine iron.

"Never mind," Mrs. Levitt said. "What do you think about this girl went missing in Orlando? The boyfriend killed her, you take my word for it." Oh, I believed that.

Listening to Mrs. Levitt talk about Irving was like sitting out back at a barbecue talking to the other cop wives the way I'd done dozens of times during my marriage. Sometimes, on those summer afternoons, I'd think Bobby was right, that I exaggerated things. I'd sit in the backyard of Bobby's friend Buddy's split-level out on Long Island, and listen to Buddy's wife, Marie, and her sister, Terri, who was also married to a cop, and Marie's neighbor Annmarie, whose husband was a firefighter, and they all made it sound like marriage was the Stations of the Cross, like that was the natural order, trial by husband.

"He can sit out there like Father of the Year, but God forbid he should bathe one of them or buy them a pair of shoes," said Marie.

"A pair of shoes?" said Terri. "What are you, dreaming? A pair of shoes? What about putting the goddamn mayonnaise away after he makes a sandwich?"

"He makes his own sandwich?" said Annmarie, and we had to laugh. Had to.

Oh, lord, the stories they told, and all of them funny and sharp, like Mrs. Levitt's. About how Terri was so tired from the kids one night that she fell asleep in the middle of sex. About how Buddy showed up at one of the girls' birthdays drunk and passed out on the couch, where the party carried on without him, around him, how someone put a butter-cream rosebud on his nose and he never even stirred. About Annmarie's husband, Kevin, and the toast he gave at his brother's wedding that was so full of profanity and references to the groom's previous girlfriends that the bride burst into tears.

"Honest to God, it's like having five kids, and the girls are easier," Marie said.

The working girl, they all called me. Hey Fran, they'd say, what's up in the real world? And I'd tell stories about the hospital. About the girl who came into the ER ten centimeters dilated and named her baby Benedetto because she kept staring at my name tag, yelling and cursing and using her long toes against the laminated footboard of the bed for leverage while she pushed. About the gunshot victim who tried to grab the bullet as a resident held it high on the blade of his retractors and raised a ruckus when we wouldn't let him have it for his collection. "I got five of those suckers on the headboard of my bed, man," he moaned. "Five, all lined up nice. Gimme that one." About the couple who came in hemming and hawing and finally managed to say that somehow the condom got lost. A female resident put on rubber gloves and retrieved it. "You're supposed to unroll it as you put it on," she said to the guy.

"Damn," he said.

We'd sit in the kitchen and I'd tell those stories and they'd howl, those women. Never the men. The men sat on the patio under the awning in the summer and downstairs in the finished basement during the football season. They got the big screen TV, we got the kitchen table and the fridge.

I don't think I exchanged more than five words—"Fine, thanks," and "Take it easy"—with Buddy in all the time I knew him. We were barely inside the door, Bobby and me, before he'd go in one direction and I in the other, to the kitchen with the women. It was like we were different species.

None of the women worked. None of their husbands wanted them to work, they said. They all said it as if they were a little curious, like they wondered how come Bobby let me, like they'd discussed it among themselves, like they were waiting for me to let them in on the secret. None of them knew that there were ways in which Bobby made me pay for the luxury of working my butt off at South Bay five, sometimes six days a week.

"I got enough to do around here," said Marie.

I remember wondering whether that was it, whether if I stayed home and made silk-flower wreaths and decoupage boxes Bobby wouldn't be so mad at me all the time. Except that it didn't seem that Bobby was mad at me, exactly, just that he was mad, and I was the one who happened to be there.

Annmarie went home early one evening, before the rum cake and the coffee, and Marie leaned toward us and said, "That poor girl, I tell you. He's had someone on the side for two years now. She thinks his family is still pissed about that toast at the wedding, but they can't look her in the face because he knocked the girlfriend up."

"Get out!" said Terri.

"Swear to God," said Marie.

"Why doesn't she leave?" I said.

"Where would she go?" said Terri. "She should screw up her life because her husband is a pig? She just repainted the whole house. She papered the hallway."

I told them about Patty Bancroft, too, when she came to the hospital. They'd already seen her on television, talking about how a woman could get lost in the great expanse of America with a little help from the right people. "We're better than the Witness Protection Program," she said on one afternoon talk show.

"All Buddy would have to do would be to raise a hand to me once, and I'd knock him on his ass," Marie said.

"You don't know," said Terri, and I looked at her, looked at her brown eyes with their thick fringe of mascara, like spiders around them. She didn't look back at me, and I wondered. But wondering was all any of us would ever do. We'd put on silky cocktail dresses and blow-dry our hair and walk into the weddings and christenings and confirmations, our husbands checking the coats, slipping the tickets into the pockets of their suit jackets, and we'd look like happy couples, and some of us maybe were, and lots of us likely weren't, but none of us would ever talk about it. I'd been stupid when I got married, figured it was just like an extended dating relationship, one dinner and movie after another, sex in a real bed or even on the kitchen floor. I should have known by the way the photographer made us behave for the wedding pictures—"Now look down at the ring . . . look up at him . . . hold up the flowers"—that a lot of it would be putting up a good front, day after day, week after week. Until if we were lucky, if there wasn't cancer or a car wreck, our grandkids would someday toss us a fiftieth anniversary party in a catering hall and toast us, their eyes wet, for the simple fact of our stubborn marital longevity, confusing it with love.

And yet, and yet. At Robert's First Communion party Bobby and I sat side by side at the table as our son thanked everyone for coming, solemn at age eight in his little navy blue suit and his first tie, red-and-blue striped, and my right hand found Bobby's left, and I looked at him and saw the father of my son, the beginning of my grown-up life, the person who slept every night on the right side of my double bed, whose shorts I'd folded in a plastic basket for fifteen years. It was like there were two Bobbys, two Frans, two couples, and one was sitting at that table, knee nudging knee, breathless with love for our child and so, by some process of osmosis, for each other. The other Bobby and Fran stayed home, waiting for nightfall, she afraid of saying the wrong thing, he—well, I never knew what he felt.

Sometimes when I went to Cindy's house I looked at the pictures of her and her husband, Craig, and wondered whether there were two of them, too, the daytime and the nighttime couple, like masks of comedy and tragedy. And Mrs. Levitt and Irving. And strangers I saw in cars, sitting next to each other at stoplights, looking straight out the windshield, never at each other, living parallel lives.

"That princess and prince now?" Mrs. Levitt said. "There's a marriage that spelled trouble from the very beginning. And now, all of a sudden, here's the girlfriend and who knows what else."

"Remember how wrinkled her wedding dress was when she got out of the coach?"

"The princess?" Mrs. Levitt raised her hands to the sky in mute entreaty to some greater power. "I said to my friend Flo in Chicago, I said, Flo, you sit on silk and look what happens."

If Irving hadn't had his stroke only three weeks after they'd moved into the Lakeview, if she'd had time to make friends with the other women in the building, Mrs. Levitt would have gossiped about the super and the single woman on the ground floor, the dry cleaner and his nasty wife. Instead she talked about the people in the papers: the princess and her divorce, Streisand and Sinatra—"not a happy woman," Mrs. Levitt said about one, and "not a happy man" about the other—the president and the first lady. Mrs. Levitt got the tabloids when Mrs. Winkelman down the hall left them with her recycled newspapers; she would listen on Tuesday evenings for the sound of the Winkelman door and then sneak down to the incinerator and ease the *Star* and the *Enquirer* out from the twine bundle. "Look, Irving, here's that one you liked from *Dallas*," Mrs. Levitt would call across the room. "She's not holding up too good."

"Irving," she would say as she smoothed the blankets, "you remember how you lost all our vacation money in Vegas on half an hour at the blackjack?"

"You think I didn't see you that time with Mamie in the wet bar of their place?" she said as his mouth gaped.

"You were always cheap, Irving," she mused as she went into the drawer and took out fresh pajamas, laundered so often they were soft as silk. "Twelve years it took me to get a decent stove. And even then I had to hear about it for the next twelve."

Sometimes Mr. Levitt made a sound like a groan or a wheeze, and she would say, "Yes, yes, yes." And something in the way she said it made me believe she had been saying it for years, that she had said it when her husband said, "Look at how fast that crazy man in the Chevy is driving," or "It's gonna pour any minute," or "This is one tough piece of meat," that Mrs. Levitt had replied "Yes, yes, yes" just as she did today. I hate to say it, but the two of us ignored Mr. Levitt, paid him less mind than the television set or the coffeemaker. But I had the feeling Mrs. Levitt had been doing that for quite awhile.

"You listening, Fran, or am I talking to myself?" Bobby would say sometimes, late at night. God, how I wanted to say, you're talking to yourself, Bobby. But I wouldn't have dared.

"He was a good worker," Mrs. Levitt said as I irrigated and then reconnected Irving's catheter, both of us looking dispassionately at her husband's slack penis. "He made a good living. Sales. He sold automobile parts. I never even learned to drive. Too busy to teach me, right, Irving?" She smiled. "Something like that," she said. "You want tuna on toast for lunch?"

"You don't have to go to any trouble for me," I said.

"It's no trouble. I made lunch for the last girl, and she was colored. Not that I minded, but I think Irving wasn't so happy about it." She opened the refrigerator and took out a loaf of wheat bread. "Were you, Irving?" she called into the other room, and put the bread in the toaster. "But I have to say, she wasn't rude. We had one before her, she handled Irving like a sack of potatoes. I called the agency, I said she had to go. I think they sent me the colored girl for spite. Not that we minded, right, Irving?"

"Do you need anything?" I said as I was leaving each day, and Mrs. Levitt said no until I'd been there two weeks. I suppose by then she'd decided she could trust me. She put her head to one side, a girlish gesture, put one finger beneath her chin. Then she reached for her purse, a black tote bag with big white polka dots. "I'll give you the money, you'll bring *People* magazine," she said.

"I'll get it," I said. "Don't worry about the money."

"And some other time you'll bring a Big Mac," she said. "Big Mac is Irving's favorite fast food. Big Mac and senior coffee. A large coffee and only a quarter if you're over sixty-five. Which we are, right, Irving?" She straightened his covers, tucked him in as though he was a child. No children, Mrs. Levitt had told me, making a vague motion toward her midsection and moving on to some movie star's marriage. Just her and Irving, forty-eight years and counting.

The supermarket on the strip up the street from our apartment was as big as a football field, so brightly lit that it bleached out the skin of even the tannest women pushing their kids around the aisles in carts. Jets of water sprayed the peppers and plums so they seemed irresistible, more like art objects than produce. In one corner was a pharmacy, in another a bank, in a third a bakery section that gave off the smell of cinnamon unexpectedly as you came upon it, like one of those perfume inserts in a magazine. It was as though they'd put an entire American small town in an airplane hangar and then arranged and lit it to best advantage. It made me think of how I'd imagined heaven when I was a kid, white light and something for everybody. People were always hollering to their kids to find a second cart, as though they had been seduced into soup and cheese and instant pudding without meaning to be.

Robert and I could only buy as much as we could carry, but for the two of us that was usually plenty, and I was careful about how I spent my money. We'd been in the apartment for almost three months and I still hadn't paid any rent, didn't even know how much it was. It was another one of Patty Bancroft's mysteries; "We'll take care of that end of things" she'd said when I asked how long the rent would be taken care of. So I opened a credit union account with the home-care company, putting away some money every week just in case. I wore my uniform and my hand-me-downs; mainly I spent money on treats for Robert, trips to the arcades with Bennie, weekend fast-food lunches, sometimes a shirt or a comic book. I didn't want him to feel deprived, to feel poor as well as rootless. Twice he'd had nightmares and I'd sat with him until he fell back suddenly into sleep; he couldn't, or wouldn't, say much about the dreams, just that there were bad guys, that he was running, that there was darkness, falling, fear. Twice he'd asked to stay home from school with a stomach ache. Once beneath his bed I found a piece of looseleaf paper: "Dear Dad" in his scratchy, back-slanting penmanship, "I bet you are very surprised to—" Then, nothing.

Perhaps I'd told him dinner was ready, knocked at his door. Perhaps he'd heard Bennie calling from downstairs. I threw the paper away.

"You hungry?" I said as I found a cart whose wheels worked. Robert shrugged. He shrugged a lot, too, these days. Are you tired? Shrug. Do you want to watch a movie? Shrug. How could he care about anything at all, when in an instant it might disappear, when the outlines of our life were as faint and transparent as the picture on the old television in the living room. It was like that Etch-a-Sketch he'd gotten from Santa, year before last. You drew the picture and then turned the toy over, and the image was gone, nothing but gray, waiting for the next one, just as fleeting.

I didn't know how much I'd be able to buy him for Christmas this year, or how in hell I'd ever get through it, get through the tree and the meal and the goddamned carols. I pushed the cart and stopped thinking. I'd gotten good at that, at just cutting thoughts off, as though I was changing channels. From Christmas to chicken cacciatore.

The one thing I wouldn't scrimp on was food. Once the heat began to wane a bit in what, up north, passed for the beginning of winter, once I began to feel the least bit at home in the windowless kitchen in the apartment, I'd begun to cook the Italian food that Ann Benedetto had taught me to make years before. I figured it would make Robert feel more at home, the way it had made me feel as if I was making one, really making one, all those years ago.

"My mother needs a daughter," Bobby had said, "and you need to learn to cook a decent meal." Every Sunday he dropped me off, when we were first married, at his mother's house, in his mother's kitchen so clean that a spot of red sauce looked like blood. I took a shower before I went, did my makeup, but sometimes I thought she could smell it on me, what we'd been doing before, while Ann was at nine o'clock mass.

Her cooking was a list of don'ts: don't buy cheap cheese, don't put the sauce on too high, don't use garlic salt instead of real garlic, don't layer the lasagna more than three times no matter how deep the pan. A list of don'ts, a list of Bobby doesn'ts: Bobby doesn't like the hot sausage, Bobby doesn't like the thin spaghetti, Bobby doesn't like the bread from Emilio's bakery, only from Marie's. Most Sundays she had a new shirt for him, a soft, fine double knit with a collar in a dark color. "I was at the outlets," she always said. Later she bought things for Robert, polo shirts and oxford button-downs. "Rags," she called T-shirts and blue jeans. "Garbage," she called frozen food.

"She came from nothing," Bobby's grandmother

hissed when Ann went to the bathroom. "You just remember that. Don't take any crap from her. She's half Polish, for Christ's sake. My son, God love him—she gave him such a time." Bobby's grandmother always liked me, until the day she died. She gave me her cameos, that I'd had to leave behind in the rosewood jewelry box on my bureau. God, I'd thought to myself, Bobby'll really kill me if I take Mama's brooches. Mama, we always called his grandmother. Ann, I called my mother-in-law. She never asked me to call her anything else.

But she made me a cook, and so I could make Robert meatballs and braciola, pasta e fagioli and lasagna, little pieces of home at this flimsy table 2,000 miles away. He invited Bennie for dinner, and the two of them hunched over their plates without speaking until finally their mouths were shiny with tomato sauce and grease. Bennie's mother did the same for Robert: beans and rice, chicken with a sauce of tomatoes and onions. Bless our boys, talking with their mouths full.

"You want chicken cacciatore?" I said as Robert and I traipsed down the endless meat aisles in the supermarket, and he nodded, bent over another video game, which he'd traded his old one for to some boy at school. This one was soldiers and kickboxing. It made little grunting noises when one man hit another with his booted foot. *Unh. Unh. Unh.* We went past pork and beef to poultry. At the front of the store a bulletin board held flyers with pictures of missing children. The faces changed twice a month. I knew because I always looked at them while I was pretending to get a cart with wheels that really worked. All the kids looked happy in the pictures, as though they didn't care that they were missing.

"Don't put mushrooms in it," Robert said.

"You don't have to eat the mushroom."

"Can I go look at the comics?" he said without raising his head from his game.

"Where?"

"I don't know. They're over there. I'll find them."

"I'd rather you stayed with me."

"Mom, I'm not a baby. I'm all right. Just let me go."

"You come back to me in ten minutes," I said as he trotted away. I still hated to let him out of my sight. Each afternoon when I heard the school bus pull up I stood behind the screen, a peeping Tom of a parent, making sure he got off the bus and in the house safe and sound. Sometimes I wanted to hold Bennie and say, thank you, thank you, over and over again, thank you for being an ordinary boy, for making my boy seem ordinary, too, for going everywhere he goes.

"Where's your father?" I heard Bennie ask Robert one day, but nicely, softly. There had been a long silence from the bedroom, or maybe it just seemed long because I was holding my breath. Then Robert's voice came, low: "He and my mom are split up."

"Jonathan's mom and dad split up last year," Bennie said. "Allyson lives with her mom. I don't know where her father is. Sean, too. His parents got divorced when he was real little. He stays with his dad every weekend in East Preston." It was as though he would go on and on with his litany of fractured families, of kids walking on the broken glass of their parents' lives. "Your mom cooks good," Bennie had said after a moment.

"I know," said Robert. "She cooks really good at Christmas." I held the back of my hand against my mouth and a little saliva ran over my fingers with my tears. Everything we'd lost, everything I'd forced him to leave, seemed somehow to be in that simple sentence. She cooks really good at Christmas. In that moment I thought of going back, of walking in through that familiar door just so I could see the look on Robert's face. All my life I'd tried to make my boy happy, and now to keep him safe I had to make him sad. And angry, too. I could see that in the set of his mouth, sometimes. I'm not sure he knew who he was angry at. One night, doing his homework, he'd thrown his math book onto the floor and hit the wall with his pencil and I'd stood up from the couch, but stopped, so still, because the jerky choreography of violence and rage was so familiar to me that I couldn't come any closer, even when the object was long division.

"This is so stupid," he'd shouted. "This is all different than what we learned last year, and besides, it doesn't make any sense, the way they want us to carry things. And she makes us show all our work, and there's not even enough space on the page."

"What about using another piece of paper?" I said quietly.

"We're not allowed, Mom," he screamed, and tears were beginning to run down his face. "You don't understand. We're not allowed. We have to do it on this sheet or we get points off. This is so stupid." And he pushed over the chair, ran upstairs, slammed his door so hard that I swear I felt an answering vibration in the living-room floor, like the aftershock from an earthquake.

"You want to talk about things?" I said that night as I sat on the edge of his bed.

"Nah," he said.

"It might make you feel better."

"I feel okay."

"You didn't seem okay when you were doing your math homework."

"It's really stupid, the way they do it here," he'd said.

I watched him walk away in the supermarket, his

head still bent over the video game, skirting the carts intuitively, the way I imagine a blind man negotiates his living room. The long bones in his legs had begun to grow, so that he had that Tinkertoy look a boy has as he becomes a young man, sticks and knobs precariously held together. He would be taller than this father, and better looking, too. He had my nose, not the hawk beak that made Bobby look so terrifying sometimes, his black eyes predatory above it. What else was it that boy, Tyrone Biggs, had said from the witness stand? "That cop, man, he scared me."

"Did he threaten you?" his stupid defense attorney had thundered, breaking the rules, asking a question he didn't know the answer to.

"No, man. He just looked at me. Looked at me real cold."

The way some mothers look at their kid for birth defects when they're babies, try to suss out signs of stupidity as they learn to walk and talk, so I watched and waited to see that dark, lowering look on my boy's face, the look the sky has before the rain comes down in gray sheets. Three months I'd watched him for signs of colic, finally relaxed into motherhood when the danger period passed. It'd take longer this time, looking not for gas but for the early signs of rage. It was why I tried to draw him out, so that he could vent that way instead of the other. "Use your words," I used to say when he was little, and most of the time he did. But once, walking away from St. Stannie's in the morning, I'd heard a group of boys calling him Robert the Hobbit, of all things, no more than a silly singsong following him down the street, Robert the Hobbit, Robert the Hobbit, as he trudged along the pavement with his head down. And then, almost without breaking stride, he'd turned and hurled himself at them, his arms pinwheeling, his eyes big. "Shut up!" he shrieked as he hit and hit and hit, the other boys stunned, backing away, putting their hands up palms out. "Shut up!" until I pulled him away, screaming myself, "For God's sake, Robert, stop. Stop it!"

"Daddy said you have to fight back," he'd said as I hectored him on the way home. And when I complained, Bobby just waved his hand and shrugged. "The trouble is, Fran, that you don't know about boys," he'd said.

Moving away from me down the long market aisle, Robert looked just as Bobby might have as a boy, except that there was something defenseless in the way he held himself, a kind of roundness to back and shoulder. And I wondered whether Bobby had ever been like that, defenseless, before biceps and bravado and badge. Before me. Or whether Robert had learned to walk like that from me, from all the years that I'd made myself small, trying not to attract notice, give offense. Suddenly, as though he'd felt my eyes on his back, Robert looked over his shoulder and smiled, a smile that on that dark pinched face was more than a smile, was a hand, a hug, a kiss. That was the smile Bobby had had, too, when he saw me when we were both young, that made my spirit levitate, warm from the inside out.

"You know what, Frances Ann?" Bobby had said, sitting next to my bed in the single room on the hospital's maternity floor, Robert's misshapen little head cupped in his palm. "We got everything."

Jesus, I loved him. There, I said it. It makes me feel stupid, sometimes, feeling my scars, the spots where you can just make out the damage and the ones where the bruises and hurts live on only in my head. I loved Bobby, and he loved me. Anyone who heard him say it once would never disbelieve it. In the beginning I loved him, loved him, loved him pure and simple. And then after a while I loved the idea of him, the good Bobby, who came to me every once in a while and rubbed my back and kissed my fingers. And I loved our life, the long stretches of tedium and small pleasures that marked most of our time together. Our life was like a connect-the-dots drawing, and those were the lines, the bad things only the haphazard arrangement of dots they connected.

And now all the love goes into what's left of that life,

one boy, his basketball shoes too big for his little body. I watch him and I'm afraid my face looks the way Ann Benedetto's face looked when she watched Bobby, like a hungry cat when it hears the can opener, all eyes and appetite. I'm afraid that I'll wind up the way she did, with nothing but the casual, almost charitable, almost condescending affection that a grown man has for his mother once he's moved on to another woman, another source of intensive care. Alone in that spotless house, with the photographs on top of the television, Bobby at four, his foot tucked under him, his chubby fingers wrapped around his knee. Bobby at twenty-six, in his dress uniform. Across the living room, on the wall unit, was the photograph of her husband in his own police blues.

"My old man was some piece of work," Bobby always said. He'd been shot, Robert, Sr., by a junkie who didn't know how to wave a gun around during a bar robbery without having the thing go off. It was two months after we started going out, and I cried at the funeral, not for Lt. Benedetto, who I'd met only once, but for his son. The sound of the bagpipes was like strange birds, and the cops were like an army, blue with black swipes of elastic over their badges.

That's all he ever said, *some piece of work*. Never an anecdote, or a word of affection or even anger. His father was the stone in Bobby's heart. And maybe his own father would be the stone in Robert's. The patterns, the patterns, as inviolate as a clan tartan. Red, green, black, blue, father, son.

I'd been standing staring into the depths of a half-filled cart, and when I looked up a tall man had stopped Robert at the end of the aisle and was putting a hand on his shoulder. Suddenly I felt my stomach empty out, felt as though I might faint. I pushed forward, but there were two elderly women crowding the aisles, peering at coupons, and by the time I got past them Robert wasn't there. The man was looking at chickens, or pretending to. Looking too hard, I thought, like a bad actor, so that he didn't look up until I'd planted myself in front of him.

"Excuse me," I said. "What were you saying to that child?"

"What?"

"That boy? The one with the dark hair? What were you saying to him?" I realized the two women with the coupons were looking at me. My voice was too loud, even to myself.

"Robert Crenshaw? I teach him PE. At the elementary school."

The relief in my posture, the surrender to the safe and commonplace in my shoulders, head, face, must have been so profound that he peered at me perplexed for a moment, then smiled. "You're Robert's mother," he said. "And I just scared the heck out of you. I am really, really sorry."

"No, no, forget it. It was silly. It's just—"

"—that you have to be more careful today than when we were kids. Hey, in my job I know." He stuck out a big hand, thick-fingered. My own disappeared inside it, then reappeared as I pulled away, like a small fish released from the maw of a big one. He was a bigger man than I'd thought, seeing him across the parking lot and lawn of the school that first day, big and bulky, flushed and friendly, with thinning blond hair and light eyes behind aviator glasses. What kind of animal does your gym teacher remind you of? I'd ask Robert walking home, another game we played. And the answer would be something good-natured, plodding, big and bighearted. A bear maybe.

"Mike Riordan."

"Beth Crenshaw."

"I know," he said. "You and Mrs. Roerbacker work in the library."

"Sorry. I missed meeting you somehow."

"I'm a gym rat," he said. "I'm practically mildewed. You from New York?"

"No," I said, feeling my shoulders tighten again. "Delaware."

"You sound like New York," he said. "I've been meaning to call you about Robert."

"Why?"

"Hey, he's fine. You know, he's new. He'll open up more when he gets used to the drill here. There's no problem. I just want him to play on our soccer team. No big deal, no high pressure, two practices a week and they're before dinnertime. I never yell and scream, and I give them off the day before a big test. But we start next week and he'd need to stay after school and either walk home or have you pick him up. He's new and he didn't seem too sure it would be okay with you. Bennie Castro's playing, if that makes a difference."

"I'll talk to him. It's fine. It would be good for him."

"Great. Great." He paused. "I'll send home a permission slip and some more information. You can call me if you have any questions. I'm the vice principal, too, whatever that means. Call about anything, the school, the homework, whatever." He hesitated, looking into his cart. "Would you mind if I asked you something?"

I shook my head.

"How much do you know about chicken?"

"Chicken?"

"Cooking chicken."

"I've cooked a lot of chickens, if that's what you're asking."

"You know those things that you can put inside the chicken, sort of holds them standing up so they cook faster? They've got them back with the pots and pans and things. They're metal, shaped kind of like a big golf tee. Do those things work?"

I laughed. "I don't know," I said. "It never occurred to me to buy one. A chicken only takes an hour anyhow. Why rush it?"

"That's what I thought. Thanks," he said, staring into the meat case.

Suddenly I heard Gracie's voice, as clear as if it was coming over the loudspeaker instead of John Mack Carter's tips for using exciting, exotic cilantro in a variety of dishes with an international flair. Where were we sitting, Grace and I? Was it that coffee bar on Lexington Avenue, where the counterman always called her "Professor," or the Greek restaurant in the Village with the homemade pita that made us both so full we would groan all the way to the subway? The Greek place, I think, and Grace talking about the tall man she kept running into at D'Agostino's, who wanted to know about tarragon, about potatoes, about sour and heavy and light cream. "As though I wouldn't know that asking a woman about how to cook is the oldest pick-up line in the book," Grace said, shaking her head.

"I didn't know that," I'd said.

"When was the last time somebody picked you up?" she said.

"Almost twenty years ago," I'd said. Bobby, in the bar where Tommy Dolan had introduced us. Bobby, one black apostrophe of hair over his forehead, saying, "Hey, Fran Flynn. I guess if everybody likes you I might like you too." Bobby, leaning against the bar, a perfectly natural pose, his elbows back, his big forearms knotted, his pelvis thrust forward, which was the whole point.

"Well, good luck," I said to Mike Riordan, and then felt myself turning hot, and red, the same way I'd colored that first time I met Bobby. I felt foolish as I strode off to pick up parsley, tomatoes, and garlic. Soccer season. Rules, practices, uniforms. Maybe while Robert was at practice, after I got home from the Levitts, I would do something to his room, cheap bright curtains and a new quilt, some more posters, a desk. I thought there had been an old desk in one corner of Cindy's basement. Vermicelli, chicken stock, tomato paste. The cart was getting too full; Robert would complain about the weight of the bag all the way home, particularly if he had a comic he wanted to be reading instead. It was time to check out, head home. A stockboy sent me seven aisles over, to where the comic books shared an aisle with greeting cards and paperbacks, but only one elderly woman was there, reading birthday cards with her face close to their gaudy surfaces. I walked slowly, snaking through aisle after aisle, thinking about how big the market was, bigger than any I'd visited in the city, looking for Robert. Looking and looking. I began weaving through other shoppers, past cans of soup and coffee, cases of Coke and Pepsi, stacks of paper towels and toilet paper, back to the comic aisle, empty now. Part of my mind kept thinking that I needed paper towels, and the other part was saying, shouting, screaming over and over again, "Robert? Ba? Baby? Where are you?" I turned in aisle sixteen, dairy, and made my way back again. "Have you seen a boy, about ten, in a green T-shirt with a tiger on the front?" I began to ask the other shoppers, and "No," they said, no, sorry, no I haven't. Of course they haven't, thought one part of my mind, because he's in a car now, driving down the highway, saying, hey Dad, I missed you Dad, how's Grandmom, where we going, when are we going to go back and get Mommy?

I was moving so fast that I bumped into someone's cart and knocked a box of cereal from it. I came around the corner in frozen foods and almost collided with a man holding a box of macaroni and cheese, reading the back, and I saw that it was the gym teacher again but I suddenly couldn't recall his first name, only that he wanted Robert to play soccer, that I needed paper towels, and that my son was gone. He knew right away, as he looked up, saw me, smiled, then frowned, that something was wrong.

"I can't find Robert," I said, my voice an octave higher than usual, almost falsetto.

"Calm down," he said. "Calm down." He took my arm at the elbow and led me toward the front of the store, leaving our two carts next to the freezer cases, glass and chrome and foggy windows like the cases in the morgue at the hospital, where we nurses tried never to go if we could help it. I could tell by the feel of his hand at my elbow that he was used to taking charge. "He can't have gone far," he said, like it was something he'd said before. At the window where they cashed checks he stuck his head inside. "Excuse me," he called, and then I remembered that his name was Mike. A heavy girl with bad skin came to the window. CUSTOMER SERVICE, said the sign over her head.

"I'm on break," she said.

"We've lost a child," Mike Riordan said. "Can you do a page or something? Robert is his name, Robert Crenshaw."

"I can't page without the manager."

"Where's the manager?"

She called into the back "Where's Lenny?" and there was a mumbled sound, and then she came out of the booth and I started to cry, my hands over my face. "Kids get lost in here a lot," she said, as if to be helpful, and then, calling over to the closest register, "Pete, where's Lenny?"

"Hold on," Pete said. "I got a price check."

"Where's the paging equipment?" Mike Riordan said pleasantly.

The girl pointed back toward the booth, and he said, "Use it right now or I'm going to go in and use it myself."

"Don't have a spas, mister," she said. "Your wife should have been watching him."

"There's Lenny," Pete called, and Mike turned toward a dark man in white shirt and pants. HERE TO SERVE YOU: LENNY said the tag on his shirt.

"Please," I said.

"They want me to page for their kid," said the girl. "They can't find him. I told them I couldn't page without you saying so."

"He's ten," I said. "He was supposed to be in the comic aisle. Where the cards and magazines are."

"Skinny kid?" said Lenny. "Dark hair, green shirt?"

"Yes," I said, knowing the worst, knowing what Lenny would say next, describing the man who'd left with the kid as dark, nice-looking, big through the arms and shoulders, looked like the kid, looked like his dad. And Mike Riordan would want to call the police and I would want to die, right here in the supermarket, rather than go home to that apartment alone. Or back to Brooklyn.

"I just threw him out on his butt. He's probably still out in the parking lot."

"What?" Mike Riordan said, but I was already halfway to the doors. The pavement between the store and the parking lot was full of people loading groceries into the backs of their cars, but off to one side, where the gum machines and the little automated horse ride stood, Robert was sitting on the ground, his arms held tight around his knees, his head down as though he was one of those little black bugs, the ones that roll up into a ball to protect themselves when they're disturbed.

I ran to him, touched his arm, and he jumped, then jumped at me, almost knocked me down as he threw his arms around me. Neither of us spoke and I just held him, held him tight, saying nothing, trying to stop the shaking in his back and shoulders. Then I heard a voice behind me say, "Hi, Robert. You okay?" But Robert shook his head and kept it pressed to the front of my body, although his arms had fallen to his sides.

"That bastard, excuse my French, says that he thought Robert was alone and that they have a rule against unsupervised kids in the store," Mike Riordan said from behind me. "Apparently they've had some problems with vandalism, shoplifting, and he just throws kids out if they're by themselves."

Robert's head snapped up, and spit flew from his mouth as he cried, "I told him and told him that my mom was there and I could find her. I told him I wasn't unsupervised. He just kept saying sure, sure, she'll find you outside. He wouldn't listen to me."

"Oh, sweetie," I said, holding him tight, but he pulled away.

"He wouldn't even let me look for you. I told him where you were, and then you weren't there. Where did you go? Where did you go?" He was so loud now that an elderly man came over to peer at him, at us, as though to save him from being abducted by the woman in the faded blue shorts and white polo shirt, the man in the blue button-down and the aviator glasses. "He's fine, he's fine, he's just upset," Mike said.

"I told him," Robert said, crying, and I reached for him again but he pushed me away. He slumped back against the big glass window at the front of the supermarket.

"I told that guy I'd be writing to the head of the supermarket chain," Mike Riordan said. "That was the most stupid, sadistic thing I've ever seen. All he had to do was walk him around the market."

Robert mumbled something, and I leaned in to listen. "I don't care what you said," he said. "I told him that my dad would kill him. I told him that he'd shoot him with his gun."

"Let's go home," I said.

"I'll drive you," Mike Riordan said.

That night Robert and I had frozen pizza for dinner. We'd left all our groceries in the store; so had Mike Riordan. "I hate this place," Robert said, and I did not reply.

I was frightened then, and no amount of paint, no optimistic plans, no hours in the school library, no TYs from Jennifer nor "Sit, Mrs. Nurse" from Mrs. Levitt could take that feeling away. No framed prints hung between the windows could change the fact that the blinds were drawn, sullen and mute. That moment in the supermarket, when I was certain Robert was gone, saw only emptiness in the space where he had been, was like a dress rehearsal for disaster. Afterward, adrenaline was always in my blood, as though I swallowed it down every morning with my vitamins. It was like those times years ago when I went to police funerals with Bobby, and felt, as the sound of taps floated over the cemetery, as though I was rehearsing the agony of losing him. It was the greatest pain I could imagine. But I was young then.

Coastal storms blew across the state all through the end of October, and the dried and yellowed branches of palms would slither across the roof over my bedroom sometimes late into the night, the wind blowing gravel from the center courtyard with a sound like bullets spraying the brick walls outside. The storm windows shook in their frames, and I lay on my back staring at the ceiling, waiting for the surreptitious sound of the front door opening. I went over it every night in my mind, how it might have been different, how I could have saved us all: me and Robert and Bobby, too. Sometimes I'd lull myself to sleep with memories of the two of us pushing Robert in his stroller around the neighborhood, Bobby's brawny arm brushing against my own, the hair rising on both, his black and thick, mine pale and downy. Or I'd see Bobby in my mind in the backyard in September, picking tomatoes, looking at each one carefully before he put it into a colander Robert was holding solemnly, proudly, at chest level, as though he was a little acolyte, a backyard altar boy. I guess it told me everything I needed to know about my past life, that I'd lie in bed crying while those pictures passed before my mind's eye, feeling the ordinary soft sweetness of those summer days, and yet listening at the same time for the noise of someone coming into the apartment to get me, to push me around, to punch me out, to take me out. I was lonely for that other Bobby, the one who whispered in my ear in bed so he wouldn't wake the boy, who sometimes held his hand over my mouth so I wouldn't make too much noise when he was on top of me. "You'll scare the kid, Fran," he'd say close to my ear, and I could tell by the sound of his voice that he liked that, liked that he made me squirm and scream that way.

But he made me scream those other ways, too, or at least moan and cry: please, no. That was my marriage: please, yes, sometimes; please, no, the others. If only I could have stayed with one Bobby and left the other.

"You had no choice," I said over and over to myself. Sometimes I said it out loud in the little box of a bedroom.

After that day in the supermarket, Robert was scared, too. I could tell by the way he behaved in the daylight, truculent and distant, when he'd kick a book across the floor or sit alone in his room, staring at the yellow aluminum siding of the house next door. I could tell by the way he behaved at night, trembling and clingy. He said the bathroom plumbing was keeping him awake, gurgling and burping through the thin wall, and asked if he could sleep in my bed. I wanted to let him, so much, if only to have someone I loved next to me, to help me sleep. But I knew it wasn't good for him. It reminded me of when he was a baby, when I'd had to let him cry himself to sleep, to teach him not to keep getting up in the middle of the night, to keep him from being so cranky during the day. Bobby held me down, the first night, when Robert wailed for twenty minutes straight and I wanted to go to him. The next night it was ten minutes, and the next he fell asleep before I'd even gotten down the hall. I thought about that all the time now, how sometimes you have to do hard things to your kids to do the right thing for them in the long run. But I still felt the way I'd felt that night, ready to give up, give in, at a moment's notice.

We struck a bargain, Robert and I. We dragged his mattress into my room, next to my bed. I draped my arm over the side and held his hand. He slept there for four days, then dragged the mattress back. It's easier to heal, I guess, when you're ten. I still hear noises in the night, the plumbing, the wind, the cars, the past.

I hurry down the dusty streets of Lake Plata, my walk just this side of a run, and wait for Robert to come home from school every day. Sometimes I hear him out in the courtyard talking to Bennie, the two of them fooling around, whacking each other with their sweatshirts, pulling off each other's caps. Sometimes I just hear the slam of a car door when a mother has arranged to drop him off, or when Mr. Riordan has driven some of them home from soccer. "Thank you," I hear Robert call. He is never really late. He knows.

"Hi," I say as he drops his backpack just inside the door, but it is as though now my real life has begun, as though I've shopped and cleaned and tended to other people in a kind of trance. I never felt this way before, when I worked at the hospital and Robert went after school to his grandmother's for an hour or two. But my life was different then, larger. Now it has been whittled away to its essentials. I make certain kinds of foods because Robert likes them. I bake so that he will have nice desserts. The refrigerator is covered with his test papers. I even bought a baby monitor, the kind we once kept by our bed so we could hear the sounds from his crib, so that he would not even whimper without me knowing it. Now I have the receiver under Robert's bed, the monitor under my pillow. Sometimes I can hear him mumbling in his dreams. It puts me to sleep, like the sound of the ocean, knowing he is there. Knowing that if someone opens his bedroom window, I will hear it.

Often I go in and watch as he sleeps the sleep of a ten-year-old, as close to unconsciousness as a healthy human being can be. I know my greatest fear is his fondest wish. Daddy. Daddy. Daddy. He loved Bobby as I once had, viscerally, from the gut, with no regard to events. Bobby was just the sort of father that a small boy would be likely to love. "Does your dad have a gun?" his friends could ask, and he could nod, safe and secure. Once in second grade he wrote a story about what we did, Bobby and I. The first sentence was "My daddy makes sure bad things never happen."

The copy of *One Fish, Two Fish* we'd brought from home sat on Robert's bedside table, and sometimes he read it, although once or twice he said he was going to give it to Chad Roerbacker. The fish looked so friendly and familiar, smiling up from the page, their cowlicks splayed, their fins akimbo. One night Robert was paging through it and said, "Remember when I was five and you used to lie down next to me on the bed while I fell asleep?" I was sorry, later, standing by his bed, looking down at him, that I hadn't said or done more. Next night I slid out of my rubber flip-flops and lay down next to Robert, smiling, my arm over his chest.

"Mom, no offense, okay?" he said, "but I'm a little too big for this."

But before he went to sleep he would always suffer me to sit by the side of his bed, and he would ask me questions about my childhood, about whether I liked sharing a room with Aunt Grace, about whether it was scary to be home alone while my mother worked, about my father's job as a fireman and the big fires in which he'd been involved, as though he was constructing from the ground up a life he'd loved and lost, a life I'd seemingly obliterated in one trip. He particularly liked the one about the time a man with a gun had robbed the bakery on a Sunday morning when I was sixteen, in the desultory fallow period between the 9:00 and 10:30 masses, when I usually rearranged the doughnut trays and wiped down the glass cases. "You're kidding, right?" I'd said when he asked for the cash. And after I'd filled a brown bag with bills he'd demanded doughnuts, cream-filled, chocolate-frosted. "I'm not giving anybody pastry who just robbed the place," I'd said, and then Mr. Orlofsky from down the block had come in for his Sunday morning seedless rye, and the man had turned and run from the counter, clutching the bag and the gun, knocking Mr. Orlofsky down.

"Tell the doughnut story," Robert said, and then, after, "That was cool. That was brave."

"Jesus God, what a stupid thing to do," Bobby had said on our second date, when I'd told him the story.

"Tell the doughnut story," Robert said. "I told it to Bennie. He thought I made it up."

"I would have given him kaiser rolls," I said, "but not pastry."

"Tell it from the beginning." He played with my hands, with my fingers, as I told it again—the register, the bills falling into the bag like play money, the sound of the bell on the door as Mr. Orlofsky came inside. Each night, as I stood to go downstairs, he would ask one question:

Does Grandmom know where we are?

Does Aunt Grace know where we are?

Does Mrs. Selick, the third-grade teacher, or Father Charles, who gave him First Communion, or Mrs. Pinto?

And over and over I would say no. No, honey, no, Ba, until finally one night he told me he didn't want to be called Ba anymore, if I didn't mind, if it didn't hurt my feelings, no offense, but he was too old now.

He never asked "Does Daddy know where we are?" He knew that was the point. I'd sent Grace that note with the photographs because I hadn't wanted her to file a missing persons report. But I was as sure as I was sure of anything that Bobby would never do that, would know that the guys in the missing persons section almost always found a missing spouse healthier, happier, somewhere else. He would never countenance the whispers around the force: "You know Benedetto, the guy in narcotics? His wife took off on him, man. Took his kid, too."

Why had I been frightened of that young flat-faced cop at the door of the elementary school that first morning? There would be no outside interference. If Bobby came it would be on his own, slithering over the roof like a big palm frond in a high wind. But I'd be ready for him. Mr. Castro had a tangle of tools in the closet just inside the door of the Castro apartment, and one day I'd asked to borrow his crowbar, and hadn't given it back. It was under my bed. No matter when I touched it it was always cold, like a dead thing beneath me.

Robert allowed himself to be looked after now, to be babied, in his father's words. It was as though the supermarket had given him a taste of something, an inkling of terror and of loss. Our nighttime conversations were the ones he'd had when he was a smaller boy, with less scar tissue: "What if," I said at breakfast, and he said, softly, sweetly, "we went to the beach . . ."

". . . and you had a really big boogie board . . ."

". . . and got good enough at riding the waves that I could stand up like a surfer . . ."

". . . and dolphins swam up to shore and swam around you . . ."

". . . and I could understand what they were saying . . ."

"Yo, Robert," Bennie yelled from outside in the dusty quadrangle. "The bus is coming."

"We'll go to the beach soon," I said as I kissed Robert good-bye. "I promise."

It wasn't really good-bye at all, only see you soon, for every morning I followed the bus route on foot, met up with Cindy just as I had that first day. She usually brought me something: a jar of collagen cream, a crock of genuine Vermont maple syrup, tomatoes from her parents' farm. "Oh, please," she'd say dismissively when I tried to thank her. It was easier to thank her obliquely. "I love that perfume," I'd say, or "That's a good color on you," and she'd smile. Her teeth overlapped in the front, and she always smiled with her mouth closed, unless she was having a really good time, and then she forgot.

"What's in the bag?" she said the Monday morning after the supermarket, and I pulled out a jar of my red sauce, what Bobby's family always called gravy. "Bless you," she said. "I'll just dump it over some ziti tonight."

"If my mother-in-law could hear the way you say zee-tee, she'd have a stroke," I said.

"She's your ex-mother-in-law, hon, so who cares?" said Cindy. "She Italian?"

"She's a witch," I said.

"That's nice. What else you got in there?"

"Running shoes," I said.

"Oh, please," Cindy said.

That's really how I got to know Mike Riordan, by running three mornings a week, the mornings, after the library, that I didn't have coffee and muffins at Cindy's house. It had come to me suddenly, as I was trying to make things normal, ordinary, better, as I was laying shelf paper in the slightly sticky kitchen cabinets. It had come to me again as I rose from bed after those nights awake, listening, when my body would feel stiff and old. It had come to me finally in Kmart, buying white crepe-soled shoes to wear to work, stopping in front of cheap running shoes and remembering the expensive pair Grace had given me for my twenty-seventh birthday, white nylon mesh with turquoise and purple stripes and a bubble of some gold gel in the heel. "Running makes you feel young again," Grace had said.

"To hell with you," I'd said. "I still *am* young."

I couldn't think of Gracie too much now. It made it too hard, harder than it was any other time. But when I was running those first few months in Brooklyn, when I was twenty-seven and trying to get pregnant and she was twenty-one and trying to get into grad school, I thought of her every time I ran. I always imagined her making a loop around Riverside Park as I made an arc around the bayfront in Brooklyn. "I'm running with you in my mind," I said, when we talked about our best times and our injuries, our knees and our hamstrings. I worked the eight-to-four shift at South Bay and I'd get up at six and run in the morning, when the air felt as though someone had just blown it out into the Brooklyn streets, like it had been delivered fresh each morning the way they used to deliver our milk in those smooth glass bottles when I was little. The lights were on in some houses when I went out, the cars steaming in the drive-ways in wintertime, a few people already on their way to the bus stop. But the streets were quiet except for the thud of my running shoes on the pavement in a perfect rhythm that made me feel that living through any day was possible. Two, sometimes three miles, the sun coming up over the bay, painting a streak of silver across the undulating water, making me squint and stagger until I'd turn away from dead east into the narrow streets running north. I'd watch them run the marathon on television and at the start it looked more like rush hour on the IRT than running, all of them jockeying for a square foot of pavement across the Verrazano-Narrows Bridge. I never ran like that. I liked being alone. Bobby had worked evenings and nights a lot. "It's when the bad guys work, so it's when I have to work, too," he told Robert later on, when the boy was old enough to understand. So I'd do my day shift, go to bed early, run just after or just before daybreak, depending on the seasons, and come in and take a shower as quietly as I could manage, carrying my shoes out into the hallway so the sound of them on the floor would not disturb him. On the kitchen counter would be the dirty plate from Bobby's dinner the night before, that I always left on a warm setting in the oven. Ann Benedetto hadn't raised her son to get his own meals or wash his own dishes.

I stopped running when I was six months pregnant with Robert and started again when he was a year old and I went back to work. Bobby didn't want me to do either one, said we didn't need the money and I didn't need the exercise. But I worked part-time on a night shift for a couple of years, so that I was mostly at the hospital when Robert was asleep, and once he started school I was gone only when he was. But that one hour in the morning was for me. In the dark, in the dining room, I laced on my shoes, pulled on my sweatshirt, pounded the pavement until my throat burned with the effort of breathing. I even ran once with two broken ribs, just to show Bobby what I was made of. "Frannie, Frannie, Fran," he mumbled that morning as I stripped off my shorts, the bed smelling of sweat and scotch and semen, because he never wanted me more than when I was broken and bruised. "You are one fucking piece of work."

I ran in Lake Plata after I got home from school in the morning, making a circuit of the blocks around the apartment complex: Poinsettia, Hibiscus, Royalton, Largo, Miramar, the musical words that danced attendance on the flat frame houses with the attached garages. The heat was like a sock stuffed in your throat, and sweat ran from me like tears, tickling and taunting my legs and chest and arms. I left my wire-rimmed glasses on the battered chest in the bedroom and the sun made fluorescent spots in front of me and waves of black at the periphery of my vision. Sometimes, despite myself, I'd see Brooklyn in my mind, and it was as though if I ran hard and fast enough, I'd come around the corner and I'd be home, really home, up the street from the bay in Brooklyn. The towels would be soft on my body and the carpeting soft under my feet and Robert would be wandering around half-asleep, dogged by little-boy problems, lost shoes, misplaced homework. And Bobby would be—where? Somewhere else. We'd have the idea of Bobby in the house, as though any moment he might walk in. It would be like a perfume, like the smell of gravy cooking on Sunday, or the turkey on Thanksgiving. So sweet, the smell of safety. I could almost smell it over the smell of gasoline and petunias on the back streets of Lake Plata. Sometimes I cried as I ran, but it was so hot and I looked so raddled that you couldn't even tell. There was no one to see, anyhow. Everyone was inside or at work.

One morning there was a man standing at the corner of Largo and Miramar, leaning against the corner of a chain-link fence behind which a dog reared, snapped, snarled, filled with frustration at my flashing legs just out of his reach. By the front gate was a sign: BEWARE OF THE DOG it said. It seemed so completely superfluous that I almost laughed. The man nodded at me. His arms were folded across his chest, red as summer roses from the heat.

For a week I ran around the streets, different routes on different days, with certain landmarks to guide me: a trailer painted turquoise as bright as a postcard of the Caribbean, a white house with a black cat always unflappably sitting in one window, a lawn with a bumper crop of yellow plastic sunflowers with whirligig petals, occasionally stirred to a desultory turn in the still, midmorning air. Once again I saw the man. This time he was reading a paper, standing at the same corner, and he didn't look up as I passed on the other side of the street. The third time I came upon him I was coming from the opposite direction, thumped around the corner and he was sitting in a parked car, a battered white sedan. It was near the end of my run and I was tired, had gone a good distance, four, maybe five miles. The sidewalk was cracked and heaved up just at the curb line, a nosegay of dried and dying dandelions growing where the earth beneath the concrete showed pebbly and brown. I stumbled, nearly went down, righted myself and felt a pain in my ankle, tried to continue quickly past him, saw him looking at me, noticed all at once his thick arms and chest, his odd disconnected half-smile, the way he seemed glad to see me as he leaned toward the open window. The dog was hurling itself at us both from behind the fence, and I wondered how I could have been foolish enough to assume them connected, man and animal. I was hemmed in by the car and the fence and I moved past him and yet waited, in my mind, to feel his hands. Maybe he muttered something; I don't know. But as I edged past him I ran faster, faster than I'd ever run before, all the way home. Locked the doors, checked the windows for the thousandth time, changed without showering because I was afraid that the sound of the water would mute the sound of someone coming in the window or the door, though they were locked, locked tight, what did they matter, locks? Once, in the emergency room, the cops brought in a woman who'd had to be carried, naked, from a building the city was demolishing. Wrapped in a blanket, her head tucked between her shoulders like a dying bird, she'd huddled in the corner of an examining room, and I'd asked her what she was afraid of. Her whisper was so soft that at first I didn't hear her. "Everything," she finally said a little louder. It shamed me now, to remember that I'd gone out to the nurses' station and said, under my breath, "What a head case this one is." It shamed me, now that I was afraid of everything myself. I'd never found out, after they took her up to psych, whether that woman had good reason to be afraid.

The next week I didn't run. I told myself it was the ankle. "It's a filthy habit, anyhow," Cindy said. "Get yourself one of those Jane Fonda tapes." But one day I wore shorts, a T-shirt, and my shoes to school in the morning, and after Cindy had driven to pick up Chad from her mother and take him to tumbling class, I'd made a slow circuit of the track that sat, gray-brown and sunburned, between the elementary school and the big sprawling middle school a block away. It was boring, that sort of running, no store windows to offer color and light, no "Good morning" from mailmen with their breath running in a stream of steam from between chapped lips. But from the track I could see the front and back entrances to the school, and the drive leading up to both. From the track I could see Robert and Bennie and the other boys who had begun to gather in a group around them shoot hoops on the blacktop during morning recess. If I could have run all day instead of working, I would have.

Mike Riordan fell into step beside me the third morning I was out there. He was wearing an Orlando Magic T-shirt and baggy running shorts. You can tell a lot by someone's running clothes. If the colors are bright, the fit fine, the logos designer, it almost always means fraud, someone who likes the idea of running better than the act itself. Mike Riordan's shorts and shirt looked ancient, one step removed from the rummage sale. The real deal.

"Okay if I join you?" he said, and I nodded, no words, because I was already breathing hard, the way I liked to, so that I felt really alive. For the next thirty minutes we said nothing at all, until as we were pulling up, panting, cramping, he added, "I have a free period now, and this beats evenings all to hell." Neither of us were chatty runners; both of us could go for almost an hour without giving up. Or maybe he slowed down for me. Or maybe I picked up for him. My fears cooled as my flushed face did, walking home to shower and change into my blue polyester uniform shift, to make my rounds. But at night I still set a folding chair beneath Robert's window piled with boy stuff, video games and books and little bits of leftover Lego things he and Bennie worked on, things that would fall to the floor with a clatter if anyone came through the window.

I used Mike Riordan, those early days. I felt safer with him around, and I was unapologetic, unashamed about using him for protection, even though he had no idea I needed protecting, no idea that he was any more than my running partner. I'd never run with someone else before, and I was startled by the spurious and instantaneous intimacy it produced, the sound of the two of us breathing hard, ragged, in tandem, half-dressed, single-minded, perspiring and without the usual scrim of carefully arranged hair, polite smiles, makeup, and sunglasses. When I left school after my run, knowing that no stranger had entered the front office or peered through the chain-link of the playground fence, I left also knowing that no one could easily have contact with or news of Robert with Mr. Riordan standing guard. I remembered how he'd bellowed at the manager of the supermarket, and I felt less afraid for my son.

"He's sweet on you," Cindy said. "That's all I'm saying. That's it. He is."

"Oh, please," I said. "He's a friend. A male friend. Women have male friends."

"Well, now, dear heart, that's fine, except that if the good Lord had wanted women to have male friends he would have arranged for men and women to have something in common."

"You don't have men friends?"

"I have a husband. He sort of has friends. They're sort of my friends. You know the name of that tune."

I'd had a man friend once, or thought I had. Sometimes Ben Samuels and I ate lunch in the pale green cafeteria at the hospital, where everyone looked ill in the watery light from the glass-block windows. Once we went to a conference on trauma treatment in Manhattan, in the auditorium of the medical center where he'd gone to med school, and afterward he took me to a Japanese restaurant for dinner, where we sat on tatami mats, our shoes side by side at the sliding paper door, a pair of brown suede lace-ups, a pair of navy pumps. There was something about those empty shoes that suggested an indiscretion, but all we'd done was eat teriyaki and talk, of nothing, really, although both of us spoke a little more effusively than need be of our family lives.

Over tea he was surprised that I'd missed the piece in the Sunday *Times* about head injuries, more surprised when I said I didn't read the paper. "I can't believe a woman as smart as you can get through the day without *The New York Times*," he said, and I'd blushed, and been embarrassed, and replied in a flippant voice, "Cops hate the *Times*. They think it always takes the side of the bad guys. Cops spit on *The New York Times*. The *News* is the cop paper."

"But you're not a cop," he said. I've never forgotten the way he said that. It came back to me, even after he'd moved out West. "That's a good move for him," Winnie said when she heard about it, giving me a look.

I know Winnie thought I used Ben Samuels to get some of what I didn't get at home, someone to talk to, someone who took me seriously. I'd been happy in his friendship.

But happiness wasn't what I got from Mike Riordan's company. He made me feel safe, safer than I'd felt in a long time. And it made me feel safer having Robert at school with Mike there. Sometimes I think Mike sensed all that, without understanding exactly why, as he ran alongside me, stood on the sidelines in front of me at soccer games.

The first time I watched Robert zigzagging across the flat expanse of the school soccer field all I could think of, all I could watch was the stand of trees at one end. All I could think of was a familiar figure emerging from behind one of the tree trunks as everyone was staring the other way, downfield at the visitor's goal, of someone reaching out for the Lake Plata school forward with the floppy bangs and skinny legs, the quick kid who called instructions to his teammates in a surprisingly low voice as his feet churned up the turf. Bobby, motioning to Robert: come on, come here. Blink and he'd be gone, my son, floating off like a piece of ashy paper lifted from the fire by a wind up the chimney on a cold night. It was all I could do not to pull him off the sidelines when another boy went in in his place, and I think, turning and seeing me, knowing just what I looked like when I was terrified, Mike Riordan knew some of what I was feeling.

"I need a parent to go with us on the bus to Lakota, Tuesday," he said one day after we'd lost a home game 3 to 1.

"I'll be there," I said.

I'd never known a teacher to talk to, except for Grace, if an associate professor of American studies could be called a teacher. All those years of school with the nuns, grade school, high school, even nursing school, and the cool remove of their habits an instant bar to intimacy that remained when the black veils and white wimples gave way to street clothes and nurses' uniforms. Even the teachers at St. Stannie's had intimidated me, standing at the heavy school door and shutting it with a *thunk* when the last of the identically dressed children had hurried inside. I gave them my son, and twice a year they gave me a progress report—mediocre penmanship, decent spelling, an affinity for math and history. A good boy.

So for weeks I did what the kids did, called him Mr. Riordan, silly as it was, he five years younger than I, with that pink baby face and straw-colored baby hair. But it seemed to suit the circumstances. Mr. Riordan dropping Robert off after soccer practice and accepting a Pepsi at the kitchen table while he and Robert complained about the ref they'd had for the last game. Mr. Riordan taking Robert, Bennie, and two other boys to McDonald's to reward them for perfect attendance at the end of the first month of intramural practice and play. Mr. Riordan taking Robert and me to the International House of Pancakes after a Saturday morning game at which Robert had scored two goals.

"Let me say this," he'd said, bent over blueberry pancakes and bacon, wearing his yellow polo shirt with "Mike" embroidered over the heart. "You came to play today." He pointed his fork at Robert. "You came to play. And did. That second goal was a miracle."

"You looked good out there," I said, smiling.

"You looked great," Mr. Riordan said.

Mr. Riordan, the two of us sitting on the leatherette seats at the front of the bus, our conversation interrupted by the throwing of paper and the occasional muttered "asshole" from the seats behind. "Keep it clean, guys," Mr. Riordan yelled, "keep it clean." It's hard to call a teacher by his first name. Maybe that was when I started to call him Mike, on the bus. One day he had a lottery ticket in his top pocket, and when I mentioned it he blushed.

"I buy one every once in a while," he said, turning it over in his hands. "You know, you pick up the paper, some gum. Then you give the man a couple of numbers." He read them off the ticket: 19, 9, 44, 10, 21. "I don't even know how I picked these," he said.

"What would you do if you won? Would you quit your job?"

He shook his head. "Nah. Look at me. I play soccer with ten-year-olds for pay. Why would I quit?"

I laughed. "Mr. Riordan, Sean called me a Tampax," a boy named Andrew shouted from the back.

"Hold on," Mr. Riordan said, and walked to the back of the bus. I looked back, pretending I was watching the mediation, when what I was really looking for was

Robert, the sheer pleasure of seeing him sitting quiet, maybe even content, near the back of the bus. He was staring out the window while Bennie talked to him about something. His profile looked hard, adult. He glanced up, saw me, waved. Mr. Riordan stopped by to talk to the two of them for a moment and they looked up at him, tipping their heads back on the slender straws of their necks, tipping them far back as though Mr. Riordan was a giant, or God. "He's doing it again," Andrew called. There was silence, then more bickering, then the rumble of a deeper voice, then silence again.

"You Tampax," I said, when he dropped back into his seat.

"I know," he said. "I do all the disciplinary stuff and one of my biggest problems is not laughing. One of the third-grade girls came in crying the other day. I sit her down, I give her a Kleenex. She's sniffing and blowing her nose and finally she says, "Joshua keeps telling me he loves me and I just want him to stop!"

"That is a great job," I said.

"I guess most people would quit. If they won the lottery, I mean."

"I wouldn't. I love to work. My mother always worked. When I was a kid, it was my father who didn't work. It was like a life sentence—guilty of emphysema. Sentenced to the big chair in front of the TV for the rest of his life. The poor guy was like a piece of furniture. I never wanted to be like that. I had my first job when I was sixteen."

"My mother never worked."

"How many kids did she have?"

"Seven."

"She worked," I said.

Out the windows of the bus the sun was sinking behind a grove of trees and a row of shacks the migrants used when they came to Florida to pick fruit. A stray dog chased after our tires, and the noise of the boys began to evaporate with the daylight, their conversation to go gray with fatigue. They'd lost, 4–2, in a tough game. Robert had played poorly.

"How's your hamstring?" Mr. Riordan said.

"Still sore."

"You should stay off it."

"Ha," I said. "I'll be out there tomorrow morning."

"I had Robert in my office the other day," Mr. Riordan said quietly. "I kept meaning to tell you."

"Why?"

"He got into some sort of argument with two of the boys. Apparently they were teasing him about the way he looks, how dark he is or something. You know how they are at this age. And he held one of them against the wall and said, 'I'm going to get you.' Mrs. Bernsen was just a little knocked out by the way he said it. Like he really meant it, if you know what I mean?"

I knew exactly what he meant. I closed my eyes and leaned against the window. Robert the Hobbit, Robert the Hobbit, making sure that no one got over on him, just as Daddy said. It was Bobby Benedetto's song, the one he sang as he paced his kitchen. I'm going to get that sucker who sells crack in the quad at the Lincoln projects. I'm going to get that asshole who laughed at us when we stopped him the other day. I'm going to get the jerk-off who threw the tennis ball at the patrol car, opened the hydrant, put his little brother out to work as a drug runner. Getting them all—that was Bobby Benedetto's vocation.

"Hey," Mike Riordan said, "it's no big deal. We talked. Or I talked and he listened. You know he's basically a good kid. He has some problems dealing with anger. And other stuff. I think he keeps things bottled up inside."

I know, I said. The divorce, I said, the move, the new school, the new friends. He would be fine. Fine. Fine. Fine. Sometimes you say a word so many times that it loses its meaning and shape in your mouth, until it's like a piece of gristly meat and you want to spit it out, or swallow and get it over with. Fine. First Robert said it, now I did. If we said everything was fine often enough maybe it would be true.

Even Mr. Riordan did it. One day as we were running, trickles of sweat outlining the curve of both our jaws, our breath coming hard and jagged, he suddenly said, softly, then more insistently, "Don't worry about him too much. Don't worry. He's fine." But of course he had no idea.

"He's fine," I said again.

"I know that," he said. "I do think it would do him some good to talk to somebody. Dr. Stern, maybe."

What could I say? There was no kid in the world who needed to talk to someone, as people always delicately said when they wanted you to see a shrink—I knew, I'd done it in the ER dozens of times myself—there was no kid who needed it more than Robert. There was no one who needed more to speak the words he couldn't say, to look at the things he couldn't see. Someday, I swore, I'd do that for him, so that he could give up the secret, once and for all, so that he could say that his father had lied to him, and his mother, too, all those mornings when they acted as though everything was all right. Fine. Fine. But not now. That was Robert Benedetto's story. And for now, no matter how bad it was for us both, Robert had to be Robert Crenshaw.

"I'll think about it," I finally said. "I really will. I know he needs to get things out of his system more."

"He might do better if a professional could help him with that. It might give him some ways to deal that would make him feel better."

"I know. I'm just not sure it's the right time."

"Well, think about it."

"I will. And promise you'll tell me if anything else happens. Or if you notice any kind of problem. I need to know. Please."

What could I tell him, this nice man with his nice open face, to explain away what seemed to be my stubborn refusal to help my child? That if Robert talked to the school psychologist about what was bothering him the gig was up, that bottling-up was part of the plan. I knew that for Robert's sake it would be a good idea for him to take a stroll twice a week through the maze of his memories, to try to reconcile the beloved father who'd done terrible things, the trusted mother who'd lied about them, the happy home that had been rotten at the root, like one of those trees in full leaf that blows over in a storm to reveal the hollow trunk. To talk about what it felt like to be suddenly plucked, still half asleep, from one existence, and set down a day later in another strange new one. But he would have to do it on his own. It was too dangerous for anyone else to know our secret. It was too dangerous for Robert to talk about what had really happened, who he really was. If he told a psychologist, he might tell a teacher. If he told a teacher, he might tell Bennie. And pretty soon everyone would know. Everyone, and Bobby. That was how Bobby would find us, through one missing brick in the wall between that life and this.

"He'll be okay," Mike Riordan said.

"I think so, too," I said.

One of our goalies was snoring behind us, a bandanna covering his shaved head. "Shane's starting a new fashion," I said. "Head lice," Mike Riordan whispered. "We managed to keep it pretty much contained to the fourth grade." "Nearly there, folks," the driver said. Crickets were sawing away out in the muggy Florida night. It was already almost Thanksgiving.

"Do you know Chelsea Roerbacker?" I said, to change the subject.

I could see Mike Riordan's teeth in the dim gray light as he smiled. "I sure do," he said. "Speaking of Dr. Stern."

"I don't know how Cindy does it. It would drive me crazy, to have a kid of mine that frightened of that many things."

"You know what?" Mike said. "Most kids are that frightened of that many things. They're just too scared to admit it. And so are most adults. I think the amazing thing about Chelsea is that she puts it all out on the table."

"Mr. Riordan," somebody yelled. "Zachary spilled a juice box all over my pants. In the crotch."

"Go for it," I said.

He held up his lottery ticket and kissed it. "Please, God," he said.

I don't know exactly when I started to call him Mike, but I know that was the moment I began to think of him that way.

"Mr. Riordan," one of the boys moaned, "do you think we'll win next time?"

"Absolutely," he said.

For my birthday Cindy took me to the mall south of Lakota and bought me a decent haircut at a place called The Clip Joint. My birthday was November 10, or at least Beth Crenshaw's birthday was. Frannie Flynn's birthday was October 30, a hateful time to have a birthday, Mischief Night, the nasty stepbrother to Halloween, a day of soaped windows, egged windshields, staying inside, safe at home. I'd never had a birthday party, unless you counted the cake with butter-cream icing and pink roses my mother brought home in a white cardboard box from the bakery on the bottom floor of the office building in Manhattan where she worked. For my Sweet Sixteen I brought the cake home myself, from the bakery where I worked; now I knew the butter-cream was made out of shortening and sugar. "It's chocolate," my mother had said, when I cut into it, and Gracie had said, "Fran doesn't really like vanilla cake. You should have known that." She grew up fast, Grace; she always said what she thought. In bed that night she'd whispered, "What if I threw you a big birthday party at the Waldorf-Astoria . . ." But I pretended to be asleep.

Birthdays—that's how they get you. You wouldn't imagine that, would you, but Patty Bancroft said the biggest mistake people made was changing their name but keeping the same initials, and claiming the same date of birth. Patty Bancroft's people had shaved two years off my age as well, so that Beth Crenshaw, wearing a rubber cape in the beautician's chair that squeaked when you moved in it, was thirty-six years old.

"Manicure, pedicure, styling, color," Cindy said in the car. "On me. And Craig'll take the kids out water-skiing on Lake Lakota, then maybe Chuck-E-Cheese for lunch. Mine are happier than pigs in shit, excuse my language. Chad thinks Robert and Bennie are grown-ups, only more fun, and Chelsea thinks they're cute boys. Which they are. When's Robert's birthday, anyway?"

Someone who thought they knew children but didn't had assigned Robert a date of birth to replace April 30. "Fourth of July," I said.

"That's a tough one," Cindy said. "No school, so no school party. And everybody doing their own barbecues, beach trips, family deal. On the other hand, you'd always have fireworks. I guess I could work with that. You want your nails wrapped?"

I laughed. "What is having your nails wrapped?" I said.

"Oh, it's great. You'll see. They put these little pieces of linen on your nails, spray them until they get hard as a rock, file them, shape them."

"I can't have them too long."

"Don't be so negative."

"No one's messing around with my feet."

"You'll see. This'll be great."

She was right. Cindy was always right about things like that. My hair fell in soft layers around my face, a more buttery, warmer color than my own home dye job. My nails were painted with white tips and my feet massaged by a Korean woman in a pink smock who smiled all the time. It was pretty clear she didn't understand a word either of us said. It was early on a Saturday morning and we were the only people in the place except for two handsome, hard-looking, dark-haired women, the elder a shadow of the younger, who came in just as we were finishing. Between them they carried a long white box, and, setting it down carefully on the receptionist's Formica desk, they lifted out a crown of pearls and beads with a long tail of tulle the color of light coffee.

"Oh, that's gorgeous," Cindy said, watching everything in the salon's wall of mirrors, the ends of her hair falling like dandelion fluff on the shoulders of her rubber cape.

"A hundred and eighty dollars for a veil. Just for the veil!" said the older woman.

"Don't start," said her daughter as one of the beauticians began to set her hair in rollers.

"It would look beautiful with her hair up. Look at this." She held the veil out to us all: me, Cindy, the woman who was cutting Cindy's hair, the Korean woman who was shaving dead skin from my heels and smiling and nodding. "A chignon inside the band of beading, so that you could really appreciate, you see what I mean? Which would also mean a better view of the back of the dress when she's at the altar. See, they all look at the front of the dress, these girls, but most of what you see during a wedding is the back. You don't want the whole back of the dress hidden by all this hair."

"So you want your hair up?" said the beautician to the bride. The embroidery on her smock said her name was Jenna, and her small, pinched features had settled during the mother's monologue into the carefully neutral look I'd learned long ago to adopt with difficult patients.

"I told you what I want when I came in for the consult. I want ringlets. She wants my hair up, but she's not the one getting married."

"You look one hundred percent better with your hair up," her mother said.

"Ma, you want your hair up, you get your hair up. I'm not getting my hair up."

"It'll ruin the pictures."

"Chris doesn't like my hair up. I don't like my hair up. I'm not wearing my fucking hair up."

"You kiss your mother with that mouth?"

"You're done," said the woman who was blowing Cindy's hair dry. The Korean manicurist handed us our purses so we wouldn't smear our polish. "Look at how nice her nails look," said the mother, pointing to my hands. "I told you you should have gotten a French manicure."

"Ma, don't start," the daughter said. Cindy and I waited until we were at the escalator before we began laughing. "What do you bet she winds up with her hair up?" Cindy said.

"You think?"

"Oh, honey, I know."

My head smelled of flowers, and my hands looked elegant, smooth, like they belonged to someone with drawers full of sachets and closets with padded hangers. "They were so Brooklyn," I said.

"So what?"

"Never mind. It's just an old expression. You were right about the pedicure."

"I know I was. Happy birthday, honey."

Those were the times I felt bad about what I was doing, the times when I spoke aimlessly of a life in Wilmington that seemed an empty invention to my own ears, the times when Cindy patted my hand while she was telling another story of another friend getting screwed in divorce court. Cindy thought I was having a wonderful birthday, when my real birthday had been a week before and I'd cried most of the evening, thinking about Gracie somewhere, crying too. Gracie always helped me blow out the candles on my cake, even when I was a grown-up. I hated lying to Cindy, hated that I did it more or less every day just by letting her call me Beth. It was all I could do, sometimes, not to tell her everything.

"I bet Mr. Riordan'll like your hair," Cindy said, pulling the minivan onto the highway.

"I bet you've been waiting half an hour to say that. Ever since I got out of the chair."

"Tell the truth, I wanted to say something in the shop, but that Jenna lives in Lake Plata so I decided to protect your privacy."

"Thanks so much."

"So what is the deal here?"

"Cindy, you watch too much TV."

"You may be right, hon, but I can tell you that on TV the soccer coach and the player's lovely single mother wind up together. After many misadventures. Plus, I don't see too many other stars on your horizon. Except for Jim. He's a real romantic guy. That last time you ran into him leaving our house, I heard him say to the other guy in the truck, 'Man, would I like a piece of that!' What a sweetheart."

Jim was one of the laborers who worked for Craig's pool service. He was tanned from all those hours in the sun, and he took his shirt off every chance he got to display muscle definition that made him look like a Saturday morning cartoon superhero. The ends of his Fu Manchu mustache were always a little wet, and I had thought about what it would be like to sleep with him the first moment I saw him, balancing a shovel across the tight shelf of his shoulders, looking enough like Bobby Benedetto to be a first cousin. He smelled like sweat and chlorine, and I tried not even to look at him, those few times I'd run into him at the Roerbackers. But once he'd smiled at me, real slow, and I knew he knew what I was thinking.

"Like I said, you watch too much TV," I said to Cindy. "Mike Riordan is a very nice man. That's all."

"Oh, no. A nice man. That tears it. Remember how in high school, your girlfriend would go, oh, him, he's such a nice guy. And what that always meant was that she was dying to go out with the guy's nasty friend."

"Well, thank God high school is over."

"Oh, please. Life is high school, except everybody's either ten pounds lighter, or fifty pounds heavier."

I started to sort everyone I knew into one group or another. "You're right," I said.

"I am right, and I'm right about Mr. Riordan. And please don't tell me you're holding out for Mr. Right, because he ain't coming. He never comes."

"And this from a happily married woman."

"I'm happily married because I'm real realistic. The statute of limitations on finding them irritating as hell is four, maybe five years. It doesn't matter how good-looking they are or how much money they make; that's when you start to notice how they can't ever manage to put on a fresh roll of toilet paper or put dirty clothes in the hamper. You've been married, you know the drill: Honey, where's my shirt? In the damn closet, dear, where it always is. Couple years gritting your teeth, and then you just got to get on with it. Or not, I guess." She looked over at me. "What got me going on that?"

"Mr. Riordan."

"Oh, never mind Mr. Riordan. Let me do your

makeup when we get home. I got these new neutrals that'll look great on you."

Usually I resisted Cindy's sample case, but for once I went along with her. She made bacon, lettuce, and tomato sandwiches for us both, and then went to work on me with pencils and foam pads, powders and creams. Except for a mouth that was too big for the rest of my face, I looked good when she was finished. "Not a day over thirty," she said. Instead of thirty-six. Or thirty-eight. Another secret to keep straight, my very age.

"God, I wish you had a hot date tonight," she said. "Can I buy your clothes, too? No offense, hon, but you tend to play down your best feature. Your bod cries out for short white shorts and a crop top."

"You're the first person I've heard use the word *bod* since junior year high school."

"Or one of those little T-shirt dresses would be nice, too. And they're cheap. Dress Barn has them for forty bucks. That's where I got this." Cindy was wearing royal blue shorts and a print blouse with a ruffle down the front, white sandals, and a matching white belt.

"Can I ask you something without pissing you off?" I said.

"Shoot."

"How come you do all this—the makeup, the clothes? Don't you get tired of having to look perfect every day?"

And Cindy sat down heavily in the chair across from me, all the makeup piled on the glass table between us; with her face sort of sad and serious she looked like exactly what she was, a former prom queen who'd grown up, gotten married, and fought the good fight against losing her looks. "God, I'm sorry," I said. "I can't believe I said such a shitty thing."

"Don't rub your eyes," she said, "or that mascara will be all over your face. It's okay, anyhow. You're the only friend I've ever had who would ask me a question like that. Plus I think you're the only one I've ever known who I'd know how to answer. You know, most people, I'd just say, well, a girl's got to look her best, doesn't she? or one of those dumb-ass things you learn to say." I'd never heard Cindy swear before. I wanted to reach across the table for her hand, but she kept it curled up in her lap.

"I think it was the farm, you know it? It was just so dusty all the time, and the dirt came in the windows, so that no matter how often you'd dust there'd be this little bit of dirt that was always on the sills. And my mother would go out to make her deliveries and she'd smell so good and look nice, even though she's a kind of plain woman, you'll see when you meet her at Christmas. Then next morning she'd be up in a pair of men's overalls helping my dad out in the barns, and she'd smell like manure. And after a while I think I got like Scarlett

O'Hara in the movie, you know? 'As God is my witness, I'm never going to be dirty again.'

"I fell like a ton of bricks my sophomore year for a boy named Jackson Islington, can you believe it, from some little place past Lakota. He was a senior, light-headed boy, but dark eyes, you know how nice that looks sometimes? And you'll know how crazy I was about him when I tell you I was only fifteen and he was already putting his hand up my skirt in the car, and I was letting him. He dropped me off one day and he was talking to my dad for the longest time and then my dad came in for dinner. I can still remember we were having macaroni and cheese and stewed tomatoes, and my daddy says to me, 'That's a nice young man. You don't meet too many anymore who have their hearts set on farming.'

"Lord, you should of heard that boy when I asked him about it next day coming home from school. Talking about the earth and watching things grow and the air in the early morning, making it sound like planting ten acres of feed corn was like being a priest or something. And then he started kissing me and he kissed my neck and then lower, the way he always did, I think that was what got me going in the first place, and then he kissed me on the mouth, stuck his tongue in the way he had a million times before, except I could taste the dirt, just taste it, so that I almost gagged.

"Even now sometimes I think, Cynthia Lee, what was wrong with you? Because when you're fifteen you're supposed to be able to just overlook those kinds of things, get all carried away and loopy in love. But I felt his hands on me and all I could think of was me all scrawny and dark the way my mother was, and dirt on the dining-room tablecloth. And that was that. That was that." There were tears in her eyes, and Cindy dabbed at them with one carefully bent knuckle. Then she laughed, the sort of shaky gasping laugh you laugh when you're trying to shake tears away, a laugh I'd laughed myself sometimes, talking to Grace about things.

"First date with Craig, I say to him, 'What do you think you'd like to do for a living?' He was seventeen, must have thought I was crazy. He said, 'I'm going into business.' The pool business gave me pause, with all the digging around, but he put that shower in the basement, right by the outside door, and he's clean and smelling of Christian Dior before he ever comes up those stairs." And with that she lifted her chin and smiled at me, the kind of brilliant smile one woman gives another that might as well be a punch in the nose, so little is it to be messed with. I looked down, fiddling with the tubes and pots on the table, looking at their labels: Terra Copper, Autumn Leaves, Sweet Peach, Sable. Almost despite myself I started to talk.

"I had this nun in eighth grade who wanted me to apply to this really good private school. She kept saying that she thought I had potential. Potential. I got to love the sound of that word. It sounds like somebody shot you out of a cannon. And then I talked to my parents about it, and my mother looked at the brochure I brought home. It was on this great paper, I remember, soft and shiny and there were beautiful color pictures of the kids in their uniforms, in science labs and reading in this big library. And my mother looked at it, and then she just said, 'Why?' That's all. It was like my whole life in one word. And it just stayed like that—when I wanted to go on a trip to Spain with the language club, or go to college. The answer was always the same: why? What's the point? I knew it was because they didn't have any money, with my father on disability and my mother working as a secretary. But it didn't feel like it was about money. It felt defeated. I'd look at this picture of the two of them on their bedroom dresser, thin and nice-looking and all happy and smiling, and it was just like defeat had taken over the whole house, until I didn't see the point either. I went to the local parochial girls' school and then I went to the local nursing school and then I got married and I guess I was just grateful for anything I could get.

"I didn't even really think about it until my sister got older. Because they did the same thing to her, except that she didn't pay any attention to them. What's the point, Grace? Take shorthand and typing, Grace. Dr. Edgar the dentist is looking for a receptionist, Grace. She'd just laugh at them sometimes, when we were in our room, make fun of them, even. She got herself a scholarship to private school for high school, and she got jobs and grants to work her way through college, and she rented a U-Haul so she could drive cross-country. My mother asked her why she was going all the way to Chicago for school. And she said, 'Because I want to.' Like it was the most natural thing in the world, to do what you wanted.

"Sometimes I'd see her looking at me and I could tell she felt sorry for me. God, that just about killed me, that little Gracie, whose diapers I'd changed, who I sang to and read to, who would yell 'Where Frannie?' running around the house, her diaper all droopy around her fat knees, who I taught all the line dances and how to roll her uniform skirt after school, that she would wind up feeling sorry for me. But, you know, I had no one, and Grace had me. That gave her confidence. Or at least a lesson in how not to do things." I shrugged. "She just made herself a completely different life. Just made it up, from scratch."

"Well, that's what you did," Cindy said.

"What?"

"Here," she said. "You made yourself a whole new life here. Just like your sister did."

"It's different."

"Oh, hon, that's what we all say," she said. "Of course it's different. Everything's so out of a clear blue sky that everything's always different. Like if I'd taken French instead of Spanish I might not have known Craig and my whole life would be different. Or if I'd gone all the way with Jackson before I knew what was what, everything would have been different. Scares me to think about it, it would have been so different. And if you weren't as nutty about Robert as I am about Chelsea I wouldn't have run into you and that would make things different."

"I am not nutty about Robert. He was in a new school, he was—"

"I know, I know. It was different than with Chelsea. That's fine. Anyhow, now we know everything we need to know about one another. You know how come I wear foundation and powder every day, and I know how come you don't. I thought we were just going to get our nails and hair done, and the next thing you know we're sitting here ripping our guts out."

"It's the birthday. There's something about a birthday that makes you think about your life that way. About how you got to be who you are. About whether you're happy with your life."

"I guess this might not be the best birthday to ask if you're happy with your life," Cindy said.

"I guess you're right. What about you?"

Cindy stared up at the ceiling. It was almost as if I could watch the years roll by behind the scrim of her eyes, her thinking about everything that had been, the man, the kids. Herself.

"I'm pretty happy with my life," she said finally. "But it isn't exactly what I expected."

"Amen," I said.

She leaned over, gave me a hug, put all the makeup in a tote bag she was giving away free with every order during the holidays. "Who's Frannie?" she said.

It was such a shock, but I didn't show a thing in my face. Besides, she wasn't looking at me, was looking down at the tools of her trade.

"What?" I said.

"You said your little sister called you Frannie. That she said 'Where Frannie?' all the time."

"It's an old nickname," I said, my breathing still ragged from talking, and listening, and feeling.

Cindy held out the tote bag, red with black patent trim. My mother-in-law would have loved it. "Well, Frannie, honey," she said, and just the word, that one word, sounded so good in her mouth. "Here's your new face. Happy birthday again. You're a new woman, swear to God."

"What happened to Jackson Islington?" I said.

"I haven't a clue," said Cindy. "What happened to your eighth-grade nun?"

"She left the convent, got married, and become a social worker."

"How about that?" Cindy said.

The sweet potatoes in the casserole dish on the kitchen counter looked like a photograph from some recipe in a magazine, if I do say so myself. The secret's in the bourbon, boiled down with butter and brown sugar until the whole mess is as thick as maple syrup. It was one of my mother's recipes. One of my mother's only recipes, unless you count the ones she read off the back of the can of cream of mushroom soup. At my mother-in-law's, where we always had Thanksgiving dinner, the sweet potatoes were tolerated, not welcome. The turkey, too, was more centerpiece than main course, filled with sausage and aniseed, surrounded by platters of lasagna and artichokes stuffed with cheese. At Ann Benedetto's I used to eat the sweet potatoes myself, so that my casserole would not sit untouched on the sideboard, even though the food she served was always better. In the battle between turkey and lasagna, turkey doesn't stand a chance.

The bourbon, that's what my mother always said. And the pecans. They were expensive, the pecans, almost three dollars a bag. The bourbon I bought in one of those tiny bottles they serve on the airlines. I was afraid of having booze in the house. The second week we were in Lake Plata I bought a bottle of cheap chardonnay, rough and vinegary on the back of my tongue, yet somehow it only lasted two days. After that, no more. Every bit of the bourbon went into the saucepan.

"Sweet potatoes are weird," Robert said, poking them with his finger the night before as they sat steaming on top of the narrow stove. "But they smell good."

They were crusty, brown and orange, and still fragrant if you put your face close enough, even stone cold on Thursday morning as I listened to Cindy on the phone, my heart sinking. Her voice was ragged, the static on the car phone in Craig's van like pebbles rolling around in the receiver. It was Thanksgiving, but instead of putting the turkey in the oven the Roerbackers were rolling south, down the spine of the state to the retirement village where Craig's parents lived and where, the night before, his father had had a stroke. And the

Thanksgiving plans of the Crenshaw family, such as they were, were rolling away with them.

"I am so sorry," she kept saying. "I am just so sorry."

"Cindy, stop," I said, poking the potatoes. "Things happen."

"I know," she said. "I know."

"We'll make other plans," I said. "The Castros, maybe."

"Oh, I forgot about the Castros," she said, and her voice sounded a little lighter, the static a little more raucous, until somewhere along the highway we lost one another with a rattle, a strange sonic shriek, and a still pool of dead and empty air.

But of course I knew that the Castros had gone away, too, to celebrate Thanksgiving with some cousins in Orlando who had been, Robert told me, billionaires before they found it necessary to come to America and be reincarnated, driving cabs, cleaning motel rooms, another brace of people who'd been somebody else once. That morning, when I had stepped into the quadrangle of the Poinsettia complex, just to see the sky, to sniff the air, it had had the atmosphere of a place that had been evacuated, as though someone had forgotten to tell us about the coming storm, the floods, the tornadoes. But the only natural disaster was the holiday; our shabby little horseshoe of low-ceilinged duplexes was the sort of place to leave for a family gathering, not a place in which to have one. And we were leaving, too, leaving for the Roerbackers, with Cindy's family, and Craig's. Until Cindy and Craig and Chelsea and Chad—it almost makes me smile to give all their names together like that, and I still mocked Cindy from time to time—had gotten on the road at daybreak to travel to a hospital intensive care unit 250 miles away.

"Sweetie, we have a problem," I called upstairs to Robert, trying to keep the sound of bad news out of my voice. There was no answer and I trudged up, looked in at him on the bed, reading a magazine that Bennie had given him, an expert's guide to video games.

"Remember the game I told you about, that you said was way too expensive?" he said. "If I could get a used one for half-price, could I buy it?"

"I don't know," I said, sitting on the edge of the bed and dancing my fingers up his leg. "That was Cindy on the phone. She and the kids had to go to Mr. Roerbacker's daddy's house. He had a stroke last night and they had to go right away to see him. So we can't go to their house today."

"So where are we going to go?"

"I don't know," I said.

"I have to write a composition about Thanksgiving," Robert said.

"You don't have to write it today."

"I know. But what will I say if we don't have Thanksgiving?"

How had I forgotten what it would be like, to go to a cheap restaurant on that day of all days? I knew, knew in the way a person with scars can remember the pain of surgery. The first Thanksgiving after I met Bobby he'd invited me to his mother's for Thanksgiving. Grace and my mother and father had gone off to my aunt's house in the Catskills, carrying a cheesecake and a bottle of rosé wine, and I had set my hair, shaved my legs, ironed a dress that didn't need ironing.

I didn't know that Bobby hadn't told his mother until that morning, and I suppose he didn't know that she would fall entirely apart at the suggestion that there was a strange girl who expected to sit at her table, that white phony French-provincial table with the centerpiece of wax grapes in a silver basket, the table where only family sat. He sprung it on her; that's the way Bobby put it, as though I was a small animal with sharp teeth waiting to leap at the crepey white skin around Ann Benedetto's neck. I can imagine now what she must have been like that day: cold, affronted, then tremulous, a shaking hand to her only child's cheek, begging, begging, not today, not today. And so Bobby had changed my plans. I should have had some vision of the future then, as I listened to him talk on the phone. "It's no big thing," Bobby said. "I shouldn't've sprung it on her like that. She'll get used to the idea. You know, only child, all that. It's no big thing. She'll meet you at Christmas. I'll see you tomorrow. Don't eat too much turkey."

I could have stayed at home, heated up a can of soup, read a mystery novel. Instead I'd gone up to the Boulevard, to a Greek luncheonette, and had turkey with all the trimmings at a stool at the counter, two stools down from an old man with emphysema who smoked all through his meal.

"How was it?" Gracie said when they got home, carrying leftover turkey wrapped in tinfoil.

"Nice," I said.

"They put out a good spread, those people," my father had said, wheezing, falling into his chair and breathing into his oxygen mask as though it was the Fountain of Youth.

And still, remembering that, I took Robert to The Chirping Chicken, the two of us trudging along the shoulder of the highway because there were no sidewalks, there was no need for any, everybody rode in cars except for us. The linoleum and the fake leather on the booths was the color of the sun, so that you felt blinded when you walked inside. The gravy was the color of the sun, too, bright yellow with flecks of black pepper swimming on its oily sheen. At least it was not gray. That was what I remembered about the food in the luncheonette in Brooklyn, that the gravy was the color of cardboard, and I cried in the bathroom and blew my nose on a square of gray toilet paper, rubbing off the foundation and the powder I'd put on to go to Bobby's. I told Robert that story at The Chirping Chicken, and somehow I made it sound innocuous, even amusing, like something from one of the sitcoms, something that would have a laugh track. That's how I always tried to make life sound for Robert. I couldn't bear for him to feel pathetic, to see me as pathetic, too.

"These are really good mashed potatoes," he said. "They don't have one single lump."

"Did you not really want to go to the Roerbackers?" I said.

"No, it was okay. But it's like Grandmom didn't want you to come when you weren't her family. I think Thanksgiving shouldn't be with someone else's family. I think it should just be with your family."

"What about Christmas?"

"Christmas is different."

I always did Christmas, at our house. I cooked standing rib roast and Murphy potatoes and caramelized onions and Ann Benedetto went to her brother's house on Long Island. Grace came to our house for Christmas, and Mrs. Pinto, whose children all lived in Florida. That was one of my biggest fears when I was out with Cindy at the mall, the possibility of running into one of Mrs. Pinto's daughters, with their big hair and their sharp eyes, fringed with lacquered lashes like anemones.

"Nana told me once Daddy hurt his finger on Thanksgiving and she carried him to the hospital because the cab didn't come. She said he was yelling and screaming and she was running down Ocean Avenue with him getting blood on her."

"I know that story," I said. "He needed eleven stitches in his hand. He fell on a bottle out in the backyard. He still has the scar."

"It's a big scar. When I got that cut on my head when I was five I got stitches but you can't even see." Robert raised his bangs to show his smooth, high, golden-brown forehead. There was the suggestion of a straight line across its center, as though someone had drawn faintly with a ruler. "Jesus, Frannie," Bobby had said, cradling the boy in his big arms on the sofa in the living room, running his lips softly over the bandage. "You should have called me at work. They could have raised me on the radio."

"It was only five stitches. And I got the plastic surgeon to do it."

"You know what, champ?" Bobby had said to Robert.

"When you're grown-up, girls will say, oh, Robert, how'd you get that scar? And you can make up a story. You can tell them it was a racing-car accident. Or you were in a sword fight. You don't have to say you were bouncing on the bed and you hit the headboard. Which you're never going to do again as long as you live, so help me, God; keep him off the bed, Frances, do you hear me? Hear me, buddy?"

Robert had nodded, burying his face in his father's chest. Bobby had smiled at me over the brown head, so small, so fragile somehow. I'd felt Robert's head with my fingers for years after infancy to make sure that the bones had joined over the exposed fontanelle, the soft spot.

Why at that moment, pushing stuffing around the thick white plate with the side of my fork, did I suddenly remember what Patty Bancroft had said at the hospital? Winnie was discussing a case, a case of children brought in and then scattered to foster homes after their mother had been beaten into a coma in the middle of the night by an old boyfriend. "The children were asleep," Winnie had said, and Patty Bancroft had answered, spitting out the words, "The children are never asleep. They only pretend to be."

"Daddy broke his leg when he was in high school, in a car," Robert added, eating a roll. It was as though he had permission to talk about Bobby because I had done it first, but maybe only a distant Bobby, the Bobby he'd heard about in stories, not the man he knew, the man who did things while he was sleeping. Or pretending to be.

"He almost got shot, too, when you were a baby," I said, pushing him into the present. "Some man pulled a gun on him in the park but his partner got the guy to put it down."

"Daddy said it wasn't even loaded," Robert said. "He told me once."

"But he didn't know that until it was over. They were chasing the guy because he'd grabbed somebody's bag on Fifty Avenue."

"He told me."

"Your daddy is a good cop," I said. I didn't know if even that was true anymore. There was that teenager in the projects who said Bobby banged his face against the back divider in the patrol car. There was the minister who said Bobby had used a "racial pejorative" to a member of the congregation who'd complained when the cops tried to move along some teenagers from in front of a sub shop. I was like most cop wives; he told me just enough to make it a story but not so much that it'd make it real, feel what he felt, know what he knew. After a while I couldn't tell if he was a good cop. But at least he'd never come home with money in his pocket I couldn't explain, hadn't been like some of his friends, who suddenly came into A-frames in the Adirondacks or cheesy cruises to the Caribbean. "He's working a lot of overtime," the wives always said as though they were just passing the time of day, that breezy way they lied.

I looked down into my coffee cup. "I was really proud of your daddy then, Ba. I was proud of him lots of times. And I really loved him."

"But he hit you," Robert said. It was the first time he'd ever acknowledged it. Somehow it was like a benediction.

"Yeah," I said.

"Because you did stuff he didn't like."

I sighed. "Not exactly. Not really. You know how you know the things that will make me mad, like not doing your homework or being mean to someone or getting in a fight? The thing about Daddy was, it was really hard for me to tell what he didn't like. You couldn't really tell what would make him mad. And that made it hard. And even if you don't like what someone does, you can't hit them. When you're mad at someone, you have to talk to them, not beat them up. Beating them up is wrong. It's always wrong."

"You don't hit me," he said.

"No."

"You would never hit me."

"I would never hit you," I said.

"Daddy never hit me either."

"I know, Ba. What happened with Daddy and me, it had nothing to do with you," I said. It's what we're supposed to say, isn't it, whenever a marriage is ripped apart and the kids come tumbling out, tumbling down? And I don't know why, because it's such a big, bald-faced lie that any kid with half a brain could figure it out. Robert just nodded, played with the surface of his pumpkin pie. "That was kind of a dumb thing to say," I added. "What I meant was that it's possible for me and your daddy to be angry at each other without either of us being angry at you."

"I bet Daddy's mad at me."

"Why?"

"For going with you."

I leaned forward, took hold of his hand. It just lay there, a small warm thing half-asleep. "Ba, he'd know that you didn't have any choice in that. He'd know that I made you go."

"I bet he's mad at you."

"I'll bet he is, too," I said.

We walked home then, along the highway, and somehow it was better. Somehow it was good. The wind blew trash across our path, bits of wrappers, foil and plastic, and we must have looked a sight to anyone passing by. But it felt somehow festive, our isolation, as though we were having an adventure. "I'm full," Robert said, patting his belly, smiling up at me, kicking at a soda can along the gravel verge. I felt the ghost of Bobby at my shoulder, but it was the good Bobby, the Bobby who I'd found sitting quietly in the dark by the side of Robert's bed that night so many years ago, when our little boy woke up crying, reliving the fall on the bed, the doctor's hands, the needle with the lidocaine, the operating-theater light in his eyes. "I got him, Fran," Bobby had whispered to me, and I'd gone back to bed.

We walked over to the Lakeview with a Styrofoam container of food from The Chirping Chicken for Mrs. Levitt. Her hair was every which way when she opened the door, and there was a football game on the television. The living room was dark but when she saw Robert she moved around turning on the lights. "This is a beautiful boy," she said. "He should have some soda." Robert was frightened, I could tell, his eyes ricocheting around the room, lighting on the hospital bed then bouncing away. "It's all right," Mrs. Levitt said. "That's Mr. Levitt. He likes the Green Bay Packers, don't you, Irving?"

"That's college football," Robert said, looking at the TV.

"Aah," said Mrs. Levitt, "what do I know? Besides, you don't complain, right, Irving?" Her food was on the kitchen counter, and I put it on a plate and brought it to the card table. The two of us sat on either side of her as she ate, patting her mouth with a paper napkin. She held forkfuls out to Robert, but he shook his head.

"You make house calls on holidays, Mrs. Nurse?" she said, and I smiled. We didn't stay long, just long enough for her to feel as if she'd had company on the holiday. As we left she handed Robert an old, old copy of *The Adventures of Tom Sawyer* with a dark-green cover and a gilt fleur-de-lis on its spine. Inside in faded ink was a big, round, florid signature: Irving S. Levitt. Robert clutched the book as we walked home.

There were almost no cars on the highway, and the breeze was a little cold, as though even the tropics had to pay homage to the Pilgrims' chilly feast. It's as if life stops in America on holidays. Or maybe it's that way everywhere, all over the world, all the places I've never gone, countries I've never seen. It used to be that way on Sundays, when Gracie and I were young. The newsstands and the variety stores were quiet and dark, the OPEN signs in the windows flipped over to CLOSED. The little knots of people at the corners where the buses stopped on weekdays, workdays, were gone, and the streets had a sleepiness like the sleepiness indoors, where working people dozed in their chairs and children chafed at the torpor, bored with checkers and Old Maid and the bickering of their elders. Now only the holidays—the real holidays, not President's Day, or

Labor Day—have that bittersweet air of stop time I remember from Sunday, the sabbath. It was the way life had seemed to me when we'd first arrived in Lake Plata, like falling through nothing. It didn't seem that way as we walked home, the turkey I'd asked the waitress to give us for sandwiches in a plastic shopping bag in my hand. It seemed as though we were taking it easy, having a real holiday, nothing to do, no stories to tell. Or to make up as we went along.

"I love you, sweetie," I said.

"I love you, too. If I can that video game for, like, half price, can we buy it?"

"Don't push your luck."

"Please?"

We had a good time, the rest of that desultory day. I know, because I read about it later in Robert's composition, which made it seem real to me, so real that I put the composition in my bedside drawer after it came home from school. We took out the pot of wallpaper paste I'd bought to paper the bathroom and used it instead to paste pictures from old *Sports Illustrateds* to Robert's closet door. Mattingly, Dr. J., Boomer Esiason, even the women from the Olympic basketball team. We sat cross-legged on the floor of his room, which was dingy and had a line of dirty rubber soles marks around the wall a foot above the molding, as though some kid had kicked and kicked and kicked and kicked. We made a mess,

Robert and I. We'd never made much of a mess before. The closet door was covered with biceps, long legs, faces. It was almost like company. We crammed the leavings from the magazines into a garbage bag, and Robert stood back, his fists on his hips, and narrowed his eyes.

"This is the coolest thing we've ever done," he said. "Bennie's not gonna believe this."

"It looks really good," I said.

"How will we get it off?"

"Don't worry about that now," I said.

Then we watched an old movie on television, wound around one another on the scratchy old couch, and ate turkey sandwiches, and toasted each other with ginger ale. There was an old jar of maraschino cherries in the refrigerator door, just like in an ordinary house, like my real house, on the bay in Brooklyn, the jar of cherries you bought for one guest who drank Manhattans—Bobby's aunt Mae, his uncle Thomas's wife—and that ever after sat and sat on that shelf inside the door. I put a cherry in each of our sodas.

"I used to do that for Aunt Grace when we were little girls," I said. "I'd put the cherry juice in, too, and make it a Shirley Temple for her."

Maybe that was what did it. Or maybe it was just curling up on the couch with Robert, feeling him warm and pliant beside me, smelling his hair the way I used to smell Gracie's as I pulled it into an unruly ponytail. Or maybe it was just that it was, after all, Thanksgiving.

My sister's Thanksgivings were like those horrible short stories in *The New Yorker*, that seemed to have no beginning, no ending, no point. A visiting professor from Oxford who wanted to know all about the Pilgrims. A research assistant whose husband had just left her for another man and who wept in the kitchen and drank too much wine. The couple who lived down the hall from Grace, artists who brought couscous with cranberries in it. Oh, it was funny to hear all about it afterward, and I always did, because the last thing Grace did on Thanksgiving night was to call and tell me all about it.

"And, naturally, she's sitting at one end of the table telling me how satisfying it is to work with her husband, how close it's made them, and he's sitting at my end with his hand on my thigh," she'd say, and "Have you ever made stuffing with chestnuts? If not, don't, because it sucks!" and "Tell Robert this Brit brought me little plastic Pilgrims and I'm foisting them on him when he comes to see me next week." She always called me, just shy of eleven o'clock, Grace did. And so, after Robert stumbled from the couch to his room, his breath smelling of mayonnaise as I kissed him good night, I picked up the old rotary phone on the wall in the kitchen, poured myself more ginger ale, and sat on the linoleum cross-legged, my heart going like a mouse in a cage. She knew, when she picked up; I could tell she knew by the way her voice was, soft and whispery, not like Grace's insistent alto at all. She had to say it twice—"hello . . . hello?"—because the shock of hearing her overcame me suddenly, knocked the wind out of me.

"Happy Thanksgiving, baby girl," I finally said, and my voice wasn't my own either.

"Oh, my God," she said, and she started to cry, "oh, my God. Oh, Frannie. Oh, Frannie." For a minute or two all we did was cry.

"Where are you?" she finally wailed, and then immediately, in a more ordinary adult Grace voice, "Don't tell me. Don't tell me anything that matters. Don't tell me anything that I can give away."

"To Bobby."

"To Bobby. That son of a bitch." Her voice thickened again. "He sat in my living room and he cried. He cried. I almost felt sorry for him. I would have, if I hadn't seen your face. Even then, he got to me. I wound up telling him that if I heard from you I'd make you call him."

Her words caught in her throat, part grief, part fury. "A week later he comes back and wants to know, have you called, where are you, what's your address. And I said I had no idea, I hadn't heard anything from you.

And he accused me of being an accessory to a kidnapping! I couldn't figure out what he was talking about at first. I said, Bob, don't forget that I saw her face. And he says to me, that's exactly why you don't want to fuck with me, Grace."

"Did he hurt you?"

You could hear the hum of the telephone static in the silence, in the moment when Grace tried to decide which would be better for me, the truth or a lie. She went for the lie. Don't we all?

"No," she said.

"Don't let him in again, Gracie. You can't take the chance. He just goes out of control."

"I know. I know. My God, Fran, what you've been living with all this time."

"We're fine," I said. "Robert's fine. He's getting settled. I'm working. I've got a place, and a little money."

"Let me send you more."

"I can't. I can't give you the address. Or the phone number. It's not that I don't trust you. It's just safer."

"The bastard could break my leg and I wouldn't tell him anything. That son of a bitch. My God, Frannie, I feel like such a fool. All those years you taking care of me, such good care, and you were in so much trouble and I didn't even figure it out, or do anything. Nothing. I did nothing." She started to cry again, my little sister, the way she had when she was a child, when I'd hold her head to my chest, hold it still to stop the sobs. "I didn't do anything to help you."

"You didn't know."

"How could none of us have known? I called Winnie at the hospital. She said the same thing. She suspected, but she said they all told themselves that you wouldn't put up with it."

"It's amazing how much you'll put up with," I said.

"I lie in bed at night and think about having him killed and dumped some place where no one will find him. Sometimes I can't believe it's me. I want him dead. If he were dead, then everything would be fine. You'd come back. You'd be safe. I pray that a car will run him down, or that some scumbag on the streets will shoot him."

"I'm safe now, sweetie," I said, matching Grace lie for lie. "Don't talk about killing anybody."

"Twice my mailbox has been broken into and the super thinks it's druggies, but I think it's him. I had my phone checked for bugs."

"Jesus, Grace, he wouldn't bug your phone."

"Oh yeah? You sit there and tell me you're sure he wouldn't do that."

"He might," I finally said. We were both silent again, the silence of two people who have long lived with and loved the sound of each other's breathing. That's what I wanted Robert to do, when he was grown-up, living a life away from me. I could hardly stand to think of it, but when I did I thought of telephone calls when I would just listen to him breathe over the line.

"How's Mom?" I finally said.

"The same. She told Aunt Faye you'd decided you needed a change of scene. She told me that Bobby was rude to her when he came to her house. Rude. Jesus God, what an understatement. 'He was really rude to me, Grace Ann,' she says."

"Oh, I bet he was," I said. "Never mind. Tell me the dinner story."

"What?"

"You know."

She thought I was crazy, wanting the old familiar story of her Thanksgiving dinner, the story of the strange food, the urban strays. But she did it. There'd been a defrocked priest who'd been prominent in the antiwar movement a quarter century before, who brought a bottle of good wine and then drank the whole thing himself. "It's the first time I've heard anyone actually use the word *imperialist* in conversation," Grace said. There was Grace's lesbian friend Trudi, who taught Virginia Woolf and Gertrude Stein and got into an argument with everyone else at the table about whether the Virgin Birth meant Mary was gay. There were two old women from the building who sounded like second cousins to Mrs. Levitt, who brought rutabagas that had turned out to be surprisingly good, and a graduate student from American Samoa who felt compelled to tell Grace in the kitchen just as she was whipping the cream for the pie that he loved her. "Oh, for God's sake, Ramon, cut that pie and put it on plates, I told him, and that was the end of that," Grace said in her old, wry, dismissive, strong Grace voice.

"We went out to dinner at a pretty bad restaurant," I said softly. "It was nice. We went to see one of my patients. We watched *Miracle on 34th Street* after. I think that's why I called."

"We watched it, too," Grace said. "Trudi cried and said she'd always been in love with Natalie Wood."

"We were watching the same movie at the same time. That's pretty good."

"I miss you so much," Grace said.

"I know."

"Give Robert a hug and tell him I miss him, too."

"I can't, Grace. I can't tell him I talked to you. I can't confuse him too much, about now and then, here and there. I can't stay on too much longer, either. I'm afraid. I'm afraid for you, mostly."

There was silence again. "*Breakfast at Tiffany's* is on the Movie Channel at midnight," Grace said. "You want to watch it together?"

"We don't get cable here."

"Will you call again?" Grace said.

"If it's safe," I said. "I'm with you every day in my mind. I'm running."

"I'm running with you in my mind," Grace said. I put down the phone in Florida and she hung up in New York.

I bought Robert the game he wanted for Christmas and hid it in the crawl space above the second floor. I bought Cindy a small sweet landscape I saw in a poster shop at the mall, and Mike Riordan a nylon jacket for running on rainy days. I bought presents for all my patients, although we weren't supposed to: a computer game for Jennifer, full of dragons and demons and a female superhero in a breastplate; a book for Melvin on smart investing and a romance novel for his wife; and, for Mrs. Levitt, a three-year subscription to *People* magazine. Christmas was coming, and I had enough money to buy presents. No one asked for the rent; I didn't get a phone bill. There were calluses on my heels from my running shoes. When the phone rang now I just answered it, listened to the home-care agency ask about taking on a short-term assignment, Cindy ask whether I wanted her to drive me to school for soccer practice, the school to ask if Robert could take Tylenol for a headache. Twice it rang and no one was there. That happens to everyone, I told myself. To everyone.

"You all right?" Cindy said one morning in the library.

"I'm not sleeping real well," I said.

"Ladies," Mrs. Patrinian said, "not too loud please."

"You tried taking melatonin?" Cindy said. "One of the moms at Gymboree swears by it, says she can't even manage to stay up for the news now."

When we went back to her house that morning she made me muffins and searched her medicine cabinet for sleeping pills. "Nothing but under-eye concealer, hon, but to tell the truth you could use it," she said.

"Do I look that bad?"

"You look tired. Sort of frail. I don't know, some men like that look."

"Some men like single women in their twenties with no kids."

"You just stay away from those men, and keep on running around that track."

"You got a one-track mind," I said.

"Ha, ha," Cindy said.

I told Cindy about Grace, and a little about our parents, although I placed them all in Wilmington, Delaware, along with two older brothers and the accountant from whom I was divorced. I changed the subject Gracie taught from American studies to English literature, and I never mentioned Hunter College. I told her that my father had died of cancer, not of the emphysema he'd picked up as a New York City firefighter, all those buildings with asbestos insulation and two packs of Camels a day. I told her my mother was a secretary, even told her that she was the secretary to the head of a labor union. Soon I knew all about Craig and his pool business, about how Chelsea was afraid of thunderstorms, dogs, and insects, and how Chad was afraid of nothing, about Cindy's mom, Helen, and how she was one of the people who discovered that the Avon bath oil repelled mosquitoes, since the farm had more mosquitoes than crops. She was a second-generation Avon lady, Cindy was; she showed me the story in the Avon annual report about her and her mother. Her parents' farm was somewhere between Lake Plata and Jocasta, and her mother had logged sometimes a hundred miles a day dropping off eyebrow pencil and bath-oil beads to the wives of other farmers, before the area was all built up, chock-full of retired Northerners and people who confused sunshine with gold. Cindy went along when she got older, swiping those little sample lipsticks that the Avon lady left at our apartment for me and Gracie, even though our mother wouldn't buy a thing. A sea of moisturizer managed to keep Cindy's parents' place afloat, the thirsty faces of all those women baked leathery by the harsh Florida sun.

Cindy and Craig had lived on the farm right after they were married, then built their own place in a subdivision two miles from the center of Lake Plata, in a redwood house with a lot of windows and an aboveground pool with some kind of automatic alarm on the surface so Chad wouldn't fall in and drown. Chelsea was afraid they'd all drown, in the pool, at the beach, in the tub. They lived at the end of a cul-de-sac, in an area of cul-de-sacs, as though by eliminating through roads the people who lived there could keep the rest of the world away. Every time I came for coffee I took the measure of Cindy's kitchen, envying her her no-wax linoleum and the double-door refrigerator with the automatic ice maker. But as my eyes roved around the white Formica and the oak cabinets I was really walking through my own house in my mind, up the four steps with the white iron railing, through the storm door and into the foyer with the half-round table and the gilded mirror over it, the one Bobby's mother gave us for a housewarming present. It's funny how you get about a house when you've never had one, never ever thought you'd have one. The day we signed all those papers, with thirty-years this and thirty-years that, passing around the checks like in some grown-up board game, we'd gone over to the house and wandered about like a couple of kids, our words echoing in the emptiness. Buying the house made it seem as though it was us that was so solid, made of brick and plaster so that nothing could blow us over. I remember looking up the stairs and it was like they were reaching up, not to three bedrooms and a bath with a glassed-in stall shower, but to heaven. He'd shoved me a few times by then, even hit me in the stomach once. But I never looked up those stairs and imagined myself falling down them with a fist in the small of my back.

"This is it, baby," he said, and he pulled me down to the wall-to-wall, his words echoing in the empty, stripped-down rooms. And it was. I got carpet burns on my butt that day, and I was the happiest woman in the world. People can talk about self-respect all they want, and people do plenty, usually when they're talking about somebody else's business. But whenever I thought about leaving, sometimes as much as leaving Bobby I thought about leaving my house. Balloon shades and miniblinds and the way I felt at night sleeping on my extra-firm mattress under my own roof that we'd had hot-tarred the year after Robert was born—all of it helped keep me there. And if that sounds foolish, just think about that solid settled feeling you get when you open your cabinets and there are the mugs for the coffee that have held the coffee day after day, year after year, hanging in a row from cup hooks, all the same color, the same size.

Small things: routine, order. That's what kept me there for the longest time. That, and love. That, and fear. Not fear of Bobby, fear of winding up in some low-rent apartment subdivision with a window that looked out on a wall. Fear of winding up where I'd come from, where I was right now. It took me a dozen years of house pride and seventeen years of marriage before I realized there were worse things than a cramped kitchen and grubby carpeting.

I wondered how much damage Bobby had done to our house when he'd found us gone, with no one around to bruise or break. I wondered what he'd told his mother, whether he'd told his friends, or whether he'd just quietly set about the business of finding me. He had a half-dozen friends who were on full pension and working as investigators; maybe he'd called one of them. One hundred and thirty days I'd been gone. August. September. October. November. Someone would have thought of Patty Bancroft by now. When a car pulled to the curb in front of the apartment complex at two in the morning it rocked my world. Cindy gave me a bottle of melatonin, but I was afraid to take it, afraid to sleep deep. I dozed on and off each night, lulled by the sound of Robert's breathing over the baby monitor.

It's funny; with all the elaborate preparations that Patty Bancroft's people had made, I never doubted that some day he would find us. I always felt like I was just buying time, the time it takes to raise one boy from child to adult. I never figured out how hard it was going to be to do that until I started, and then the bitch of it was that it was too late to turn back, though I wouldn't have turned back anyhow. The bitch of it was that it takes so much time and effort to make things good for them, and so little to make them bad. The bitch of it is that we're never sure whether what we're doing is right or wrong.

Some of the damage is done. Robert watches too much, is too quiet. It's better when he's with other kids, but with adults he's always waiting for something to happen, like a psychic looking down at someone's palm. When he got thrown out of the supermarket, he was angry and upset, but he wasn't surprised. It was as though he knew that grown-ups, at any moment, might go off like car alarms, loud, scary, for no reason at all. The truth is, that's the way Bobby made him. And me, too, by taking it. Robert has a look on his face too much of the time that people have when they think they've heard something moving around in the basement, heard the rumble of thunder so far away it just might be a truck in the next block. He had that look on his face that last time in Grace's apartment. That's how I think of the weeks before I left: the last time. The last time Bobby hit me. The last time I saw my sister. The last time I left my house, locking the door behind me.

The last time in Grace's apartment I saw Robert's

face change, saw it go still and watchful, realized in a minute or two that he'd heard the elevator and the footsteps before we had, had been listening for them. His eyes were huge but his shoulders hunched, as though he was trying to make himself small, smaller, tiny, invisible. *Bang,* at the door. *Bang,* and Robert shrinking into himself like a little old man. It's amazing, how furious the sound of knuckles meeting wood can sound.

"How the hell did he get upstairs?" Grace had said, and she made herself big, threw her bony shoulders back, marched in her clogs—*bang, bang*—to answer the banging at the door.

"Go away, Bob. Just go away."

"I want my wife and my son." I had been able to hear in Bobby's voice that he had been drinking, but not too much. "Now."

"Go away, Bob. You've done enough damage."

"This is none of your goddamn business, Grace. Frannie? Fran? You come out here and talk to me or I'll break the goddamn door down." I could feel Robert's shoulders vibrating beneath my fingertips, or maybe the vibrations were coming from inside me.

"How the hell did he get up here?" Gracie said, all her freckles standing out against the white of her face, and from the other side of the thick oak door of her apartment came what sounded like a chuckle. "I showed the doorman my badge, Grace." That voice again, that deep bass line, music to someone's ears, if not mine. You could just see him talking to the Russian émigré who minded the door of Grace's building, an old man in a faded blue-black uniform and ill-fitting hat. You could see Bobby flipping open the little leather case I'd given him when he made detective and the doorman falling back before him, perhaps even touching his hand to the corner of his hat. Sometimes I thought how hard it was to be a cop, to put on the clothes and be force of law and then take them off and be no more than a man with a cheap sport shirt and a stack of bills. But sometimes it made things easier.

"Let him in," I said.

"No."

"Let him in, Grace. Or take Robert into the other room and I'll let him in."

"Aw, hell, Frances," Bobby had said when I unlocked the deadbolt and the other two Yale locks, but whether it was because of my betrayal in leaving him and going to Grace or because of the look of my face, which was mottled purple and black where it wasn't covered with adhesive tape, I don't know. Maybe he didn't know how bad he'd hurt me. He'd come in after midnight the night before and banged around the kitchen and the living room looking for something, muttering furiously to himself, waking me from a sound sleep, so that I couldn't go off again. I don't know why I went downstairs. I've asked myself that so many times, no matter what Patty Bancroft likes to say on television about placing blame where blame belongs. All I know is that if I'd done what I'd done so many times before, pretended to be asleep, ignored the staccato sounds of rage from below, I'd still be sleeping in my own bed now, and my son in his. Or maybe not. If it hadn't been my nose on a Wednesday in late July, it would have been my jaw on a Saturday in September. I suppose that's true. Like a cloud to a storm to a hurricane the thing between us had gotten bigger and blacker every day, until maybe it was bound to pick us up, smash us down, leave us all in ruins. In Lake Plata.

There wasn't even an argument. Or maybe Bobby had been having an argument with me in his head all day long—on the job, in the car, while he was banging around the kitchen. Maybe it was an argument made of saved string, a big, brightly colored ball of an argument, the synthesis of all the arguments we'd ever had before. Why the fuck do you baby the boy go to your sister's ignore my mother wear that skirt work so many hours look at me like that fuck my friends your friends strangers doctors everyone anyone the man in the moon? I'd stumbled down the stairs and into the hall in my long white nightgown and the light hurt my eyes and I couldn't see his, could only see half a dozen drawers and cabinets gaping open, as though he was looking for something. He probably was. Bobby was always looking for something, and neither of us knew what it was.

"Bobby, what is your problem?" I'd said, squinting in the light, and it happened, just like that, three good punches that I remember and then I came to maybe an hour later, covered in blood, my nose and tongue numb. I'd broken one and bitten right through the edge of the other. I'd fixed myself up with Bactracin and bandages and gone to bed right beside him. I know people will find it hard to understand that, but it was my bed, I belonged there, I wasn't going to be thrown out of my own bed no matter what. I woke once to hear Bobby sending Robert off to school, pretended to be asleep when I heard our bedroom door open. I called in to work sick when Bobby was gone, waited for Robert to come home, spent $25 on a cab and took him to Grace's and let myself in and waited there in the shadows, no lights on, her apartment cheaper because it was at the back of the building. Robert fell asleep in her bedroom.

"I broke my nose," I said when Grace came in with her briefcase and her tote bag full of books.

She stood there, my baby sister, still that even if she is thirty-two, and her own face crumpled, and she sat on the arm of the sofa and took my head in her hands. She's little, Grace, but strong in her bones and muscles somehow; she lifts weights, too, just like Bobby, and when she raises those skinny arms over her head to stretch you can see all the connections in her body, everything, biceps, triceps, shoulder muscles like rubber bands.

"No, you didn't," she said. "You didn't break your nose. Don't you ever say you broke your nose. Someone else broke your nose. That son of a bitch. That bastard. I told Mom he was doing this. I told Mom about all these things that happen to you. That big bruise you had the last time we had lunch. The time you had the marks all over your one arm. And you know what she said? She said you always were a clumsy kid. Jesus God, if she could see you now."

We sat at Grace's round oak dining table, Bobby and I, while Grace took Robert into her bedroom. It was a small apartment and the table was really at one end of the living room, by casement windows that looked out over a sliver of 104th Street. "Where are you gonna sleep here, on the couch?" he said. "Where's Robert gonna sleep?"

"Look at my face," I said.

"My son should be in my house. Not in some shit hole on the Upper West Side. You don't know this area like I do. He could get hurt here."

"Look at my face," I said.

"I'm taking you home," he said.

"No."

"Then I'm taking Robert home."

"I won't let you."

Then Bobby looked at my face, looked at it good, looked at it with a cold, cold look that he, for all the things he'd done to me, had never given me before. And like he'd been rehearsing it he said, real quiet, "What are you gonna do, Fran? Call the cops?"

That's when I knew. That's when I knew that this was the last time, that I was leaving. If there was a moment when I decided that Bobby Benedetto would never touch me again, it was at that moment. He was gloating, really, although for once you couldn't read his mood in his voice. He was telling me that I was trapped, that I was chained in some basement he'd created, a basement with flowered ironstone dishes all laid out neatly in the cupboards, with silk flowers in a vase on the dining-room table. He was telling me that I'd never get away, that he could do what he wanted and I couldn't do a thing about it.

As we were leaving, Gracie pulled me back into the little foyer for just a moment. "Please don't do this, Frannie," she said. "I'll help you. I'll do anything to help you."

"How?" I said. I was asleep on my feet and my face hurt so much that the pain was all I could think of.

"I'll think of something," she said.

"He's going to take my kid, Gracie," I said.

"We can stop him," she said. I laughed then, even

though it hurt, a bitter choking chuckle halfway to a sob. "What are we going to do, Grace, call a cop?" I said.

That night I gave up and slept on the floor in Robert's room. Bobby saw the puddle of pillow and blanket on the floor and tried to put his hand out to me. I cringed, pulled away, then looked him full in the face. Once I saw a man in the psych ward reading the notebooks he'd written before he'd been given antihallucinogens, reading the gibberish he'd written frantically, fanatically, as though it was the secret of the universe. Bobby looked a little like that when I pulled back from his big hand.

I'd taken two Percocets I had left over from having my wisdom teeth out, and when I woke up, my one cheek beating with every beat of my heart, the sun was making shards of daylight across the blue carpeting and the house was empty. I ran from room to room calling Robert's name, and finally I called the principal of his school, who called the counselor at the school day camp, who said that he was in gym, playing pillow polo. There were only ten days left of day camp. We were renting a house at the beach for the first two weeks of August, a cottage on Long Island Sound. But I wasn't going.

I'd called a family planning clinic in lower Manhattan to make an appointment for the next day. Then I'd called Patty Bancroft. And I bet Bobby thought it was because he'd broken my nose and bloodied my face. He'd never touched my face before; it was as though, as never before, he'd touched my insides, who I was, who I am. And it was his threat, too, that made me understand that I had to run to hide, to get away. What was I going to do, call a cop?

But maybe it was Robert who made me run, really. It was the look on his face on the way home from Grace's apartment that last time, the look on his face as we passed under the streetlight on our corner. The look on his face was nothing, nothing at all, the look he might have if he were watching a boring movie on television or playing with his food at the dinner table. The part of a little boy that would be frightened if his father threatened his mother and his aunt, the part of him that would be scared and screaming if his mother's face was all bruised and bloodied: that part of Robert was dead. Or been driven so deep inside that you couldn't see it and he couldn't feel it. I saw it for a moment when he came home that next day from day camp and saw me in the kitchen, in the sunlight; I saw the kind of horror and fear that a normal kid would feel. But then it was gone again, his face flat and closed, as he asked me whether I'd had an accident. So many accidents during his childhood, and all of them lies.

That's why I left when I did, how I did. During the long nights of a Florida winter, alive with wind sounds and whispers, as I imagined that Bobby was on the roof, at the door, jimmying a window open, I had a lot of time to think. And that's the truth. That's why I left. I'm a nurse, you know, a Catholic girl, a mother, and the wife of a man who wanted to suck the soul out of me and put it in his pocket. I'm not real good at doing things for myself. But for Robert? That was a different story.

Oh, goodness gracious, you must be Beth. And Robert." Cindy was right, her mother was thin and dark, as though she'd been dried by the sun, a raisin of a woman with her daughter's big blue eyes and electric smile. She stood aside to let us into the house, her arm extended as though we were being welcomed to something magical.

"Merry Christmas," Craig said, getting up from the couch, a mug of eggnog with snowflakes painted on it in his hand.

"Merry Christmas," said Mike Riordan, who was sitting next to him.

"Hi, Mr. Riordan," said Robert. "What are you doing here?"

"You come in here, Beth," Cindy shouted from inside the kitchen.

When I'd been younger I'd worked at the hospital sometimes on Christmas Eve and Christmas Day, ceding the holiday to the older women with children and in-laws to cook for. But even in the lounge of the medical-surgical floor, or the emergency room, we managed to construct our own traditions, the fancy trays of meats and cheeses studded with radish roses, the plates of cannoli and cream puffs, the tiny tree with felt ornaments that one of the aides made, with each of our names spelled out on a bell or a star in glue and glitter. And later we'd made our own Christmases, Bobby and Robert and I. Christmas Eve dinner at Ann Benedetto's, scungilli and calamari and baccalà, the walk home through a cold Brooklyn night along streets bright as day with lit-up lawn reindeer and sleighs and Mr. Costanza's house, that got in the *Daily News* every year because it took $500 worth of Con Ed juice to light it for a week. Morning mass at St. Stannie's, the kids clutching whichever toy was the favorite that year, Ninja Turtles, Power Rangers, Battle Beasts, dinner in the early evening. And after the guests were gone and the dishwasher was humming and Robert was in bed, his new toys ranged around him like a bulwark, the smell of fresh plastic and evergreen in the air, Bobby would put on his Nat King Cole album and at the words "Chestnuts roasting on an open fire" he would take me in his arms and dance me slowly, seriously, around our small and narrow living room, singing along in a baritone grown a little uncertain with age. I can feel him, smell him, if I close my eyes and hum that song to myself.

It was the Florida weather that had saved me, as I'd climbed out of bed that morning to dress. It was as warm as April in New York, so that it made it hard to believe in reindeer in the snow or sleigh rides. Even Robert felt it: "It's weird to wear a short-sleeved shirt to Christmas," he'd said as he loaded new batteries into his video game. That was the new word, *weird*. "It's weird to be going to somebody else's house for Christmas," he said later, eating his cereal. "It's weird not to have a bigger tree," he mumbled, putting his bowl in the sink.

"That was the biggest tree I could afford," I said, my voice quavering. "Those were the presents I could afford. This is the kind of Christmas I could afford."

"It just feels weird," Robert said, his own voice unsteady, and I'd hugged him hard then.

"It's weird not to be with your father," I said. "And Aunt Grace, and Grandmom. It's the hardest thing in the world not to be with the people you love on Christmas Day."

"But I'm with you," he said. So sweet, sometimes, the way he would say things like that, as though just like his father he was two people, the one who hated where he was, and the one who'd made his peace with it. As I'd begun to do. I wondered, just for a moment, whether Bobby had done the same thing, whether even now he was sitting with a glass of red wine, saying "Ah, good riddance" to one of his cop friends while the wife checked on whether the ham was ready to glaze and the kids bickered over their new toys. But I looked down at Robert's shining hair and knew that that couldn't be true, no matter how much I wanted it. "My son," Bobby used to call him. "My boy." That possessive pronoun. My wife. My girl. He'd never give us up. Somewhere, somehow, I knew that he was listening to that Christmas song and seething. Robert went up the stairs of the Roerbacker house to help Chad with his new Duplo blocks and I went into the kitchen to arrange Cindy's baking-powder biscuits on a cookie sheet.

"Mama, honey, go sit back down," Cindy said, when Helen Manford followed me, pulling idly at the cord on a little Santa pin that made his eyes light up red and faintly demonic.

"I had a pin like that when I was a kid," I said. "I had a red Christmas coat one year and I wore that pin on the lapel."

Mrs. Manford smiled. Farm or no farm, dirt or no dirt, she still had a kind of beauty, with a grace of bone and posture that would forever survive sun and long hours and hard work. Next to her, her daughter, with her bright lips and hair in a curly twist, looked like a jumped-up imitation of the real thing.

"Go ahead and tell her," Cindy said, sipping some white wine, pouring me a glass. I could hear the men from the living room, like the rumble of thunder.

"I got this one when I was a girl, too. Fourteen, I think. I loved it so dearly that I managed to hold onto it. I even got the jeweler up on the highway to find some kind of new battery for it when it wouldn't light up anymore."

"Once when I was seven or eight," Cindy said, "there was a hurricane and they evacuated us all to the high school. Mama's running around, getting the picture albums and the records from the farm, bills and invoices and all that. All of a sudden she lets out this little yelp, runs back into her bedroom and comes out with her hand in a fist. 'Oh, for pity's sake, Helen,' my dad says, and sure enough it's Santa."

"You'd better take good care of him when he's yours."

"Oh, for pity's sake, Mama, you'll live forever." Cindy turned down a fruit sauce bubbling on the back of the stove. "I'm gonna kill us all with this meal."

"I don't want to hear one word about cholesterol on Christmas Day," Mrs. Manford said. "There's too much of that as there is. Cynthia Lee, it's not a good idea for you to be drinking and cooking at the same time. You'll burn yourself on that stove."

"It's a glass of wine, Mama. Want one?"

"No, ma'am," said Mrs. Manford.

"Take these spiced pecans out to the table for those guys to munch on," Cindy said, handing her mother a bowl.

"Well, they smell good," Mrs. Manford said doubtfully, carrying the food into the next room.

"There's a guest in that living room that you didn't tell me about," I said to Cindy.

"Well, since you two are such friends, I figured I didn't need to," Cindy said. "Hold this chafing dish." She poured creamed onions into it, then waved me over to the table and handed me a silver lid.

"That's all you're going to say?"

"Oh, for pity's sake. The poor man has his mama and two of his sisters coming with their kids tomorrow. He told Mrs. Patranian he was going to stay home today and straighten up his place. She was going to take him home and feed him lamb and some terrible bean stuff she was telling me about. You should have invited him yourself."

"We were coming here!"

"So, see—I saved you the trouble."

"You should have said."

"Good thing you dressed nice. You look good in green. Not like most blondes, who just look washed out." She squinted at me. "Wait a minute, wait a minute. I'm not so drunk that I don't notice you're not wearing your glasses. You finally get contacts?"

"Leave me in peace and give me something to do," I said.

"You knew he was coming after all," Cindy crowed, and I hit her with a dishtowel.

Cindy's Christmas was ham with raisin sauce and mashed sweet potatoes with marshmallows browning on top, creamed onions and baby peas, papier-mâché angels on the mantel in the living room, and a silvery white artificial tree with red lights and ornaments. "I know, I know, it's tacky," she said when I caught her buying evergreen fragrance in a can. "But I can't stand picking pine needles out of my carpet."

Craig was tending a fire in the fireplace, although it was almost seventy degrees outside and the air-conditioning was on. He and Mike and his father-in-law were talking about the football standings, pro, college, and local high school, and whether the mayor of Lakota was a crook, a smart politician, or both. Cindy's father, Ed, leaned forward and did most of the talking. He was a short fireplug of a man, while Craig was tall and quiet, a big bony man with a thatch of gray-brown hair, whose smile seemed to be a kind of muscle spasm he neither controlled nor invited. When he and Cindy were in the same room it felt as though they'd divvied up the parts of their marriage, and Cindy, along with kids and home decor, had gotten the part that controlled laughter and sociability. "He's my rock," she liked to say of Craig, and there was something stony, fossilized about him, a man prematurely old at forty. But I was inclined to like him because of the way he let Cindy clean up around him and chide him for his bottle caps and missing buttons as though nothing could be more welcome or more sensible than being chided. I liked him even more that night, when he rose beneath a brass chandelier that was bound and gagged in an endless rope of fake greenery and red ribbon, a dishtowel tucked in the waistband of his pants, raised a glass of white wine, and said, "Merry Christmas to all. Thank you for joining us, Mike and Beth and Robert."

"Thank *you*," I said.

"Don't speak too soon, Miss," said Ed Manford, bent over his plate. "You haven't tasted any of this yet. Maybe you don't know that our girl has a reputation as a chef." He laughed, one of those short barking laughs that seem to be the specialty of small men, and that are never really mirthful. "And I'm not talking Julia Child, that's for sure."

"Here we go," Cindy said under her breath.

"You're a nurse or a nurse's aide or something, aren't you? You ever dealt with a case of ptomaine?" *Bark, bark.* "There's Pepto in that bathroom, isn't there, Craig?"

"Ed, don't start," said Helen Manford, turning her sweet potatoes over with her fork as though she expected to find something buried inside them.

"Did she tell you about her first try at home cooking?" Ed Manford added, leaning toward me until his beefy upper arm was against the side of my breast and I was back as far as I could go in my chair. "Barbecued chicken, done to a turn. Brown and crispy, like out of a picture in a cookbook. Just one little thing." The bark again, this time with more of an edge. "She didn't defrost it. Red and raw and all bloody inside. Good thing we had some bologna in the icebox."

"That was twenty years ago, Dad," Cindy said.

"She made a picnic last year for the soccer tournament," Mike said. "That was the best fried chicken I ever had. And that chocolate cake you brought. That was great, too."

"Remember that barbecue they had for the girl's third birthday, El?" Mr. Manford said, as though Mike had said nothing at all. "I was in the bathroom for the rest of the evening. I never figured whether it was the potato salad or the spareribs."

"No one else had a problem," Cindy said, but he didn't

pay any attention. "How's your ham, Helen?" he asked. "Done enough?"

"It's perfect," said Craig Roerbacker. "Everything's perfect. As usual."

"Really. Great meal, Cindy. Great meal," said Mike.

"Not a whole lot of money in teaching, is there?" Mr. Manford said.

"Nope," Mike said. "You have to love it." He smiled at me. "And have a sense of humor."

"Spoon. Spoon. Spoon. Spoon," shouted Chad from the children's table set at one end of the room.

"Pipe down, little boy," said Ed Manford, shoveling in his food.

"Spoon!" Chad yelled again, happily.

"You be a good boy, now," said Helen.

"Leave him alone, Mama," said Cindy. "It's Christmas." Over at the children's table Robert was whispering to Chad and feeding him sweet potatoes, teaching him his favorite party trick, being good, being quiet. Teaching him to make himself disappear when the grown-ups started to raise their voices.

We all had coffee afterward in the living room, the fire burning blue in the stone fireplace, Mr. Manford asleep in the recliner chair. Both Cindy and her mother took aspirin after dinner. Chelsea hit Chad with Holiday Barbie because he'd disarranged the doll's hair;

she'd been sent to her room, where she'd fallen asleep sprawled across her bed in a red lace party dress. "You're not supposed to be mean at Christmas, Mommy," she sobbed as she went up the stairs, Barbie's head going *bump-bump-bump* on the treads. Robert read *One Fish, Two Fish* to Chad—I could tell because from time to time I could hear Chad shout "Fish!" from upstairs.

"I told him if he went to sleep I'd kick the soccer ball with him tomorrow," Robert said when he finally came downstairs.

"Bless you, sweetie," Cindy said, her head tilted back in the circle of her husband's arm. From upstairs we all heard the word faintly: "Ball! Ball!" All of us laughed except for Mr. Manford, who was snoring, and Mrs. Manford, who was cleaning the kitchen, though Cindy had tried three or four times to persuade her not to.

Mike drove us home, of course. Cindy'd asked him before we'd even arrived. The lights of the strip were glowing like decorations in the mist, but for the first time since we'd come to Lake Plata, maybe the only time all year, all the parking lots were empty, as though of one accord we had all decided to take one day off from cheap hamburgers and labor-saving appliances and instead come together in our living rooms. We passed house trailers set back behind the Price Club warehouse and tiny cinder-block houses that couldn't possibly have more than two rooms, and I was certain that each had some Christmas tradition, and perhaps as much of a divide between what we felt and what we wanted to feel as there'd been at Cindy's that night. I couldn't help thinking of how Cindy had once been in love with Jackson Islington, who wanted to settle down on a farm; I couldn't help thinking of Ed Manford's stubby hands, a faint tracery of black soil etched in so deep that it would never come out, no matter how much he scrubbed. He'd eaten everything on his plate, then taken seconds.

"How in the world did that hateful man ever produce someone as sweet as Cindy?" I said in a low voice after looking in back to make sure Robert was occupied with his new video game.

"That's a good question," Mike said. "You see it all the time. Some really good kids with terrible parents. And some great parents with tough kids."

"And then you've got Cindy and Craig, who seem so grounded, with Chelsea, who is scared to death of everything. Cindy couldn't use the electric knife for the ham because it freaks Chelsea out. I've never seen the point of an electric knife. It's just as easy to carve with the old-fashioned kind. Cindy said that as soon as Chelsea hears it humming, she stats to think someone's going to cut a hand off."

"I think the fear thing has to have something to do

with Cindy's sister. I imagine that's why Cindy's parents are so strange with her, too. They probably look at Cindy and see Cathy. Although you'd think they'd be grateful to have Cindy and be a little nicer to her."

"Cindy doesn't have a sister."

"She did. She didn't tell you?" He shook his head. "That's weird. It's one of those famous stories that every town has. Sooner or later she must have known someone would tell you. Cindy was an identical twin. From what I've heard Mrs. Manford really used to do it up the way people used to with twins, twin girls mostly, curls and Mary Janes and matching dresses and all that. The story I heard was that one day their mother sent Cathy out to their cornfield to call Mr. Manford in for dinner. He was on one of those big tractors, those John Deeres with the huge wheels they use around here, where you sit up high off the ground. Apparently he never even saw her. Someone told me he thought he hit a rock."

"Jesus Christ," I said.

"Yeah. If I'd been the father it would have killed me. But I'd also like to think it would make me treasure the one I had left."

"I can't believe Cindy never told me."

"Maybe it's too hard for her to talk about it," he said as he pulled up in front of the house. "Here we are."

Robert had fallen asleep in the back, his game still

buzzing in his hand. Mike Riodan carried him inside, laid him on the couch and turned to go. Our living room had a small tree stuck in a bucket of wet sand, decorated with glass balls and paper apples I'd found at the discount drugstore, and beneath it were a few packages. I handed him one. "Merry Christmas," I said. "I didn't bring it tonight because I didn't know you were going to be there."

"I didn't know you were coming, either."

He lifted the green jacket from its box, held it up in front of him as though he'd never seen a jacket before, had no idea what it was used for or what it might be. Robert stirred on the couch, then sat up. "That's a good jacket," Robert said faintly.

"If you've already got one—" I said.

"No," Mike said. "Thank you. I really needed this." He laughed. "I'll drop your presents by tomorrow. I didn't bring them because I didn't know—you know."

"Merry Christmas, Mr. Riordan," said Robert.

"Mr. Riordan was weird about his present," Robert said later as I tucked him in.

"I think he didn't like it but he was trying to be polite," I said.

"I liked everything I got," Robert said.

"Me too," I said. "I love you, Ba." I held him for a moment and realized that he was beginning to feel different in my arms, more geometric, less soft. The tears slid down my cheeks and onto his face.

"I love you, too, Mom," he said. "I had a really good Christmas. Don't be sad."

"I'm not, hon. I'm not." In the kitchen I picked up the phone, put it down, picked it up again. I wasn't even sure who I wanted to call. Or who I could afford to call. Patty Bancroft had called me, three days before, when the phone bills came, to ask icily about the twenty-three-minute call to New York on the evening of November 24. It hadn't felt like twenty-three minutes, those precious minutes on the phone to Grace. It had felt like no time at all. "You have no idea what can be done with phone records," Patty Bancroft had said coldly.

"How could anyone see my phone records? I haven't even seen them. I don't even know where they're delivered."

"Holidays are a difficult time, Elizabeth," she'd said. "People call home during the holidays, and people who are looking for them know that. And getting a copy of a phone record, for someone who knows how, is nothing. Nothing at all."

I'd hated the tone of her voice, as though she were talking to a child, a teenage girl who talked too long to her friends, a stupid adolescent with no idea of the results of her actions. But she'd scared me. I picked up the receiver in the kitchen, then put it down, then picked it up again. The dial tone turned into the manic high-pitched beeping of a phone off the hook, and I could hear the sing-song murmur of the recorded message: "If you wish to place a call . . ." Finally I hung up, then picked the phone up once more and dialed the number on an index card tacked to the kitchen doorjamb.

"Hello," she said, her voice a little hoarse, as though she had not had cause to use it that day.

"Hi, Mrs. Levitt. It's Beth Crenshaw. I know it's late, but is it all right if I say Merry Christmas?"

In the background I heard the sound of conversation, even music. "Is this a bad time?" I added.

"Ach, no," she said. "Irving and I are watching *White Christmas*, aren't we, Irving. A Christmas movie, what can it hurt? Not like having a tree, right? That Rosemary Clooney, it's a shame, how heavy she got. She was a nice-looking girl when she was young."

"She was, wasn't she?"

"But you can tell, the ones that have to watch it when they get a little older, or next thing you know, a backside out to here. Now she wears nothing but muumuus."

"But a beautiful voice."

"Beautiful. Merry Christmas, Mrs. Nurse. I'll tell you something—Irving likes you. I can tell. This one you like, Irving, I said."

"I'm glad. Tell him I said thank you."

"We'll see you Tuesday, won't we, Irving? I have a little something for the little boy."

And then I called Cindy, even though I'd just left her. "I just wanted to say thanks again," I said. "You saved my life with that dinner, and the presents and everything." I thought of Cindy's twin, of the early years, when she'd been able to look at a mirror image without even looking in the mirror, of sitting in the kitchen, or their room, or wherever she was when Cathy went out to call Ed Manford for dinner, of her hearing the shouting, the screams. Or maybe not. Maybe just hearing a silence where a moment before ordinary life had been. It had been a good story, that story about Jackson Islington. But it hadn't been the real story. Although I couldn't complain; it had been a good story I'd told her, the story of the nuns. But it hadn't been the real story, either.

"I love you, kid," I said.

"Love you, honey," she said. "I got to go to bed. I had too much wine." And in the kitchen I poured myself a glass of water and drank it by the living-room window, looked out over the dark quadrangle hung with motley lights from a gap I made with my two fingers in the blinds. Finally I went to bed, with Nat King Cole playing over and over in my head, with my stomach roiling with wine. I thought of Ed Manford leaning so close to me, of Cindy's sister disappearing beneath the big ridged wheels of a farm tractor. And I thought of

Bobby. The Christmas before he'd given me a half-heart, cut down the center with a jagged line, hanging on a heavy gold chain. The other half he'd hung around his own neck, on the chain where he wore his miraculous medal, the image of the Virgin Mary his father had been given by his own parents when he became a cop, that Ann Benedetto had refused to have buried with her husband, had given to her son instead. I'd left the half-heart in my jewelry box, below the costume things. But I knew Bobby had found it, his heart, jettisoned, left. Maybe that had been enough. Maybe he had let me go. Maybe he was singing Nat King Cole into some other woman's ear, some woman he'd found to take my place, a woman who didn't make him angry or mean, who got all the good stuff and none of the bad. As Christmas Day darkened and deepened into the morning of the day after, I fell asleep, wondering.

The next morning Mike Riordan came by with two packages, beautifully, extravagantly wrapped, the work of a department store gift-wrapping department, all foil stars and glittery ribbon. "I thought you had company today," I said.

"They're coming at three," he said. "I cleaned up by stuffing everything in the closets."

For Robert he had gotten a Yankees baseball shirt, blue and white pinstripes. For me there was a runner's rain jacket, lightweight, deep green. It was more or less the same jacket I'd given him, except that his was size large, mine size small. The look on my face must have been funny.

"Don't tell Cindy," Mike said, "or she'll talk about it till next Christmas."

There was something called a Safe-Home party with kids, balloons, hot-dog wagons, and clowns at the school on New Year's Eve, Mike so busy that I only got to wave at him across a very crowded cafeteria, and then the holidays were over. Soccer ebbed, basketball flowed; Robert had practice three times a week after school, games every weekend, enough homework that he moved straight from his desk to the sink to brush his teeth and wash his face for bed. Jennifer got a new wheelchair and taught me to play a computer game called "Knockout"; she always won, the high score table a list of variations on her name and initials. Cindy and I ran a sale of books the library no longer needed, our hands and faces gray with the dust of years. And one day at the end of January, walking home from the

Levitts, seeing familiar lights in now-familiar windows, it occurred to me that the tedium of this life had become comforting, that it felt real and lasting in its sheer ordinary drudgery, that in the same way I found it restful to run a route I'd run dozens of times before, so it had become restful to do these small tasks that I knew by heart, that asked no more of me than a kind of rote recitation of the body.

I was less fearful, but not foolhardy. I still scanned every crowd—at the mall, at the ball games—as careful as a snitch looking for a hit man. Not just for Bobby, for his dark head, his hawkish profile, but for his uncle Gerald, or some cop now retired who'd once shared a squad car with him, or a woman who knew us both from St. Stannie's. America turns out to be a very small country if you're trying to get lost in it. Mention you're from Omaha and it's a cinch: any stranger you meet will say he has a cousin there. It's why I had been able to come to Lake Plata and be absorbed by the town as completely as a stone falling into deep water: because there was no town, really, just a collection of strangers ranged around a commercial strip. No families who had lived on one block for three generations, or even the remnants of that sort of life, a son or a daughter living in a house a block or two away from where their parents had raised them.

One Saturday we went to a carnival outside town to celebrate the first win of the peewee basketball team. Every carnival is the same carnival. Literally. If you read the name on the tickets they make you buy in vast quantities for the rides, or look at the gaudy logos painted on trucks parked around the outskirts of the glittering circle, you might see the same name in an empty field in Florida as you see in a high-school parking area in Westchester or outside a mall in Oak Park, Illinois. Westhammer Amusements, Jensen Amusements, Richter Amusements. They just hook it all up to trailers or throw it all on flatbeds, the haunted house, the midway games with their bad odds and cheap toy prizes, the Tilt-a-Whirl and Cyclone. Three days later they pack it all up and haul it to the next town. Bobby would never let Robert go on any rides at a carnival. "Look at these dirtbags," he'd whisper if Buddy or Jimmy or one of the other guys managed to drag us to one instead of just barbecuing in their backyards. "How tight do you think they made the screws on those things? Those look to you like the kinds of guys that take a lot of trouble with a wrench?" Not even the little boats that traveled in a tiny circle in a track of fetid water two feet deep, or the cars that were lower to the ground than Robert's tricycle. Someone else's children would be screaming from the Dragon Wagon, waving at us as the cars thundered up and down the track, and Robert would be standing, big-eyed, next to Bobby, a hand in his, as though my failure to recognize the clear and undeniable danger of this place removed me from them both. Crackerjack he could have, and cotton candy. But no hot dogs, or sausage and peppers cooked on a big griddle by women with tattoos. "What are you, nuts, Frances?" Bobby would say.

"You want a hot dog?" I said to Robert while I was taking food orders and we were trying to settle the boys on some splintered picnic benches. He nodded, then smiled. It felt like something to me, maybe a moving on, a moving over to some other place, where we made new rules and traditions. Hot dogs were no longer dangerous. We were living a different life. Every once in a while, at moments like this, it felt like mine. "Mrs. Bernsen asked us in school to talk about an adventure," Robert had said one night over leftover lasagna. "I talked about it being an adventure to move to a new place where you've never been before and where you don't know anyone." I'm not sure what showed in my face, but he'd added quickly, "I didn't talk about before. Just now. Like meeting Bennie and everything."

"You are the best boy in the world," I'd said.

Mr. Castro was working nights as a janitor at the paper products plant and had agreed to come along to the carnival to help Mike and me keep the boys in order. He brought Bennie's little sister Sandy, who had just turned five, as a special treat for her birthday; he held tight to her hand as she danced and smiled and cried, "Popcorn, Papa! Popcorn, please?" Jason Illing's father was there, with his video camera, just as he was at every game, filming Jason slumped on the bench, the boy's shoulders bowing to his belly like an old man, filming the two minutes or so that Mike, who played everyone, cut no one, gave Jason to play. "Hold up your burger," Mr. Illing called, but Jason ignored him and hunched over his Dutch Fries and his root beer. Cindy came with us, too, after one of the other boy's mothers backed out. She had Chad in the stroller, and I'd managed to coax Chelsea from the little niche between Cindy's torso and the stroller handle onto a picnic bench, where she ate a hot dog slowly and thoughtfully.

"I don't like rides," Chelsea said.

"Can I tell you a secret?" I said. "Neither do I. They always make me feel like I'm going to throw up."

Chelsea nodded.

"Eleven, twelve," I heard Mike muttering to himself, and I laughed. "They're all here," I said.

"It's hard to keep track of sixteen of them in a place like this," he said.

"I know. But you don't really need to keep track of

sixteen. Jason is under constant electronic surveillance, I never let Robert out of my sight, and Robert never makes a move without Bennie. Mr. Castro is keeping an eye on Jonathan, who always gives Bennie a hard time. That leaves twelve. And Cindy and I divided the twelve up on the bus. So all you really have to do is hand out tickets."

Of course, it wasn't as simple as that once the leavings of their lunch were bundled into waxed paper and tinfoil and chucked—underhand, overhand, Jonathan Green from behind his brawny back, and why was I so happy when he missed by a foot?—into the metal drums used for trash. "Tilt-a-Whirl!" Mike yelled, and as of one accord most of the group would move toward the ride and some would scatter, to knock down weighted milk bottles with a hardball, to buy junky jewelry or sugar-coated nuts, to look at the Army Reserve tank.

"Can I put you in charge of stragglers?" I asked Cindy, who was trying to get mustard out of her shirt with a paper napkin and a cup of water she'd wangled out of the homemade lemonade stand.

"Not with herself hanging onto my midsection," she said, looking down at Chelsea. "I'm straggling myself."

"Chelse," I said, bending down, "will you come with me and we'll make sure the guys are okay on the rides?"

"I don't want to go on."

"Me neither. That's why I need your help."

Her hand in mine was sweaty, but sweetly curved. Cindy had put her hair into a French braid and she was wearing pink shorts and a matching shirt with ruffles of lace around the legs and sleeves. "You look so pretty today," I said.

"So do you," Chelsea said. "You look nice in a dress."

"It's a T-shirt dress, not a real dress. Your mom bought this for me for Christmas."

"I know. She likes to buy people clothes."

"They're making me go on," Mike shouted from a car on the Tilt-a-Whirl, wedged in between two of the smaller boys, his arms around each one.

When he came off he was rolling his eyes. "The only way you keep from throwing up is by fixing on one stationary point and staring at it," he said.

"Really?"

"That's my theory."

"Did it work?"

"So far," he said. "I just stared straight at you."

I could feel the color come up in my face, see it in his. "What next?" I said.

"How about dinner and a movie?" We both looked down. "Never mind. I can't believe I said that. Jesus, Riordan."

"Beth, I have to go to the bathroom really bad," Chelsea said.

"We'll be at the House of Horrors," Mike said.

When we got back they were all still in line. Jason's father was panning the row of boys, calling "And your name is . . ." to each. A group of retarded children and their teachers were ahead of them. The children were wearing name tags and smiling, dancing in the sunshine, rolling their eyes at the demons and ghouls painted on the outside of the House of Horrors. "Are you sure?" one of the teachers kept asking, and they all nodded. But once inside we could hear shrieks and wails, and the ticket-taker flicked his cigarette into the grass and swore. "Keep your people back," he barked at Mike, who threw out his arms as though to restrain a regiment of unruly soldiers.

"Bring them back out," he yelled into the House of Horrors, and a moment later the teachers and the children hurried through the black door and down the up ramp, the adults rosy with embarrassment, the children drenched in sweat as though in an instant every bad thing they had ever imagined had come at them by the light of the cheap strobe, ready to rip their hearts out.

"Wow," said Chelsea.

"Go ahead," the ticket-taker yelled at Mike.

"Are you guys still up for this," Mike said, turning around.

"Oh, for Christ's sake," said the ticket-taker.

After that there was the Viper, and then the bumper cars. Chelsea thought about the bumper cars, but then she saw sparks fly from the tether to the ceiling when one of them hit the wall. "Are you gonna go on anything at all?" said Cindy. "Anything? They have pony rides."

"Maybe in a little while," she said.

"Pretty girl," said Mr. Castro.

"Thank you. Say thank you, hon," Cindy said, a little too loudly. Then Christopher Menendez threw up, and Mr. Castro took him to the men's room.

"Oh, my Lord, please don't put him in my car on the way home," Cindy said.

"This was a bad idea," Mike said.

"No it wasn't," I said. "This is just one of those things that sounds a lot better before and after than when you're actually doing it."

"That's what I like about her," he said, turning to Cindy. "Most women would say, yeah, it was a bad idea, let's get out of here. Or they'd say, no, it was a great idea, we're having a great time, and you'd know it was bull. Instead she said what she just said, which happens to be true and accurate."

"That's what I like about her, too," Cindy said, in a voice that sounded as though she was playing the ingénue in the school play.

"Ferris wheel and then call it a day?" Mike said.

"Sure," I replied.

Cindy looked at her manicure and then at Mike's back as he plowed through the crowds to the place by the bumper cars where he'd told the boys to assemble after their fifth go-round. She rubbed the nail on her index finger with a frown as though she'd found a flaw in the finish. Chad was splayed in the stroller fast asleep. "I'm not going to say anything," she finally said.

"Good," I said.

Both of us lapsed into the tired silence of adults who have been with children from morning to night. It seemed to me heroic that someone like Mike Riordan or Mrs. Bernsen did this every day, and with good humor. Even now, as he stood at the back of the group waiting for the Ferris wheel to empty, I could see that he was bantering with the boys, keeping them in line without hectoring them as I would have done. The Ferris wheel filled with children just before our group made it to the head of the line, and it began to spin slowly, a blur of smiles and antic waves to the parents and friends below. It was only late afternoon but the lights were already on around each rim, two circles of blue lights in the lengthening, darkening day, heavy clouds settling over the fields so flat around us.

I looked down. Chelsea's face was tipped back, her

mouth a little open, watching the other children go up and around, and I thought I saw in her eyes the kind of sadness you sometimes see, as a nurse, when a child in a wheelchair watches other children run. And then there was something else, wonder and shock, too, and a tearing noise I thought at first was the sound of one of the rides, until I looked up and saw that one of the cars of the Ferris wheel was half hanging in the air, and dangling from it was a child, making a high-pitched noise, something like a cry, something like heavy breathing, *ah-ah-ah-ah-ah.*

I ran forward, dragging Chelsea with me, and saw that another child had already fallen to the packed dirt at the side of the Ferris wheel, a boy in blue shorts and one of those buzz cuts Robert kept begging for. "He's dead," Chelsea whispered as I knelt next to him, adults and children surging around to see. There was a terrible scream, and I heard the noise as the second child's body hit something and then she fell, remarkably, only a few yards from the other.

"All right," I cried, half turning, and in that instant I was myself again, Frances F. Benedetto, RN, taking no shit in the emergency room. "Here's the deal. This child can go under, big time, or I can help him. But to help him I need all of you to move back."

"Oh my God," a woman started to shriek, in a familiar timbre. "Oh my God!" Mike came up behind me, and I said, "Tell Cindy to get ahold of Mom or Grandma or whoever the hell that is and take her someplace and calm her down. Tell Cindy to lie to her. Tell her I'm a doctor. Tell her the kids are fine. Do you know CPR?"

"Yeah."

"No, I mean really know CPR. Not one class at the Y."

"I really know CPR."

"Then come right back." I looked up and raised my voice. "I need a tie or a scarf," I called. Then, looking around at the women in T-shirts and frayed shorts, the men in jeans and singlets, I added, "Or a belt. A belt would do it."

CPR, done by someone who knows how to do it, is like a calisthenic, like push-ups or leg lifts, a series of quick, synchronized, monotonous movements. Mike did it just right. The boy, who was probably concussed, began to wheeze and moan. The little girl had a compound fracture of the left leg, the bone poking jagged and white from just above her knobby, scabby little knee. But the tourniquet kept down the bleeding. She was in shock, staring straight up at the sky, whispering to herself, "Mommy, Mommy."

"You're okay, sweetie," I whispered back. "You broke your leg."

"I tried to hold on," she said.

"I know." Two ambulance attendants wheeled a gurney over in a cloud of dust. "I'd figure on a couple of busted ribs," I said. "Luckily the car they were in wasn't that far up. If they'd been at the top—" I shrugged.

"Nice work," one of them said. There was blood on my dress and my hands.

In the hospital I'd learned that there are really two kinds of people in the world, people who go hard and efficient in times of terrible trouble, and the ones like, it turned out, Grandma, who scream, shriek, go limp, sink to the floor, become patients themselves. PITAs, we called them in the ER, short for Pain In The Ass. All of the adults with me had fallen into the take-charge group. Cindy had managed to convince the grandmother that the children would be fine and to get her to breathe into a bag and drink an orange soda. Mr. Castro had rounded up all the boys and taken them to a tent filled with video games at the back of the fairgrounds.

And Jason Illing's father had taped the whole thing. While we were dropping off the boys, explaining to parents what had happened and assuring them that all of us were fine, he went to the local news station and sold a copy to them. Six months of being careful, dying my roots, talking about goddamned Delaware, feeling my breathing quicken at the sight of a patrol car and feeling it slow as my son slept silently in the next room. Six months, and that idiot, that moron, that fool maybe ruined it with his sorry little Sony, that he loved to hoist on the palm of his hand. "Weighs less than a sack of sugar," he liked to say.

We went to Cindy's house, where she brought out tortilla chips and salsa, perhaps in a salute to Mr. Castro, and beer in deference to the aftershock of the day's events. When we turned on the television, we were the lead story on the evening news, and there I was in the center of the film clip, a red flag to Bobby's bull.

The fear I felt as I watched was worse than it had been while I worked over those children. There was the little girl, her leg bent at a horrid acute angle, and there was Beth Crenshaw, using a brown leather belt as a tourniquet. You could scarcely see my face, except for once when I turned to look back, straight into the big eye of the camera. I was glowering the way I always did when I concentrated, so that a nursing professor had had to take me aside once and tell me that it was important not to look as though I was going to throttle the patient while I was threading an IV line. I could imagine someone watching the television news, someone channel-surfing in a motel room at Disney World or in the living room of a time-share in Delray, some cop's wife, some friend of Ann's from Sodality at St. Stannie's, seeing me in that instant and saying, "My God, that woman looks a lot like Bobby Benedetto's wife, doesn't she?" I closed my eyes and let my face fall forward into my cupped hands.

Bobby, I could hear them saying, I saw Fran on the news in Florida. Some little town up north, what was the name? At a carnival ride, taking care of some kids, a terrible accident. What's Fran doing in Florida? Lakota, that was the name of the place.

"You didn't look so bad," Cindy said, patting my arm. "Considering."

What a ghoul Illing was. He'd panned the crowd and come to rest on Chelsea, her eyes dilated, her mouth ajar. But the terror I'd seen there for a moment was gone, and in its place was a great overwhelming calm. Probably anyone else watching would have thought the child was in shock, but I had no doubt that she was at peace, having seen that she was not crazy or strange but in fact prescient, correct, that the world was indeed as frightening as she had always believed and that it was possible for children to eat funnel cake, stand in line, wave to their friends, and then simply fall out of the sky. And the look on Robert's face, when the ambulance finally wailed off down a dirt track and into the distance with a dust cloud behind it, was just as easy for me to read. He might as well have said it aloud: Daddy was right. Daddy was right.

"Are you okay?" I'd asked him in the car on the way to Cindy's house, and he'd nodded. Of course. Of course. He'd seen worse without ever admitting to fear, giving way to nightmares. The blank eyes again, the blank stare. My heart sank. It was like he'd traveled back in time, to a place where he wouldn't let himself feel a thing. "Those kids who fell will be fine," I'd said.

"I know," he'd said.

When I went upstairs to use the bathroom I found him in Chelsea's bedroom, Cindy bent over him, her arm around his shoulders. Sobs shook him and made it hard for him to talk, so that the words came out in the funny little burbles he'd babbled as a baby. There were tears and dirt mingled into a streaky mess on his face, and a wad of tissues in his hand. Cindy patted his back twice and then slipped past me and out of the room. She patted me, too, on her way out, and I took her place next to Robert and held him as he sobbed some more. Finally he managed to say, "It was just so scary. It was so scary." I held him and rocked him and my heart was so light, laughing almost inside me, because my boy knew to be afraid, to be frightened, to cry at blood and guts and pain. It was like he was normal. It was like something was alive inside him, something that could see terrible things and know them for what they were. It had been a real accident, this one, but he hadn't even used the word. He could tell a bad thing when he saw it, and I admitted to myself that I thought he'd lost that simple gift forever, until that moment.

Later, when Mike took us home, the telephone was ringing. "Let it go," I said, "let it go." But Robert picked it up, then handed it to me. "Irving and I saw you on the news," Mrs. Levitt said. "Next time you are being a hero, don't wear a dress so everyone can see your tushie. Your fanny. Ah, you know, your rear end."

"I know what a tush is, Mrs. Levitt." Mike Riordan was standing in the doorway, laughing.

Robert had gone upstairs. I could hear the water running. "He's fine," I said to Mike. "He's upset."

"It's good for him to get it out now. Better than bottling it up, you know?"

"I know," I said. "I know." He stood up and moved to the door. "You were good today," I added.

"So were you," he said. "You were great. Unbelievable. Plus I'm happy to hear you know what a tush is."

"I'm sorry I was so snotty about the CPR thing. There are just a lot of people who think they know how to do it from watching TV."

"I was a community ambulance volunteer for five years."

"I didn't know that, see."

He took a step toward me, with a funny little embarrassed smile, and took my face in his hands. Then he kissed me, very softly, the way a boy I'd liked in eighth grade who had braces top and bottom had once kissed me, as though he was afraid something harder would hurt me, or him. There were footsteps from upstairs, and he dropped his hands and moved away, toward the door.

"Boy," he said.

The phone didn't ring for three days, and when it finally did my hand lingered over it as though I was afraid the receiver would give off an electric shock. My heart pounded as I listened to the electronic tympani: *clink, bang, rattle, buzz, buzz, clink*. I was surprised that it had taken so long for Patty Bancroft to come looking for me. I had become her bad child, her prodigal daughter, the kind of person, like Maeve Banning at Queen of Peace, who always wound up in the principal's office, in the hot seat.

"Maeve Banning," Sister Eucharista would say over the intercom after morning prayers and the Pledge of Allegiance, "please come to the office." And we'd scarcely look up. Maeve Banning, the mothers would whisper, would wind up—well, you know. She hadn't. Of course she hadn't. Grace told me she was a lawyer now, a partner in a big law firm, helping corporations stay out of trouble.

I was Patty Bancroft's Maeve Banning. I made unauthorized phone calls. I wound up on the evening news.

"Elizabeth?" she said.

"Beth," I said again. She could never remember that that was the name I went by, and suddenly it occurred to me that it might be because they made us all Elizabeths, that huddled in apartments and small houses and trailer parks around the United States there was a great community of Elizabeths, like one of the medieval religious communities, committed to poverty and obedience. And silence, of course. Patty Bancroft was our public face, our voice, our leader. You could tell that she enjoyed that, that it made her feel good, to have gone from being powerless in her own home to being powerful in the world. I realized that that was what had always bothered me about her, that she enjoyed her work so much.

"We're working on relocating you to another part of the country," she said. "Perhaps next week, if we can set the arrangements in motion."

"What?"

"I gather that you were on television. That was a very, very foolish thing to do. And that your picture was in the newspaper. The impulse to be a Good Samaritan must be deeply ingrained in someone from your professional background, but I beg of you, not just for your own sake but for the sake of your own child and many others, don't yield to it in a public place ever again."

"Next time I see a kid bleeding to death I'll remember that."

"There's no point in sarcasm. You've only made things difficult for you and your son. Someone will let you know next week about the relocation."

"My name wasn't on TV. My name wasn't with my picture in the newspaper."

"That's not the point."

"We're not leaving. I'm not uprooting my boy again."

"I'm afraid that's the price you will have to pay. It is not unusual for us to move one family three or four times during as many years. Particularly if they call attention to themselves or are not assiduous about breaking off their ties with the past."

"Let me tell you something about myself, Mrs. Bancroft," I said. "I like to care of my own business. I'm someone who's made her own way all her life." And the moment I said it, I knew it wasn't true. I knew that my feeble minimum-wage jobs had only been a pathetic hedge against the unpredictable life my parents made for Grace and me, a life of settling but not settling down, of moving around but not up. And my life outside of the home we shared, Bobby and I, had been a stage set, a sham. The real Fran Flynn hadn't been the woman everyone saw in the hospital, in charge, in control. She'd been a punching bag, a marionette. And now I was one of Patty Bancroft's puppets, a woman scared to run around the block, scared to let her son go alone to soccer games, a woman who'd take what she could get.

"Let me ask you this," Patty Bancroft said, "Do you want to stay alive?" It was her trump card; I could tell by the way she said it. The fact that Patty Bancroft and Bobby Benedetto so often said the same things, so often made me feel the same about myself, made me hate Patty Bancroft at that moment, no matter how much good she'd done me and Robert. But she was playing out of her league when she conjured up the worst that could happen. I'd heard it all before. I'd heard it from the master. I'd heard it when he found the card of a matrimonial lawyer in my pocket two years before I left. He'd driven across the Verazzano-Narrows Bridge from a wedding reception at 2:00 AM. dead drunk, snaking the car in and out of the lanes while I held onto the edge of the seat, the sullen gray of the water framed by the slender silver cables that held the roadway miraculously aloft. "You want to get home alive, Fran?"

Bobby had said over and over, like there was a right answer and I hadn't gotten it yet. The next morning he made me waffles for breakfast. Waffles and pancakes, that was all he could cook. But he made good waffles, even hungover and pissed off. Death threats and Belgian waffles with bacon. What a life.

"What I'd like," I said to Patty Bancroft, "is to start paying rent on this apartment. I don't like being a charity case. I'd like to pay my own phone bills. I'm putting some money away. I don't need handouts anymore. I need the name and address of the landlord."

She was quiet for a long time, and for some reason I thought she was on an airplane, flying over her empire, the hidden world of women who had ceded the right to speak for themselves, even fend for themselves, to a woman who took the podium and the microphone to speak for them, fingering her pearls. Patty Bancroft talked about herself wherever she went, of how she had been married to a prosperous banker in a town in Indiana, of how he mostly beat her about the body, not on the face, so that no one ever saw when she was wearing a suit to a country-club lunch or a cocktail dress to the club for dinner. I'd realized, hearing her tell it at that hospital, that it sounded less like a life than a story. If Patty Bancroft had ever been a victim, it was long, long in the past. She enjoyed being on top. The way I was enjoying, at that moment, demanding custody of my own life for the first time since I started living it.

"I appreciate everything you've done," I added, "but we like it here. My son is settled in, I have a little bit of money put away. Just tell the landlord to come see me and I'll pay for this place."

"You make me very nervous, Beth," she said quietly.

"I'm sorry to hear that," I said. But I'd heard that before, too. I'd heard that from Bobby. "I don't know if you understand this," I finally said to Patty Bancroft, "but I can't worry anymore about how I make other people feel about me. I have to worry about how I feel about myself."

"You have to worry about staying safe. And keeping your child safe."

"That, too," I said.

Chastity is the other vow nuns take. Maybe that was why I was scheduled to go to another town, another house, another school, another identity, because Patty Bancroft, who said over and over again that she had finally been beaten senseless by her banker husband until her face had had to be rebuilt by one of the plastic surgeons who worked for her now pro bono, had never remarried. Maybe she knew about Mike Riordan. Maybe I'd known about Mike Riordan all along. Maybe I'd tried not to notice how awkward it was for him to look at me, even in the school library or on the sidelines of a game. Maybe I'd convinced myself that I wouldn't be seduced by how comforting it was, just to know that someone bigger than me was looking out for my son. That's what had first gotten to me about Bobby, the idea that someone would keep me safe and sound, look out for Frannie better than Frannie could look out for herself. The feel of his arm around me. The way he held my coat. Jesus Christ, the illusions you manage to sell yourself, better than any car salesman. I'd done it again with Mike Riordan, except that instead of convincing myself that he was everything, the way I had with Bobby twenty years ago, I'd convinced myself that he was nothing at all.

There was no lake in Lake Plata, just a sluggish reservoir and a community pool, but Mike took us to the ocean the Saturday after the trip to the carnival. He came with a cooler full of soda in the back of his Toyota, and an armful of old blankets; I made fried chicken and potato salad.

"Can Bennie come?" Robert asked.

"I think it would be better this time if it was just us," I said.

"Just us, like me and you?"

"And Mike," I said.

"I can't call him that," Robert said. "I have to call him Mr. Riordan."

"I think when we do things like this with him you can call him Mike."

"What do you mean, when we do things like this?"

"When we all go out together."

"Are we going to go someplace together after this?"

"I don't know," I said.

"I'm calling him Mr. Riordan," Robert said.

He compromised. He called him nothing at all. When we arrived at the beach, Robert ran toward the water, kicked his shoes aside at the tide line, and went in up to his knees while we struggled with the blanket. When Mike joined him in the surf, he moved away, as though the two were magnets, naturally, inevitably repelling one another. When I went into the water, he positioned himself between Mike and me almost unthinkingly. To anyone watching from the long crowded stretch of white beach, flat and glittering slightly in the midday sun, our movements must have looked like choreography of a strange sort. Our conversation was like that strange, dissonant modern music I picked up from time to time on classical stations, fit and starts with no melody. Mainly Mike talked to Robert, and Robert ignored him:

"I hear that that team from Lake Oijda is going to be good."

"Your mother makes good fried chicken."

"I brought a Frisbee if you want to play."

"Robert, you're being rude," I finally said.

"I just don't feel like talking," he mumbled, and ran back into the sea.

I stood to watch him pushing out into the deeper water. The swell of the waves, the air making a floating bolster of the seat of his striped trunks, the working of the wings of his shoulder blades as he fought the current—he looked as though he was trying to fly, to rise up, to take off. He was a good strong swimmer, my boy, although he'd been afraid of the water at first. But he did it to please his dad, when he was three, went to the Y in downtown Brooklyn, dipped his little pointed face below the surface of the water as though he was going into a cave.

I shouldn't have come to the beach. The beach was Bobby to me. The smell, the sharp sun, the sand. I could see his shoulders, the muscles working as he pulled his shirt over his head and swam out so that he was only a dark divot on the horizon. The lifeguards would blow their whistles and demand he come back, and slowly, arrogantly, he would. He would walk over to the lifeguard stand and speak to them and then go back out, and this time they would leave him alone, as though he had some special dispensation from the everyday rules of safety and common sense. When Robert was smaller he would stand at the water's edge and watch, the whole line of his back rigid, and when he was older he would swim up and down in shallower water, parallel to the shore. And I knew he was just waiting for the day when he was brave enough to strike out after Bobby, shoulder to shoulder into water so deep that there was no imagining what was underneath your feet.

I can't swim. Never could. My skin burns and I keep my clothes on over my suit for all but a few minutes on the beach. My parents took us to Coney Island, when we were children, my mother carrying the rented umbrella and the bag of towels. It was a lot of trouble for nothing. Grace and I huddled in the shade, running in our T-shirts to and from the water like nocturnal animals woken up in the middle of the day. My insteps, peeking out from the broad shadow of the umbrella, burned so badly they had to be covered in salve as white as their natural color.

Bobby and Robert never even wore sunscreen.

"I think we've ruined a beautiful friendship here," I said.

"No we haven't. We're still friends."

"Not you and me. I don't know, maybe you and me. But definitely you and Robert."

Mike Riordan squinted through his sunglasses and shrugged. He was like me, already a bright, feverish-looking pink. An Irish tan, we'd called a sunburn when we were kids. "What would you have felt like if someone took your mother out?" he said.

I laughed. "It's not imaginable to me that anyone would take my mother out," I said.

"There you go," said Mike Riordan. "Sometimes I think it's the strangest thing—we grow up in our families seeing our parents as completely sexless beings, and then we're supposed to know how to have relationships."

"My parents were completely sexless beings."

"In your mind, maybe. That's what we all think. My parents used to send all of us to nine o'clock mass on Sundays and then they'd go to the eleven o'clock together. I was twenty-three years old before I finally figured out why they fought us so hard when one of us wanted to sleep in and go to later mass."

"I bet your mother just needed the sleep."

"Nope. I asked her one day. She said, oh, grow up, Michael, you have six brothers and sisters."

That was our first date, I suppose. At least that was what Robert seemed to assume. He appeared to know instantly, almost chemically, that Mr. Riordan had gone from being a friend to being a threat. I suppose I'd had a chemical reaction, too, the first time we went running together after the carnival. The sound of us breathing sounded different to me, and when we brushed up against one another accidentally, bare arm to bare arm, we had dozens of times, we now both lurched back to our own side of the dusty track. No matter what Cindy said, and said, and said again, I wasn't attracted to Mike Riordan, didn't have a jones for him, as Clarice Blessing, the pretty, smart-mouthed black nurse in the ER on my shift, used to say about any good-looking man who came in with a broken bone or even a bullet wound. Once, I remember, Bobby came in when he'd had to get my signature on some bank papers and Clarice had been behind the front desk. "Tasty," she said, before someone told her who the dark guy in the pressed jeans and the white shirt was. "Tasty but dangerous." That's how I thought of my taste in men: tasty but dangerous. Mike Riordan was the least dangerous guy I'd ever known, and every time I thought to myself, well, Fran, he's just not your type, I had to remind myself that my type was the type who left marks.

"Bennie asked me if Mr. Riordan was your boyfriend," Robert said one day after school.

"Oh yeah? What'd you say?"

"I said you didn't have a boyfriend."

The next week Mike took us out for pizza and a PG movie. One Saturday we went bowling and then ate Chinese at a cinder-block place back behind the supermarket that turned out to be pretty good. Robert pointedly asked for chopsticks, while Mike used a fork. "You will have a great dinner with two people you really like," Mike read off his fortune cookie. "Let me see that," said Robert. He squinted in the dim light of the restaurant, hung with red-and-gold paper lanterns and signs for Chinese beer with a dragon curled around the bottle. "The journey of a thousand miles begins with a single step," Robert read accusingly. "Yeah, that too," Mike said. "I think that's what we're looking at right here, a single step."

"I hate fried rice," said Robert. "Fried rice isn't real Chinese food."

"Eat the dumplings," I said.

"Or whatever," said Mike, shoveling in fried rice with his fork. You had to admire his patience.

The beginning of March, the air softening, turning warmer, Mr. Castro took Bennie and Robert to a jai alai game at an arena an hour and a half south of Lake Plata, and Mike took me to a restaurant in Lakota named La Caravelle, where they set everything on fire at the table except the wine. I was starting to look at him differently, the way you do, seeing the pale hairs on the back of his hands, the places at the corners of his brow where his hairline was beginning to inch back along the crown, the *V* of his shirt where his throat met his chest. The fourth time we were out—Robert away for the night, me in a dress and heels—I was afraid of him. I kept my knees from nudging his beneath the table.

"Can I ask about your divorce?" Mike said when they had put the cherries flambé in front of us.

"Do you have to?"

"Robert seems like he thinks that you and his father will get back together."

"Did he say that?"

"Not exactly. He does seem to think that you won't be around here for long, like you're going back to where you come from. Which I guess means he believes you're going to get back together."

"Don't all kids say that?"

"Lots of them. Sometimes it's true."

"In this case it's not. I stayed with him a lot longer than I should have because eventually I thought I'd get perfect enough to make things better. I figured just by being nice, or being quiet, or being pretty, or sweet, or stupid, I could make things all right. I was wrong."

"For the record, I already think you're pretty perfect."

"Don't say that. That's what screws everything up, that *perfect* crap. Because the people who don't stay, they leave because its not perfect, because they think it's supposed to be. Or my sister. She gets involved with one shitty married guy after another and she's managed to convince herself that it's because she's working out this, that, or the other thing. But really it's because if she met some nice available man who loved her she'd have to settle. He'd be nice but not smart enough, or smart but not handsome enough, or something. No one likes to settle, even though we all do."

Mike looked down at his hands. "Sorry," he finally said.

"Jesus," I said. "What set me off that time?"

"I said you were perfect."

"Well, there you go," I said, and we both smiled and then looked down at the table again. The check lay there like a message, as though if I picked it up instead of a scrawl of abbreviated entrées and numbers there would be some words, some warning: Fran Benedetto, Fran Flynn, Beth Crenshaw, whoever you are, whatever you call yourself, why the hell are you doing what you're doing, out of the frying pan into the fire, you're not single, you're not ready, you're not interested, you're not who this man thinks you are, you're not who you think you are, you're not.

I looked at his hands. I couldn't help myself. They were big, the line of the knuckles knobby and square, and I wondered what he would say if I asked him if he'd ever hit a woman, and knew that I didn't need to ask. Whatever it was that had made me soft and wet and warm whenever Bobby Benedetto whispered in my ear was part of whatever it was that made him twist my arm and slap my face. I'd been seduced by the danger I only faintly divined when I was twenty years old and the danger was being caught by the cops with my jeans around my ankles on a bench along the beach in Far Rockaway. I looked at Mike Riordan across the table as he took his credit card from a brown leather wallet and knew that he was maybe the safest man I'd ever met, and that that was his bad luck, and mine, too. Patty Bancroft used to talk about how her husband had been two men, really, one mild and avuncular, the other a purple-faced monster. But Bobby was all of a piece, and if anyone had asked me, when we both were young, if I thought he could ever do what he did, I would have said, no, my God, are you crazy? and deep inside a part of me would have known, not that it was possible, but that it was inevitable.

"You look a little tired," Mike said.

"I am."

Cindy likes to lecture me about how different dating is today than it was twenty years ago when we did it last, but she gets most of her information from daytime talk shows and the dark hints she picks up from single mothers to whom she sells Avon on her evening calls. She keeps telling me that men now expect you to put out—she still says put out, Cindy, as though sex is transactional—on the first date. But that isn't the problem. The problem is that there is less to do on a date when you are a grownup. Dancing at bars seems silly, and there are no more of the kind of Saturday-night parties where you can French kiss in the corners. As we left La Caravelle, the owner in his rusty tuxedo bobbing and grinning and urging us to return, I realized that Mike Riordan and I were running out of restaurants.

"Love is lovelier the second time around," Cindy liked to say.

"How the hell would you know?"

"Oh, don't be so touchy," she said. "You know how few single men out there are really interested in a relationship?"

"I'm not interested in a relationship," I said.

"Oh, please," Cindy said.

"Please come inside," Mike said when we got to his place, in a condo complex out by the city limits. And when we were inside, in the living room with a couch and matching love seat that looked as though they'd been arranged in exactly the same way they'd been arranged in the furniture store, he said, "Please stay." I wasn't used to a man who asked, a man who said please, and, later, thank you, bashfully, boyishly, and something about it irritated me. But still I went along, maybe to prove to myself that I could love a nice man, a good man, a man who would look at his hands when I gave him a hard time and not use them against me. I went into the bedroom, listened to the sound of zippers coming down and shoes hitting the floor as though they were sounds from some dumb show on the radio, sound without pictures. I tried to be there, I really did, but it was as though the wine and the dark numbed me, sent me into a trance. I was watching myself doing what I was doing, envisioning the curve of my back above the slight swell of my hips, looking at the cesarean scar that his fingers found hidden beneath the hair. I kept my eyes shut, but it was as though my eyes were in his hands. He kept whispering my name, and the sound of it was soothing, almost hypnotic. Beth Beth Beth Beth, and "yes" I finally said, and perhaps it was that that made me open my eyes, and remember all in a rush suddenly the last time I had had sex with another man, so vividly, so detailed that it might as well be happening again, in this strange bed with the plaid sheets and the dark wood headboard. It was like having a ghost there, hanging over me, pushing his knee between my own, holding me down with the weight of his chest, his chest hard and furred with black hair, his harsh guttural whisper, like a knife at my throat: "Come on. Come on." Using himself as though his whole body was a knife, cutting into me, breathing fire and Canadian Club into the side of my face, his jaw set so hard that I could feel the stone of the joint digging into my cheek.

"Beth," Mike Riordan whispered again, and I had to look up at him, had to keep my eyes open, to remind myself that it was not Bobby, that Bobby's hair was not light, his shoulders not sloped that way, his face not soft like this. Mike looked back at me and he must have seen something in my face. Maybe I was wearing the look I'd had that last night with Bobby, as he raped me. There ought to be a different word to describe what it is when it's your husband who does it, when it's a man you've invited, longed for, loved, hated, feared, known, desired. But there's only that one. I remember sitting with a college student one night who'd been pulled into an abandoned building near the subway and sodomized by a teenager with a gun. "It's like he stole my soul," she sobbed, eloquent in defeat. Maybe Mike looked down and saw the face of a woman who'd had her soul stolen, who was broken and empty, sere as a seed pod in autumn. Whatever was in my face, he couldn't go on.

"Are you all right?" he said.

"Yeah," I said.

"I was hurting you."

"No. It's okay."

He fell back against the pillows, his forearms crossed over his face. He smelled like lemon cologne and his voice cracked like a boy's. "Oh, God," he said, "please don't say that. Don't say it's okay. For four years I lived with a woman who forced me to pry everything out of her with a crowbar. I'd say, Laurie, what's going on? What's the matter? It's okay. That's all she ever said."

"I'm fine," I said. "I'm tired." I could not look at

him, nor he at me. I could still feel Bobby on me, like a weight on my chest.

"Beth," Mike said as I got out of the car at my own place.

"It's okay," I said over my shoulder, and went inside and took a shower.

I love to look at Robert when he is pushed and sleepy, his face a little crumpled, his eyes half-closed. Sometimes, after Bobby hit me, I'd go in and look at Robert and make myself feel better. Make myself settle down and shut up. When he's headed toward or away from sleep, Robert's face looks innocent, unmarked, as though nothing bad has ever happened to him. Will ever happen to him. He looked that way standing by my bed, holding an old earthenware bowl with a few greasy kernels at the bottom. "Could you make us some more peanut-butter popcorn?" he said, so nicely, even though he knew the answer was yes.

Only Robert and I knew that it was his eleventh birthday. He'd always liked the story, of how the pains came but the baby didn't, of how they'd taken us into an operating theater and put up a screen at my breastbone to shield Bobby and me from what was happening below, of how Bobby stood up to straighten out the crease in his pants legs and caught a glimpse of the incision like a big red mouth and the blood around the edges of the drape, of how he sat down hard on the metal stool at my head. "Are you okay?" I asked. "Bobby? Are you going to be all right?" The OB nurse, who'd been a class ahead of me at nursing school, gave him a big clean whiff of oxygen. Robert laughed, to think of his father so helpless. He liked that story. Loved it. I'd told it a hundred times. Bobby couldn't handle the sight of blood. What a laugh.

Robert's birthday was July 4 now, or at least Robert Crenshaw's was. But on April 9 we invited Bennie and three other boys from the basketball team for a sleepover in the living room. They came carrying sleeping bags and video games. Chelsea was on a sleep over that same night, her first, with a little girl named Melissa Erickson whose room, Cindy said, was entirely pink. She had been an in vitro baby, and her parents acted as though anything, from a playground spill to a B plus to a mosquito rattling around the stall shower in her pink bathroom was what my mother used to call "a federal case." It was a good beginning for Chelsea, who seemed less fearful now since the carnival, since she'd seen the worst with her own eyes. Melissa Erickson's parents were as fearful of life as Chelsea was. Maybe more.

It was Robert's first sleepover, too, unless you counted the nights he'd spent with Grace and his grandmother, Ann Benedetto bringing him back to the house with new sneakers, a new shirt, a toy, a book, a pocketful of candy and change. He'd spent the night at the Castros' a couple of times, but he'd never had a friend to his house overnight. Bobby had thought that that was fine. He didn't like strangers in the house. "I don't get all of this sleepover stuff," he'd said. "I never had anybody sleeping over at my house when I was a kid." And I'd never had anyone except Gracie, breathing in the next bed, her freckled legs tangled in the brown blanket. Robert always said that he didn't want any kids to stay over at his house anyway. Maybe he was afraid of what they would hear, of what they would say: Robert, what's the matter with your dad? Why's he yelling like that? What's that noise? Maybe he was afraid to let them into his nighttime life, those kids who hadn't learned when you needed to be deaf and blind. Maybe it was the dim memory of that night, when he was three, when he came downstairs, his face soft and pink, his eyes squinted shut against the light, and said, "Why you crabby, Daddy?" It was the first time he'd ever come downstairs when we were fighting. It was the last time he ever had. "Get back in bed, Robert," Bobby had said, his supple voice hard, not loud but mean, mean. "Don't you ever get out of your bed or come out of your room unless I say so."

"How come?" Robert had said.

"Get . . . up . . . stairs."

I stayed upstairs reading during the sleep over, listened to the murmur of the boys' voices from the living room, read and dozed and read some more. When I came down to make more popcorn they were halfway through the second *Star Wars* movie. "The guy who is Luke in the movie had a car accident and they had to, like, put his face back together," said a boy named Andrew Kovacs as the five of them lay on the floor, comic books and video cartridges around them.

"You can tell," Bennie said. "His face looks different after a while. Like his eyes are different sizes."

"I never had peanut-butter popcorn," said An Li Thong, a Vietnamese kid who was the goalie and whose school name had, naturally, become Goalie.

"His mom is a really good cook," said Bennie, as though I wasn't even there.

So normal, the long black velvet evening, the stars bright over central Florida, a moon almost full rising outside the bedroom window. It was hot during the days already, but at night it was only warm, a soft warm that felt good when I stepped outside before bed to look at the sky.

"Gentlemen," I said as I handed them a second bowl of popcorn, "here's the deal. I don't care how late you stay up"—Goalie cheered softly—"but if you wake me up, you're all going home. Hear me?" "Yes, Mrs. Crenshaw." "Thanks, Mrs. Crenshaw." "We'll be quiet." "We understand." The heavenly host, boy voices hovering between soprano and tenor, their words slurred by the popcorn in their mouths. Upstairs in the dark I could still hear them talking, hear the sound from the television, but it was muted, as though someone had thrown a blanket over them all, the way sound came through the walls when the couple who lived next door to my parents' apartment—the fourth one, I think, or maybe the fifth—would play the stereo late in the evening and fight with each other next to the bedroom where Grace and I slept. Gracie held a glass to the wall the first couple of times, to hear what they were saying, but it was dull. "She says who does he think she is, his mother?" Grace whispered to me. After a week or two we learned to sleep right through it.

In the pale blue light from the window I could make out the furniture in my room, the big scarred bureau, the landscape over it that I'd gotten from Cindy's basement, the rocking chair, the darker shadow of the closet door. And I realized, as one of the boys belched loudly downstairs and the others laughed, then chastised one another in loud whispers, that it had become my room. I knew its contours in the dark. To know the streets nearby, where Royalton met Poinsettia, where Miramar met the highway—that was one thing. To know a bedroom in the dark was something else, something final, something fine.

Even when I heard the sound of someone below, at the living-room window, I knew enough to feel only tired, tired and happy. I could tell by the whispers, a little louder than the whispers of the occasional tropical winds around the building, that the group of girls who were staying at the Castros', Bennie's sisters and their friends, had come to hassle the boys. One giggled, another squealed. The boys heard them, too. The movie was shut off, there were mutters from below, and the sound of the door opening. The crowbar beneath my bed seemed ridiculous, like a prop left over from another movie on this same set.

I opened the window and looked down on the five girls gathered in a little knot. I remembered doing this with Dee Stemple and some other girls once, when a group of the boys from Holy Cross were camping out in Mr. Dolan's chop shop, sleeping on the linoleum floors in the office. Two of the girls below were carefully holding something in their hands, like gifts. I coughed, and one of them dropped hers, and water arced up, little sparkles in the air.

"If anyone throws a water balloon into this house,

you are in big trouble," I whispered, and they screamed and scattered.

Just after three I went downstairs to turn off the lights. All five boys were sleeping with their mouths open, their hair askew. Andrew had his thumb in his mouth. Goalie's little video game was still on; football players running at one another constantly, falling down, getting up, sending the ball in a spiral across the screen. I had met his parents at soccer games; they alternated, one staying at the restaurant while the other stood, silent, on the sidelines. I turned off the little game, turned off the lights, pulled the cool sheets over myself. This is the life I always wanted to have: five boys asleep on the floor, with nothing to wake them except the giggles of little girls. It felt so ordinary.

"God, you look chipper, considering," Andrew's mother said as the boys spilled out of the kitchen and toward the front door, climbing into her van to head out to a day-long basketball clinic at the middle school.

"In this case, looks are deceiving. I'm going back to bed."

But I never made it. I was stacking the cereal bowls in the sink when the phone rang. Again there was no answer, only breathing on the other end of the phone. All the ordinariness of the night before, the sense of being settled and secure, of my boy being an ordinary boy—all of it just slipped away.

"Bobby," I whispered, defeated, and then there was a cough, a gasp, a sob. "Mrs. Nurse?" came a small voice, and I leaned back against the counter.

On my way to the Levitts', I stopped and bought an extra-value meal from McDonald's, large fries and a Big Mac. Mrs. Levitt was sitting in the dark of an apartment in which the blinds had been neither raised nor opened. She smelled of perspiration and sleep and dirty clothes, and she did not speak as I opened the door with the key she'd given me and moved past her to the bed, stopping only to lay a hand lightly on her shoulder. It was the first time I had ever been in the apartment when there had been no sound, the television still, Irving's stertorous breathing silenced. Even the big Seth Thomas clock had wound down. Irving's body was a little cool and beginning to stiffen. Mrs. Levitt had pulled the sheet down to his ankles, as though one last time she wanted to look at what, for so long, had been the scarcely noticed landscape of her life, even more than her own body, which required a mirror to see.

"You waited for me," I said, taking her hand. She nodded. "That's good," I said. "Can I call now for someone to take care of things, or do you want to wait awhile?"

"A minute or two," she said, and shuffled into the kitchen in her house slippers. I could hear her open the bag I'd brought, then the sandwich wrapper.

"What time was it?" I called.

She carried her lunch to the card table on a cookie sheet. "Nothing for yourself?" she said.

I shook my head. There was a box of matzo on the card table, and I remembered that it was Passover. "I hope I didn't bring the wrong lunch," I said, looking at the box.

Mrs. Levitt saw me looking, and shrugged. "You think God's gonna be upset that I ate a hamburger?" she said, handing me the ketchup package to open.

She was silent, eating, and finally she patted her lips with a napkin. "I was watching the cable news around midnight, maybe," she said, "and I fell asleep on the couch, and then I woke up around six. Some kind of report on geese, they had, and the sound they made woke me right up, and I said to Irving, they'd wake the dead, those birds." Her shoulders rose high and fell, just one dry, strangled sob. "I was changing the channel to the one on NBC with that young girl I like, the one that just had the baby. Then I couldn't hear nothing from the bed." She said something else, one more sentence, but it was in German, Yiddish, or Hebrew. I couldn't tell the difference.

"I got to go to the bathroom, sweetheart," she said vaguely, and shuffled out of the room.

She looked better when she came back, more alive. She crossed to the hospital bed. "Take that thing out, sweetheart," she said, and I went over and removed the catheter tube. Then Mrs. Levitt pulled the sheet up over Irving, up to his bony chin, that stuck up now like the prow of his body, proud and hard. Then she leaned close to his ear and whispered something, then patted his shoulder.

"I was hungry," she said, sitting down and looking at the debris of her lunch.

We called the Jewish funeral home in Middle Lake, and an hour later two men came, black suits, soft voices, a collapsible gurney that came up and went down on the freight elevator. The hospital bed stood empty by the window, and as I opened the blinds, finally, the sun fell full upon the white sheets that Mrs. Levitt and I had changed only two days before.

"I can have this stripped and out of here in an hour or two," I said. "Or I can leave it just as it is. Whichever will make you feel a little bit better."

She sighed. "Leave it, sweetheart," she said.

"Is there someone I should call?"

She shook her head. "Irving had two older sisters," she said. "They treated him like a prince. His mother, too, like a king. They're all gone now."

"For you, I meant."

"I had two brothers and a sister. They're all gone a long time ago." She sipped at her soda, going warm and watery. "Almost fifty years we were married. It's a long time."

"It is a long time."

"Forty-eight years last month."

"How'd you meet him?"

"Ach, everyone wants to hear the story. He liberated me," she said, and I smiled and rubbed the thin skin of her hands, crosshatched, age-spotted.

"The fifth of May, they told us after. We didn't keep track of time. One girl who slept on the shelf above me, she made marks with a piece of stone on the wall. She died of something, coughing, coughing, you know, and then sometimes we didn't know what month it was, not even what year after a while.

"You could smell from a long way those little white flowers, so sweet. There were none of them so you could see, but you could smell. When we woke up all the guards were gone, and one lady who helped them, she was going down the road, looking back like she was afraid we would come after her. There was nothing to eat. There wasn't anything to eat for maybe a week or two. Two of the girls were dead, but we waited for someone to take them. They died all the time. You'd wake up in the morning and see that someone wasn't moving from their bunk and then you'd know, so that after a while it was nothing, like seeing a rat or the sun or anything else. Just someone dead again. A lot of them died with their eyes open. That's not so nice." She looked over at the hospital bed. "Otherwise it looks more like you're sleeping.

"We went outside because of the smell. You'd think after all that time we wouldn't notice. They soil themselves, see. Well, you know that, with the nursing and all. So we went outside. Sada, the girl I sat with, she was from a farm somewhere. She talked and talked always, at night, in the morning. She was a big fat girl when she came but she was skinny then like the rest of us, with no hair on her lower place, no bubbies either, either of us. We were modest when we came, like young girls, you know, but not after a while.

"We saw dust coming and she said it was the guards coming back. I thought maybe she was right because I saw the trucks and the uniforms. But then they got close and we could see that they were different from the guards. Then we saw the flags on one of the trucks, and we knew. One of them, young, with brown eyes and a little mustache, he came and stood by me, and he said something in English. But I didn't know it was English, I didn't know English. I said in German that I couldn't understand, that I couldn't speak English. Then in German he said, it will be all right now. He looked like he was crying a little bit. I said to him, we are Jewish, sir. You should know that I am Jewish. And he said, 'Yes, miss, so am I.' "

She waited a moment, as though always here in the story the audience had had something to say. But I was speechless.

"Sergeant Levitt. I never heard of such a thing, a Jewish soldier. And they had food. Sada stuffed herself and then was sick, right on the ground, like a dog. They took us to a special tent and gave us something for the bugs. The clothes were not so good." Her eyes shone suddenly, and she smiled. "But I was a pretty girl, even in ugly clothes."

"I learned the word later. Liberated. He liberated me. Everybody like the story. One soldier, he put it in a special soldier's newspaper they had. Sergeant Levitt liberated me, and he brought me home and married me. His mother and sisters, they weren't so happy. There was a girl around the corner they liked better for him. Sophie, her name was. But he married me."

She pushed back the sleeve of one of her cardigans and there was the identification number. "You see?" she said.

"I see," I said, and nodded. I was crying, and Mrs. Levitt smiled and shrugged and patted my hand.

"Everybody likes that story," she said. "But, you know, after that, then we were married. Everybody thinks because of the story, it's like a fairy story. That's what one of Irving's nieces said once. Like a fairy story. I don't know. You got to live in the time you're living in. The past is the past, right, Irving?"

"It's an amazing story," I said.

"It's just a story," she said. "It's a long time ago, now."

"Are you going to bury him in the veterans' cemetery? Or Arlington, in Washington?"

Mrs. Levitt shook her head. "I already talked to the people at Perlman's. They'll cremate him. Then I can take him wherever I go." She looked over at the hospital bed. "You know what would have been the best thing for Irving? If he'd just gone home and married Sophie. She never married, that girl. She taught fourth grade in the public schools until they made her retire. Irving would have married her and thought about me, and I would have married somebody else, or maybe not, and thought about Irving, how he saved me." She sighed. "Ach, well. I don't know what I'll do with myself now. Maybe I'll move down to Miami. Two of my friends from home live in Miami. Both widows. Ruth and Esther, if you can believe it. I used to feel sorry for myself, tell people all my family was dead, they took them all away, my mama, my papa, my sister Rachel, my brothers. Now everyone I knew is dead. They got old. They got sick. Whatever." She lifted her hands to the sky. "Ah, what are you going to do?"

At the door I hugged her. "You look tired," she said.

"My son had four of his buddies spend the night last night. They stayed up, you know? They were good, but you still don't sleep. You could have called me earlier."

Mrs. Levitt smiled. "My sister and I, we did that. Rachel. She was the pretty one. I was smarter. Both of us in one big bed, the sheet over our heads, talking about the boys. You know, this and that. Our mama would yell at us, go to sleep. Go to sleep." She was smiling, Mrs. Levitt, but her eyes were full of tears. "Maybe your boy will want to take up golf," she finally said.

"Maybe," I said.

"Just so you'll be ready, I need to warn you that Mrs. Bernsen makes them all do family trees in fifth grade."

Cindy handed me a cup of coffee. "Is she out of her tiny mind?" she said.

It's exactly what I had told Mike Riordan when I picked Robert up after he'd been held in after school because of what Mike called "a verbal altercation" with the despised Jonathan Green, who had said that the New York Yankees were a bunch of losers. "We've done some talking about keeping your temper and agreeing to disagree," Mike had said, handing over Robert's backpack, trying not to look at me, or me at him, the horrible see-and-slide we'd both done with our eyes ever since we'd slept together. And Mike and I had

had to agree to disagree about the genealogy lesson with which Mrs. Bernsen proposed to galvanize the fifth grade during the waning weeks of the school year, a lesson that might have made sense when she'd started teaching thirty years before but today was as perilous as walking down the center of Route 18. What would little Hillary Thompson, who stuttered like a jackhammer, do with her two stepfathers and their five collective children? What about Brittany McLeod, who had been adopted from Paraguay and was as small and dark as her parents, now divorced, each remarried, were big and fair?

"She says that this always gives the class a lift," Mike said, shrugging. "All I can tell you is every year I get complaints, and every year I hear afterward that it worked out fine."

"She's out of her mind," I said.

There was no spring in central Florida, just as there had been no real winter, no hiding the ungainly edges of its strip malls and ranch houses beneath the white hillocks of snow that lent charm to even the most charmless Northeastern town in the months that seemed to stretch endlessly between Christmas and Easter (or, as Mrs. Levitt informed me when I complained about the lack of seasons, between Hanukkah and Pesach). The change of seasons might touch the tired foliage in the farm fields and the shades of green on the development lawns, but on the narrow streets with their yards of yellow-white gravel and their struggling shrubs where I lived and worked, the seasons were visible only in the displays in the store windows, the green of Christmas giving way to the red of Valentine's Day and the purple of Easter and now the pink of Mother's Day. Robert walked to the strip and bought me a box of candy and a stuffed bear holding a balloon that said I Love You. Cindy made lasagna, but Mrs. Manford couldn't come, had stomach flu or some such. "Thank God it didn't happen the day after, or my dad would have sworn it was my cooking," Cindy said.

The next day Robert had no school, some teacher's conference or another, and he went with me to visit Mrs. Levitt. The television was on, as it always was, and the noon news featured a story about a police shootout in the Bronx, four officers dead and two wounded, the greatest carnage in twenty years for the New York City Police Department. As though still corded together my boy and I sank down side by side on the sofa and leaned toward the television, as though, face-to-face, it could tell us more than the sketchy story a woman in a bright red suit and matching lipstick was reading from a TelePrompTer. We didn't have cable in our apartment, couldn't afford it, but the Castros did, and Robert knew to flip to other news channels. For an hour we waited, watched, as though we were those people I'd seen so often in the public areas of the hospital, mouths agape, half-asleep in molded chairs, waiting for the doctor to bring them news. Finally there were names, and we sank back, exhausted. I put my arm around his shoulder.

"You know people who are police officers in New York?" Mrs. Levitt said softly, placing another cup of tea in front of me. "Family maybe?" And Robert looked into my face with fear and yearning, too, and I squeezed his shoulder.

"We have friends in the department," I said. "None of them were hurt."

"I'm glad Daddy's not dead," Robert said as we began walking home.

"Me, too," I said. "Really. I'm really happy that he's okay."

"Is he okay?" Robert said. "Do you know he's okay?"

"You heard the news."

"But I mean really okay, like every day."

"I hope so," I said.

How many times had I wished Bobby would die? I lost count years ago. It was my biggest fear when he was first a street cop that the phone would ring, that the chaplain would come to the door, that I would have to hear those bagpipes again that I'd heard wailing at his father's funeral, that all I'd have left was a piss-poor pension and his badge in the bottom of my jewelry box. Even on those days when he'd first twisted my arm, or shoved me into the wall, I still woke and peered at the digital clock and then lay back to wait if he was even a half hour behind his usual time. I'd be awake when he dropped his clothes in the corner, the belt buckle making a *ka-chunk* in the quiet house, when he slipped between the sheets, smelling of scotch and beer, tasting of it too as he put his arms around me and eased my nightgown up, hand over hand, like he was climbing a rope up into me.

And then there were the nights when I began to dread the sound of the door opening softly downstairs, two or three hours past the time he got off, the sound of his stumble on the stairs or the loud bangings of cabinet and refrigerator door from the kitchen, semaphore for discontent, an investigation going nowhere, a witness who'd been arrogant or uncooperative, even a car nosed a little too far toward the entrance to our driveway. The nights when he would pick a fight, throw open the bedroom door to say "Where the hell is the bread?" or ignore the regular breathing I learned to fake and come over me, into me, no matter what.

God forgive me, but there were so many times he

went out to work and I would think the best thing that could happen to me was the call, the chaplain, the casket with the handsome cop I'd married inside it, who would never ever be able to lay a hand on me again, a fist in my face or rough fingers that opened me up as though I was a tunnel through which he was entitled, as a matter of right, to pass. When I was thinking about it rationally I knew it was no solution, that for my son his father would become a martyr, a man he would idolize and about whom he could never be told, never stand to hear the truth, the whole truth, nothing but. But often I was not thinking rationally, and I wished with all my heart that some lowlife's bullet would find a soft spot on Bobby's body, one of the soft spots I had lost the ability to find myself, with my hands or my tears or my words.

"Why did you say Daddy was a friend?" Robert said a week later, out of nowhere, as he was working on his family tree. "That day when you were talking to Mrs. Levitt? When the other police got hurt."

"Well, he sort of is," I said. But that was never true. Every time I saw a woman describe her husband as her best friend in some magazine or another, I always wondered what in the world she was talking about. Bobby and I had never been friends, ever, or I could never have loved him so completely and let him treat me so badly.

Hunched over a sheet of gleaming poster paper, Robert began to sketch out his family tree for Mrs.

Bernsen, and as he did I thought of how little he asked about the past and the future. Any other child would have been at me constantly with questions, about when and whether we were going back. Any other child would have slipped up at school, told his friends where he was really from, boasted that his father was a policeman, pointed to the map of Italy during social studies and made a lie of the nondescript middle-American last name that he carried. But as I watched Robert spread his left arm wide around his work as though to hide or shelter it, I realized that he had been in training for this subterfuge almost his whole life, learning to ignore what was in the next room, to hide what he knew from others, to refrain from asking the wrong questions. His parents had always been in disguise; it was just a different disguise now, a different sort of false mustache, funny hat.

"Do you want help?" I asked nervously from the kitchen.

"Not yet," he said.

I made some macaroni and read a magazine and the new Avon catalogue and there was still no sound from the room. Then he appeared in the doorway, smiling, nodding his head, taking my hand and pulling me to the card table.

"I figured out how to do this," he said. "Like, once I don't mind what I call people, then it can be just like it really is. Here's Daddy, only I called him Robert Crenshaw. And here's Daddy's Daddy, and I called him the same thing. It's just the same, only with different names."

And so it was. As I filled him in on the generations that had gone before, I made amendments, but few were necessary. There was one telltale Giuseppe, Robert's paternal great-grandfather, but I named him Joe. My mother-in-law's maiden name was Stanowicz; I let her keep it. And mine? Pick one, I told Robert, making a game of it. Give me a name before I was married. He made it Wynn. Elizabeth Wynn. It sounded sort of grand.

"What about Grandmom?" he asked, and my mother went in true to life, O'Donnell as she'd been born and raised, too far out on a limb to shatter the disguise of our new existence.

"See, I know who they are," Robert said. "That's enough, right? That I know. Like everybody in the class will be looking and it will say Robert Crenshaw and I'll know what it's supposed to really be."

"That's right," I said.

"I know. Like, remember how Daddy took me that one time to the place where he was working in Central Park? There was this big policeman there, I can't remember his name, but he was really really big."

"McMichael. Captain McMichael. He was the station commander there."

"That was him, I think. And he kept looking at me and saying you're not a Benedetto. I know you're not. I knew your grandfather and I know your father. Nah, I can tell, you're not a Benedetto. And I think he was saying it like a joke, because I looked like Daddy, but I was only a little kid, like five, and I didn't really understand that it was a joke. I thought maybe he was right, that I was adopted or something, like that Korean kid in my old school who was always telling everybody he was Italian just because his name was Russo, and everybody thought he was really stupid. And Daddy could kind of tell that I was upset and when we went out to get ice cream from the Good Humor truck in the park we were sitting on this bench and he said to me, see this. And he pointed to that really big vein in my arm." He held it out, thin and bony, and pointed to the blue artery that ran behind the elbow, his grubby finger outlining it for me. "And then Daddy showed me the one he had. It was really big, and it kind of bulged out. And he said there's a part of me in you. And there's a part of you in me. And there's a part of me in all the kids you'll have, and their kids."

"That's true," I said.

"I know," he said, picking up his pencil again and coloring in some leaves. Then he asked casually, as though he was only wondering whether he should use a forest-green or a medium-green pencil, "Remember that time that Daddy busted Nana's mirror in the hall and then he said he was really, really sorry and got her another one? If he did that to you, would you say it was all right?"

"I don't know," I said.

"I don't mean like go back," he said, not looking up from the paper. "I mean like accept his apology."

"I don't know, sweetie," I said. "A lot of bad things happened with Daddy and me. He did a lot of things to me that he shouldn't have. He shouldn't have hit me. Ever. No one should ever hit another person. And he did, a lot. I know it's a hard thing to understand, why he did what he did. *I* don't even understand it. Maybe someday I will."

"I need to finish this," Robert said, his pencil point coming down hard on the poster paper.

Sometimes I felt as if I'd spent my life sitting on the closed lid of the toilet seat with the water running while I cried, and I wondered whether Robert, sitting downstairs working away on his project, heard the sound of the cold-water tap at full throttle as somehow soothing, the background noise of his childhood nights, as familiar as the rumble of the furnace coming on. It took me a long time to finish this time, to throw cold water on my wan face, to blow my nose and then use a little concealer to veil the flush of emotion. Then I folded laundry and changed sheets. Cotton had always helped me get over the humps.

By the time I went back downstairs the names were all neatly printed and Robert was working on his tree, a mighty oak by the look of it, many branched, thick-trunked, sketched in with colored pencils. And as I admired it, exclaiming over his neatness and the careful attention to the leaves, I realized I would have to tell Mike that Mrs. Bernsen was wiser than I, at least in this case. For there was Robert—just ROBERT, I noticed, with no surname at all—at the bottom of the trunk, at the roots, the base, the center of it all. He had not colored the leaves in yet, and the trunk and its branches looked for the moment less like a tree and more like a great brown river, the Nile, the Amazon, the Benedetto and Flynn river of blood, and there at its isthmus was this one child, so that it seemed that all of these people, from Poland, from Italy, from Ireland and the Bronx and Brooklyn, had come together for no other reason than to someday produce Robert Benedetto, in an event as meant, as important as that one in Bethlehem that he had learned about in catechism class at St. Stannie's. There was Robert, the reason for the collision of these incongruous constellations, the savior of us all.

"Is it all right?" he said.

"It's beautiful. It's perfect. I'm really, really proud of you."

He'd been proud of himself, too, I could tell. He'd rolled the poster paper carefully, tying it at each end with a bit of twine, and he'd carried it out to the bus in both hands. The way he stood with it reminded me of when he was four, in blue satin shorts and a white satin tuxedo shirt, the ring-bearer at the wedding of one of Ann Benedetto's godchildren. It reminded me of the way, his face solemn, he'd carried the blue satin pillow, held close to his narrow chest, down the long aisle of the church. Bennie was the same, the way he carried his. It was as though they had their lives in their hands, these beautiful dark-faced displaced boys. The look of them, so serious, so proud somehow, stayed with me all day, while I scolded the dialysis patient for eating too much junk and shopped for the woman with cerebral palsy.

"Hi," I said casually when Robert came back home that afternoon, letting a great cloud of warm air into the dim air-conditioned cool of the apartment. There was a laundry basket on the couch, and I was folding more sheets, matching corners, my arms spread in a kind of benediction, so I did not immediately see his face, and when I did I couldn't at first believe it, couldn't take it in. I stood holding the sheet across myself, like a curtain, my eyes and mouth wide above it, a cartoon woman.

"My God," I said, and pulled him into the light from the window.

It looked worse than it was. His upper lip was swollen

on one side, purple and misshapen, and the area just below his left eye was beginning to color. There was a ribbon of blood beneath his mouth, but I discovered as I used my own spit to remove it, not taking the time for towel or water, that there was no wound beneath it. Maybe the gum had bled and had stopped bleeding.

"What happened?" I said.

"Jonathan Green is a jerk-off," he said, and his voice quavered deep in his throat like a birdcall.

"Sit down," I said. Ice, aspirin, tissues. I put them on the flimsy coffee table and put my arm around him. A shudder ran through him, and then he looked up, his fingers going to his lip. The colored pencils were still spread out on the kitchen table, a rainbow lying awry.

"Wait," he said, and went upstairs into the bathroom. I knew he was looking at himself in the mirror.

"This wasn't my fault," he said. "I pushed him first but he deserved it. He's had it coming all year. He's a jerk. The biggest jerk in the school. I hope I broke his nose. He called Bennie a spic. You know what a spic is?"

I nodded.

"We were talking in class about where we were from, and he started it then, he was starting to talk about how you shouldn't be allowed to live here unless you could speak English. He was saying that America was too small for Americans and all these other people were coming here and taking stuff away. He goes, like, oh, they can't even speak English. And Goalie was really embarrassed, I could tell, and this girl named Christie, you don't know her but her parents are Greek or something, and they can't speak English that good, I don't think. And I said that there were lots of people who couldn't speak that good English but were nice people."

"Didn't Mrs. Bernsen say anything?"

"She said I was right. She said her parents were German and it took them a long time to learn English and now look at her, she taught English. But then we got dismissed for the day, and we got outside, and Jonathan comes up, with Bennie right there, and he says I only said what I said because of my spic friend. That's what he said, 'Your spic friend.' " I just shoved into him as hard as I could. He called Bennie a spic. Then he hit me. Then I hit him." Blood was beading up on his lower lip again, and I handed him a tissue. He pressed it to his mouth, hard.

"I sat on him and made him take it back," he finally said. His words were muffled by his lip, which was getting bigger. "Put some ice on that," I said.

He slumped down in the sofa, his back bent, his elbows on his knees, avoiding my eyes. There were lemon Popsicles in the freezer and I gave him one, two birds with one stone, the ice and the unexpected before-dinner treat.

"Jonathan is a jerk," I said. "He's been goading you

from day one. And he's got a mean mouth on him. So now you know that he's mean down to the ground. Now you know that the only way to deal with Jonathan is to stay away from him. You're going to meet people like him your whole life. They're ignorant and spiteful and they call names because they figure it makes them big if they can make someone else small. Makes them high if they can make someone else low. Bennie is such a star, everyone likes him, and he's so good at sports and school that Jonathan had to pull him down. So he calls him a spic. So it tells you more about Jonathan than it does about Bennie."

"I said that," Robert said. "I said he didn't know what he was talking about. He didn't even know what a spic was. I knew from Daddy. Daddy talked about spics with Mr. Hogan and Mr. Carter. He said the spics live like animals and that they killed that policeman in Washington Heights. The one that Daddy helped train, when you went to the funeral. The spics killed him."

I winced. "Don't use that word, Ba," I said. "Spic is a word that people use to talk about people who are Spanish. Puerto Ricans, Cubans like Bennie. They're Latino, but people who don't like them call them spics."

"That's not what Daddy said. Daddy said the spics messed up the city."

"Maybe you didn't hear him right," I said, hearing the whole rant in my head, the way I'd heard it a dozen times. They breed like rabbits, they won't learn the language, they put their women to work filling nickel bags, the girls dress like whores, the boys can't keep their pants on, why the hell don't they stay where they belong? They were like the words to a song that I'd heard so many times I scarcely noticed it anymore, the words all blurred together.

"I thought spics were bad guys. Like robbers. Or guys who sold drugs."

"No," I said.

"So what are they?"

"Spic is a word that some people use to describe people who come from Spanish-speaking countries. The way people who don't like black people call them niggers."

"So when Daddy was talking about spics he was talking about Puerto Rican people? And Cuban people?"

"Ba," I said, and then, when I saw his face twist, "Robert. Sometimes police officers get very frustrated with all the bad stuff they see around them. They want to say bad things about bad guys and sometimes they use words they shouldn't use. Your daddy would tell you that if he was here."

Robert sucked on his Popsicle and stared into the middle distance, one eye beginning to close up into a shining slit, his other focused on nothing. For a long time we sat there, side by side, not touching. Finally he stood wearily, like an old man, sore and tired.

"I'm going up to do my homework," he said.

"Ba," I said. "It's all right."

"I don't really like to be called that anymore," he said.

Fifteen minutes later the bell rang, and Bennie was at the door. I could see tear streaks on his face. He was carrying a comic book. "Don't punish him," he said when I told him Robert was up in his room. I fried chicken, boiled rice, wondered how we would talk to each other at dinner. But when I went upstairs to call Robert he was asleep on his bed, his face turned to the window, soft and bruised like overripe fruit, a sweet peach, a golden plum. I left everything on the stove to keep warm.

I had to say this for Bobby: just like the other horrid things he did, he never did that one in front of the child, at least knowingly. He'd kept nigger out of the conversation, and whore, and all the rest, or at least he thought he had. But so much had taken place just within the range of Robert's peripheral vision, things I might never really know, things he might never admit to himself, things that made him what he was today, sleeping upstairs in his clothes, twitching slightly.

He slept through his favorite television program and Bennie stopping by, again, with a video game and another comic. There was a glossy moon, cut from the silver paper of early summer, outside the bathroom window as I got ready for bed, and its light shone across Robert's bed and spilled onto the floor of his room, where his schoolbooks, covered in brown paper, covered with doodles, lay in a motley pile. I stacked them on the floor next to his bed, but he never stirred. My own sleep was like clouds scudding across the sky, the white numbers on the digital clock looming out of the dark as I raised my head, 12:27, 1:12, 2:14. There was the sound of a siren someplace outside, wailing and then waning, and then I heard the sound of voices from downstairs. Underneath my bed was the crowbar I'd taken so long ago from Mr. Castro, and I closed my fingers around it and slid out of my room, down the hall and down the stairs.

"I know," I heard a voice say, and realized it was Robert's. He was in the kitchen, and when I reached the bottom of the stairs I could see through the door that he was on the telephone. He was sitting cross-legged in the clothes he'd slept in, his back against the refrigerator. In the moonlight I could see a stack of Oreo cookies on the floor, like pieces to a game, checkers maybe, or gambling chips.

"I know," he said again. "I want to, too." The silence seemed to vibrate. The crowbar felt heavy in my hand, and I wanted to put it down.

"Then why did you?" Robert said. And then, "I am. I'm playing soccer and basketball and baseball. I play third base. I'm getting pretty good." He rubbed his eyes, winced when he touched the bruises by mistake, pulled an Oreo apart and licked the cream. "I watched it, too," he said. "I knew you were watching it."

I should have moved sooner, but it was only then that I was sure. I stepped out of the blackness in my white nightgown and Robert dropped the receiver, staring at my face and then at the crowbar in my hand. The receiver bounced on its long cord three times gently against the wall, and then I picked it up with two fingers and dropped it into the cradle, but not before I heard his voice on the other end, deep and sleepy: "Robert? Hey? Robert?"

"Put the cookies back," I said.

"You lied to me," he said, rising to his feet, his eyes only a little lower than my own.

"About what?" I said.

"About a bunch of things."

"I didn't lie about anything, Robert. You did something really really foolish tonight. And if you ever do it again we'll have to move and start over someplace else. No Bennie. No Cindy. New school, new friends."

"I want to see my dad," Robert said. "You lied to me about him."

"About what?"

"About a lot of things. He said you lied about a lot of things."

"Tell me what he said."

"No. You'll just say bad things about him. He loves me. He misses me."

"I know that. I never denied that."

"He loves you, too, he said."

"Did you tell him where we were?"

"No," Robert said, his voice cracking.

"Did he ask you?"

He nodded.

"And what did you say?"

"I told him I wasn't allowed. He said he never meant that about the spics, that he had a friend in narcotics who's Puerto Rican. He said it was good that I stood up for my friend. He said sometimes you have to do that."

He said, he said, he said. It was like having him there in the room all over again as the words came at me, the old familiar justifications and accusations, all in Robert's voice, still high and light.

"Ba," I said, then stopped. "I didn't lie to you about anything." I touched his face. "Do you remember when my face looked like this? Only worse. My nose broke. I'm lucky my jaw was okay."

His tears shook him, so that he bounced in my arms almost the way I had bounced him as a baby, trying to lull him to sleep. The front of my nightgown was wet. There was a little blood mixed with the tears.

"I didn't tell," he finally said.

"I know, honey."

"I wanted to ask about the spic thing," he said.

"I know."

I left the crowbar by the hall closet and together we climbed the stairs. An hour later, when I was certain he was asleep again, I went downstairs and pulled a business card from behind his baby picture in my wallet. It was an answering machine, I knew, and after the beep I said, "This is Elizabeth Crenshaw. I need to speak to Patty Bancroft immediately. She has my number."

After he'd left on the bus in the morning, more than a little proud of his raddled face, Bennie's arm around his shoulder, I walked over to the school. Mike Riordan was at his desk when I tapped at the door. When he saw me he looked the way I must look when Robert opens the door at the end of the day. It made me hate myself, that look—such happiness, such shamefaced yearning. To cover up he lobbed a wad of looseleaf into the toy basketball hoop stuck to the wall next to his desk with suction cups. There was a poster next to it of a cat trying to hold onto a high bar. "Hang in There, Baby!" it said underneath. We'd had it in the nurses' lounge at South Bay, too.

"I need help," I said, and I sat in the straight chair on the other side of his desk.

"Okay," he said.

"To begin with," I said, "my name is Frances Benedetto, and I'm from New York City." It was ten minutes to nine when I started, and nine-thirty by the time I was done. How short a time it took to tell him everything, to feel the secret fall from my shoulders like a yoke.

He drove me to Cindy's house the first Saturday after school let out, half a dozen foil containers filled with food slithering from side to side on the backseat. "Don't take those corners so wide," I said, "or you're going to have barbecued riblets and chicken wings all over the car." He frowned slightly into the sunlight and took his foot off the gas, until his little car was going maybe ten miles an hour and an elderly woman had edged around him and then pulled in front. "Ha ha ha," I said.

I'd been cooking for two days, and I'd had to smack the boys with a dishtowel on their shinny dark brown legs as they filched potato pancakes and mahogany-colored riblets. "You're a good cook, Mrs. Crenshaw," Bennie said politely. "Don't try to get around me with sweet talk," I said. Robert only smiled. The marks on his face were gone, and maybe it was only my imagination that he seemed quieter. He'd always been so quiet, anyhow.

"I understand him so much better now," Mike Riordan said to me after I'd told him our story. "Thanks. It makes it easier for me."

It had made it easier for me, too. The notion that the man had seen me naked, had put his tongue into my mouth, had unbuttoned my dress—none of it meant anything compared to the fact that he knew where I really came from, what my name was, what I really did for a living, what my son had had to live through. Even his smile seemed to have knowledge in it, and understanding, and it had made me feel more myself and less afraid with him than with anyone else, even Cindy. That day when I came to talk to him he had leaned forward, asking no questions, looking me straight in the eye, and when I was finished he had come around the desk and sat in the chair the dads usually sat in, when Mike was having parent conferences. He had taken my hand and he had rubbed my fingers hard, as though they were cold and he was trying to bring back the blood into them. "You're amazing," was all he said.

He looked over at me in the car, speeding up and smiling now. "Robert's fine," he said, reading my mind.

"I know."

"No, you don't. But I do. He's a smart kid. He'll work all this out."

But I do know. I know it's not true. Children are resilient, some of the shrinks like to say, and everything marks them, say some of the others, and both things are true. Sometimes it seems as if Robert never called Bobby on the phone that night, never took his side over mine. Sometimes it seems as if Mike Riordan and I are no more than a boy's coach and a boy's mother, as though I never chose him over Robert. But Robert has scars as surely as I do, and his are more dangerous, because he cannot see them and so can believe they are not there.

"You think too much, Fran," Bobby told me once, when I was analyzing this or that. And he was right. I guess I do. What I'm thinking is that I can hardly hear his voice anymore, Bobby's voice, that ruled my life, that made me jerk like I was at the end of a leash. Even on the phone, it had sounded like the voice of someone I'd once known, a while ago. You think too much, Fran. I can't quite hear him say it.

He was right about that: I do think too much. If you're a good nurse you always do think too much, see too much, know too much. You look at the cleaned-up junkie with pneumonia who's telling you it's just a cold, a cold, man, a little vitamin C and some sleep and I'll be good as new, and you know, practically without double-gloving and drawing the blood, that he's slipped over the border from being HIV positive to having AIDS and is skidding toward the finish line of death. You see a little kid come into the waiting room with her mother, see the child do a slow and subtle lean back when the mother turns toward her, and you know, you just know, that the mother hits her. The X rays will only tell you how hard. Winnie used to say that she knew what some of them would tell her before they even opened their mouths from the set of their shoulders, the slant of their gaze. She used to say that it was like being a priest, sometimes. I felt the same way.

I call Grace now and I know that something is wrong. Suddenly there is an answering machine on her home phone. The message is curt, anonymous: "Please leave a message after the beep." Three times I've said, "Gracie, it's me." But I am afraid to give her the number here, afraid of who else might hear it, see it written by the phone on a scarp of paper. Twice I called her office, but it is the same thing there, the recorded voice, the honk at the end. "We're good," I said the last time. "We're fine." She's not. I can hear it in the cold timbre of her recorded voice. The cold in her makes cold in me. That, and Robert's phone call. And the television news program after the carnival. And what I know about

Bobby, how good he is at finding out what he wants to know.

I look at the hump growing larger between Mrs. Levitt's perpetually slumped shoulders and I pretty much know that if she takes the slightest tumble two or three years from now, it'll be a broken hip and a nursing home, a walker if not a wheelchair. "Take your calcium pills," I say, banging the plastic bottle on the tiny kitchen counter. "Ach, they bind me up," she says, eating Chips Ahoy. I bring another kind of calcium, one that doesn't cause constipation. "You need to build up your bones," I remind her, and she looks at me pityingly, as though to say, Mrs. Nurse, what do you think happened to my bones those four years they fed me mealy grain and dirty water and did whatever it was to my insides that meant I would never have a child. I see Mrs. Levitt now always in terms of her great secret, the numbers on her arm, the story of her marriage, and I realize that everyone has, her whole life, ever since that May day half a century ago. I hid my wounds because I was ashamed, ashamed of Bobby and ashamed of myself for staying with him, but now I know that I was also afraid of being reduced, of becoming in the minds of all who knew me that poor woman whose husband beats her. Or used to. I have begun to think of myself as someone who used to get beat up by her husband. I am a recovering battered woman. God, I hate that term, all those classifications that seem to reduce our wounds to the same status as eye or hair color, that make us a type, a cover line in a magazine.

"The Holocaust survivors," Mrs. Levitt said savagely one day when she saw a story on the news. "Like a club. People have no shame."

I see and I know. I know by the dandelion yellow of my patient Melvin's skin that if he does not get a kidney transplant in the next ninety days I will be attending his funeral instead of taking his temperature. I know that my cerebral palsy patient is lonely for love and romance because of the name she uses when she goes into chat rooms on the computer: Sexyjen. I wonder how she describes herself when she is no more than a line of black letters on someone else's screen, wonder if she makes herself tall and lithe, with muscles that run smooth beneath the surface of tanned skin instead of arms and legs that shiver and shake in an uncontrollable dance. She wants to be someone else, somewhere else, and I can't blame her.

I know that Mike Riordan has decided to try to make things right by making them lighter. Robert plays baseball now, just like he told his dad, and Mike takes us out from time to time afterward. Bennie usually comes along and Robert measures the distance between his coach and his mother with his eyes. It is considerable. The week after we'd gone to bed together I had bought myself some contraceptive sponges, but I'd done it the way you buy aspirin in case some Saturday night you have a headache. Things are back to where they were. No more flaming steak or tuxedoed headwaiters. Still, whenever Mike brings us home, if it happens that Robert goes down the pavement to Bennie's or upstairs to start his homework, Mike steps inside the apartment, puts his arms around me and kisses me, less gently than he had that first time. Once, when we met in the Roerbackers' basement during a school swim party, he coming out of the concrete shower stall in his shorts, his hair wet and raked back with the marks of Craig's comb still in it, me in the blue tank suit Cindy lent me, smelling of coconut from the sunscreen, he had reached for me, held me for a long time, finally pushed back, groaning. "I'm a patient person," he said.

"You're being cruel to that poor man," Cindy had said next day as we watched the kids swim.

"I don't mean to be. He'd be better off if I stayed out of his way, but that's hard, under the circumstances."

"I like him," Cindy said.

"I like him, too."

"Then what's your problem?"

"I like you, too."

"And, honey, I'd have you in a minute if we were so inclined. But we're not. How come all of us are attracted to girlfriends who are nice and smart and helpful and love us and we're all attracted to guys who are mean and give us a hard time?"

"Craig's not mean."

"Craig's different. So's Mike Riordan. Which is the point I'm trying to make. You want to try this new scented insect repellent we're coming out with?"

"What's it smell like?"

Cindy sniffed. "Musk."

"No, thanks."

"Plus he loves kids," Cindy had said.

I knew when Cindy got pregnant almost before she did. Her hair went limp and one day, in the library, as we sent out overdue cards, she snapped at Mrs. Patrinian, "We know what we're doing here." Mrs. Patrinian turned red, and so, I think, did I. In April she started drinking herb tea in the morning instead of coffee, and when we all had burgers and beer out back she drank soda water. The buttons on her white blouse, the sleeveless one, bulged a bit, showing a patch of skin between her breasts. For some reason she didn't tell me right away. There were long pauses in our conversation, and she was dying to fill them with this, the most exciting news that any woman ever has. Or sometimes, the worst.

"My son misses his father," I had said to Mrs. Levitt, taking her blood pressure as she ate a frozen yogurt with her free hand. After Mr. Levitt died her doctor had given her a physical and pronounced her hypertense, overweight. The diagnosis had enabled him to continue sending me to the Levitt apartment. Nothing has changed there, except that the hospital bed is gone and Mrs. Levitt keeps the door to the terrace open, although the freshening warm breezes of a Florida spring will soon blow hot. "The air should come in," she had said the first time I noticed the sliding glass doors ajar. "You smell a little cold in the morning, you know it'll be a nice day. Too cold, with that hard feeling, snow. At least in Chicago. You need the fresh air." Irving is in a stainless-steel jar on an occasional table. It rattles if you shake it. Robert once asked what it was. "Ah, a knickknack thing," Mrs. Levitt had said, rolling her eyes at me.

"It is hard, for the children," she added quietly, licking a vanilla mustache from her upper lip. "Life is not easy."

"I feel foolish complaining, to you of all people."

"Why?"

"Your life."

Mrs. Levitt shrugged. "You shouldn't have told me it was yogurt," she said, looking at her cone. "I would have thought it was ice cream." She licked, then said, "The big things, eh. It's all the other things. Like now, whether to keep the cable, to move, what to do between breakfast and lunch."

"You're lonely," I said.

"No, no," Mrs. Levitt said. "Filling the hours when

you're an old lady—it's not a feeling, just a job. Sometimes now I still talk to Irving. I'm entitled."

"I still shouldn't complain."

"You call that complaining? You don't know complaining. Anyway, other people's troubles don't take away yours. But don't be foolish and think somebody else is having everything fine."

Of course that was exactly what I had always thought, as a child walking home in my school uniform past the homes where it seemed reading lights shone yellow from the window to illuminate the evening hours of handsome and lively fathers, warm and sympathetic mothers, children who were tucked in tight beneath their blankets each night in rooms bright with wallpaper. There were even times, as an adult, when I had thought it of myself, of Bobby and Robert and me, eating beneath the brass chandelier in the small dining room, the dishes and glasses shining as though they'd been given to us as prizes, the flowered plates plaques to commemorate our love for one another. If it would all stay like this moment, I would think to myself. And then, as we cleared the table, stacked the dishes, darkened the house for the night, the feeling would be gone, as bright and ephemeral as the lamplight.

"Things will happen to a boy that you cannot help," Mrs. Levitt added.

"You sound like a fortune-teller."

"Just so. They always say these things that you can say about anyone. Life will be good and bad. You will meet people who can help you. Someone you love will die. Big deal."

"Did you take your calcium?"

She held out her cone. "Better than pills," she said. "Even better if it was chocolate. They make chocolate yogurt?"

Cindy eats frozen yogurt now, drinks milk, stops at the farm stand every day for fresh vegetables. I remember doing the same not long ago. A year ago. Only a year. A year ago I had a secret inside me, and, just like Cindy, I kept it a secret. Even Bobby didn't know I was pregnant. Even Grace. A good nurse would have known. Winnie had cocked her head on the side one afternoon when we were slow in the emergency room, put her hands on her big hips, screwed up a corner of her mouth. "How are you feeling?" she said. The way a woman walks, flat-footed, her toes turned out a little, her pelvis thrust forward as though her body's proud of itself—a good nurse knows.

I knew everything when I went to the clinic two days after Bobby broke my nose that last time. I lay on the table with the sheet over my knees and saw the bottle and the hose in the corner, and knew exactly how they would use it.

They were kind at the clinic.

"Let me tell you about the procedure," said the counselor, who kept looking at my battered face, at the bandages and the telltale perimeter of black and blue and red.

"I'm a nurse," I said. "I know."

When I'd assisted at abortions myself I'd told the patient there would be some cramping. Now I know that wasn't exactly true. It hurt. I was glad it hurt. The more it hurt the more I knew I had the guts to get up from the table and leave Bobby Benedetto. I wanted to know whether it was a boy or a girl, but I didn't ask, and it wouldn't really have made a difference. A boy to learn that a man can keep a woman in line with the flat of his hand; a girl to learn that men love you and hurt you in equal measure. None of the above, I kept thinking, none of the above, one of those pieces of nonsense that gets stuck somewhere between your mind and your mouth when you're having a hard time. The machine made a noise like the window air conditioner in our bedroom. I stared at the ceiling, my eyes dry and gritty. They gave us Lorna Doones and apple juice in the recovery room. "You'll get your girl," Bobby had said after my miscarriages. But he was wrong.

"We're done here," the doctor said.

Maybe that's what I felt when Mike Riordan came inside me, not Bobby, but the doctor, the speculum. I'd lain on the table and fiddled with the adhesive tape that pulled when I moved my mouth.

"What happened to your face?" the doctor said.

"I was in a car accident," I said.

I don't think about it very much anymore, what it felt like on the subway as I went from the clinic on the east side of Manhattan home to Brooklyn to make Robert a snack after school. That night I fell asleep planning my escape, and had a dream. I was running on the Coney Island boardwalk and I saw a little girl in a lime-green, ruffled bathing suit struggling in the waves. I ran to the edge of the ocean but two police officers were already there. "We'll handle this, ma'am," one of them said, and smiled at me. I turned around and started running again without looking back. It was quiet in my dream; there was no sound of the child, or the policemen splashing through the water.

She'd be six months old now. She'd be sitting up and babbling and laughing at her big brother's funny faces. I can't think about that too much. It's the worst thing that Bobby did to me, or that I did to myself because of him. But I can think about it more now than I could before, when I just let my mind drop a curtain over it. And I couldn't stop thinking about it in the car on the way to Cindy's baby shower. I couldn't stop thinking about it all day long. I thought about it as Mike and I brought the food in through the cellar door, Craig meeting us, Chelsea behind him hauling Chad around like a sack of grain, limp and pale. "Let me down!" he shouted, but Chelsea paid him no mind.

"I put so much soda on ice I had to use a second tub for it," Craig said. "The cake came and I put it in the fridge but it takes up all the room in there."

"It has a sugar umbrella on it," Chelsea said. "Can I have it after?"

"Absolutely," I said.

"Where's Robert?"

"He went on a camping trip with Mr. Castro and Bennie. Down to the Hidden Forest Game Preserve. Bennie's dad said they might see alligators."

"I don't like alligators," said Chelsea.

"Me neither."

"Hi, Mr. Riordan," Chelsea added.

I let Chelsea have what she wanted that day. The umbrella made her sick, what with the ribs and three cans of Coke, but I let her have it anyhow, even though it was pure spun sugar. We ate nearly all the food I'd made, the PTA mothers, two high school friends from Lakota, Mrs. Manford and two of her sisters, Cindy's aunts. Cindy had been out shopping with her mother and when she came in and saw the pile of boxes and the white lace umbrella hanging over the recliner in her den—I knew she'd kill me if we used the living room and spilled anything on the taupe carpet—she'd screamed and covered her face.

"I'm going to kill you for this, Beth, I swear I am," she said. But I just smiled, and smiled some more seeing her round and flushed, with the big hard swell of her belly beneath her flared white blouse, the maternity clothes a big improvement from the time when I was pregnant with Robert almost thirteen years before, when everything had had lace and ribbons and flowers, as though to have a baby you had to look like one. Five months gone she was, but she looked more, because she was carrying twins. The sonogram said it was a boy and a girl, and she'd kept her pregnancy a secret for almost three months because the doctor wasn't sure if they were going to make it.

"I could have lost them both," she told me finally, and I thought of my lost child and then put the thought aside in the face of her happiness. She loved things to be special, Cindy, and twins are special. The boxes spilled forth duplicate treasures, two pairs of tiny denim overalls, two receiving blankets in soft flannel, two embroidered samplers, one pink, one blue. Two teddy bears, one in a bow tie and top hat, the other in a dress. "Oh, I love these," Chelsea moaned, as Chad wadded up the wrapping paper and applauded every new gift.

I went into Cindy's kitchen to refill the serving dishes she'd gotten as wedding presents, probably at a shower much like this one. I remembered going to Bermuda for a week with Buddy and Marie not long after I was married, and standing in the airport looking at the cities on the departure board, and thinking that I could take the traveler's checks and just go anywhere, Seattle, Cincinnati, Paris, Grand Rapids, Montego Bay, and start a whole new life. I don't know why I thought it at that moment; Bobby and I were still in love then. Maybe everybody thinks it at some time or another, just thinks about becoming another person, giving up the law for a life as a golf pro, trading teaching for waitressing and life in the scorching Caribbean sun. I remember Bobby telling me about two cops he knew in missing persons, and how they'd gone looking for an English teacher from Queens, happy family man with a new car and a nice lawn, who just went missing one day. Two years later they found him in Australia, teaching English: he had a nice lawn and a new car and a wife named Shelley, which had been the name of the wife he'd had before.

It had seemed just a funny story then, but now I knew it was the essential truth about human nature. We'd traveled across the country, Robert and I, and in some way wound up where we'd been before. I looked at Robin Pearson, who was the secretary of the PTA, talking to Meghan Dickson's mother, whose name I couldn't ever remember. They might as well have been Marie and Terri. The thing you took into a new life with you was yourself, and so you made it so much like it had been before, used and, yes, even comfortable. When I looked across at Cindy, pulling silver wrapping from a big box, I felt a spasm of pain and grief for Grace.

"Oh, look," Cindy said, unfolding a crib quilt, a pattern of hearts done in cross-stitch. She rummaged through the tissue for a card, and finally Mrs. Manford, in a tight light voice, said, "That one's from me, honey."

It made me remember Ann Benedetto then, too, remember how she had once proposed a toast at Christmas to "her boys," how she would give Bobby a cashmere sweater and a pair of outdoor boots, a book on baseball and a duffel bag, and hand me a bottle of perfume from the drugstore, even once a single pair of pantyhose in a size too big for me. I couldn't help it; my face would flush at the baldness of the insult, just as Cindy's face was flushing now, looking from the quilt to her mother and back again.

"It's beautiful, Mom," she said, but you could tell she was thinking what all the rest of us were thinking, that one blanket was an odd sort of gift for a woman expecting two babies. Especially for a woman who had once had two babies of her own. I looked at the aunts, Mrs. Manford's sisters, but they were talking about the high school bond issue.

"Charlie and Cathy," Cindy told me she was going to

name them. She'd never told me the story about her sister, the one that had surely given an entire dusty farming town a way of describing her: "Cindy Manford, poor thing, you remember, the child whose twin sister—yes, identicals too—their poor mother . . ." Mrs. Manford was reapplying her lipstick. "I find the quilting really takes my mind off things," she said.

There was a familiarity to it all, sharper, keener than anything that could be called déjà vu. It was just the way life is. Chad dirtied his diaper. Mrs. Manford asked Cindy why he wasn't potty-trained. Robin Pearson said she hadn't been able to potty-train her son until he was four. One of Cindy's high school friends said the preschool in Lakota, the good one at the Methodist Church, wouldn't take them if they weren't potty-trained. Chelsea said she was going to give the babies their baths. Mrs. Manford said she was too young. I said I'd help her. Cindy said she had to pee so often she might as well just stay in the bathroom. Her mother said she couldn't sell Avon if she had to keep using the bathroom. It had been nine days since Robert had called his father, dialing the number we had made him memorize when he was six, in case of kidnappers. It was not that the fear I'd felt that night, as I heard that voice come out of the receiver, so smooth, so shocking, had gone away exactly. It just seemed so much less real than what was going on around me, the way Mrs. Levitt's years in the camps seemed so much less real than the cans of Chef Boyardee ravioli on her shelves. Patty Bancroft had called me back, offered again to move us somewhere else, somewhere where we would be safe. But I'd realized, finally, that there was no safe place. "I'll take my chances," I'd said. I was on my own. This was my life.

"Look at all this loot," said Craig slowly, hands on hips, as he helped stack the pile of boxes after all the guests were gone.

"Bless you, hon," Cindy said, patting my shoulder. "I love you to pieces. Where's Robert?"

"Camping with the Castros."

"You got plans for tonight?"

"I'm going to bed early. This whole thing wore me out."

"I got a better idea, but I better not tell you," she said, looking into the kitchen, where Mike was eating leftover potato salad with his fingers.

"I appreciate your restraint."

"Yeah, whatever. I got to pee." She rubbed the small of her back, hunched over the pale-pink tablecloth I'd used for the dining-room table. "I'm going to need to get some stain remover on this right away," she said. "Chad, baby, are these your barbecue fingerprints here? There better not be any on the back of my couch."

"Happy birthday!" Chad shouted, spinning and falling onto his hands and knees, chortling.

"Did he drink Janice Dickson's wine?" Cindy said.

"That's her name!"

"Doesn't she have diarrhea of the mouth? Goodness, that's a terrible expression. I picked it up from Daddy."

Mike drove me home. In the late afternoon's faded light, he looked older somehow. "I'm going to have to get out to the course more if I want to get any good at golfing," he said.

"Craig's a nice man, isn't he?"

"Really a good guy. He likes you, too."

"That was fun," I said.

"You made enough noise up there."

"I think the mimosas really loosened things up. I wish Cindy could have had one."

We were driving right into the sun, the car threading its way in and out of the cars coming from the strip malls onto the strip, corrugated boxes and brown bags in the backseats, everyone cool and dry with the air-conditioning up all the way. High summer was coming on fast, and high summer was much the same here as anywhere else, punishing heat, sweat wet on the seat of your pants. Mike's hand was damp as he reached across and squeezed mine. No jones for him. Still no jones. But, Jesus God, it was good to have at least one person in the world who knew who I really was.

"You haven't asked me the $64,000 question," I finally said.

"What's that?"

"The question everyone's supposed to ask. The question we always asked at work about some woman who came into the ER all cut up. Why didn't you leave? How could you stay?"

"You did leave. I know why you stayed. You stayed because of Robert."

"Why did I leave?"

"Because of Robert, too. You must think I'm stupid."

"I think you're amazing," I said. A truck roared past us, shook the car as though there was a summer storm. "I had an abortion just before I left." The truck was so loud I didn't know if he had heard me. I could barely hear myself.

He was quiet for a long time, looking out at the road. Finally he said, "Did you say that so that I'll know, or because you think that if you tell me enough bad things I'll go away?"

"I don't know," I said.

"Why don't you come over for dinner?"

I shook my head. The sun glinted off his glasses and I couldn't see his eyes. "Not tonight," I said.

"Is there some point when you'll tell me either to take a hike or—whatever?"

"Whatever," I said, as we pulled up to the apartment

complex. His eyes were dark, hurt the way Robert's eyes were sometimes, with no attempt to hide it. "Frances," he said.

"Beth, I'm still Beth."

"Frances. Beth. I'll call you whatever you want. I don't care. I don't care about anything. You want to tell me you're a serial killer? Go ahead. I don't care."

"Don't take a hike," I said.

"That's a good sign, right?"

"Yeah," I said, and went inside.

In the middle of the night I woke to the smell of smoke and moved out of bed and into Robert's room as fast as I could until I remembered that he was camping with Bennie, that he was not there, that his room was empty, his bed made, his school books scattered across the spread. I sniffed the air, my head up like a wild animal, followed the smell down the stairs, toward the kitchen, wondering whether I'd left the stove on, whether an electric line was smoldering somewhere in the cheap Sheetrock walls. The crowbar was still downstairs, in a corner by the door, and I picked it up, heavy and cold in my hand, as I saw the tip of a cigarette glowing in the living room. Marlboros. How in the world had I missed the familiar smell?

The way he looked at the crowbar in my hand made

me flush. "Oh, what, Fran?" Bobby said, looking up from the frayed green tweedy armchair that I'd moved from one end of the living room to the other at least a half dozen times, trying to find a place where it wouldn't look so bad. "What, you're going to hit me over the head with a piece of pipe?" He shook his head. "Jesus Christ, sometimes I think you're brain damaged. Sit down."

After the first momentary taste of adrenaline, metallic and bitter in my mouth, I didn't feel much. Certainly not surprise. It seemed perfectly natural, Bobby sitting there. Made for each other, together forever: me and Bobby, Bobby and me. He was in front of me and the kitchen was to one side, and I could feel the phone on the wall where I couldn't reach it. Like always, he read my mind. "The phone's not working," he said, flicking ashes onto an old magazine on the coffee table. "Besides, what the hell are you going to tell the cops? There's a strange man who's in my place, who happens to be my husband. Yeah, what's he doing, lady? Oh, officer, he's smoking a cigarette? Hell, we'll be right over." He dragged in, deeply. "The response time here is about twelve minutes, anyhow. Sit down."

"I'm staying right where I am."

He shrugged. "Suit yourself," he said.

He looked good, Bobby. He always had. His jeans were pressed, and I wondered who was pressing them now. His polo shirt was tight and his pectoral muscles and his abs looked like an anatomical drawing. His arms were big, the muscles thick and rounded. He'd been working out hard, and suddenly I could picture him perfectly, in the basement of the house, my house, doing his concentration curls and his crunches, getting bigger and bigger, angrier and angrier, picking up my panties and my bottles of perfume, waiting, waiting. Around his neck I saw a glint of metal, and nestled in the *V* of the polo shirt, glowing from amid the fur on his chest, the old medal his father had worn. It looked different, somehow, and then I realized that it was flanked by two halves of a jagged heart, the half he'd kept himself and the one I'd worn and left in the jewelry box on our dresser in Brooklyn. He looked handsome, Bobby, tasty and dangerous, just like Clarice Blessing had said that day in the ER. Tasty and dangerous. I figured he'd come to kill me.

"How you been, Frances Ann? You got yourself a real dump here. The whole place is maybe a third the size of our house. I was gonna sell it, but your name is on the deed and the lawyer said I couldn't sell it without your permission. Jesus Christ. I needed your permission to sell my own house.

"I had to tell him a story, about how you were in Florida. That's a laugh, right? Even before I knew you were in Florida I said you were in Florida. I had to make up more fucking stories to cover your ass, Fran. First you were real busy, then your mother was sick, then you were in Florida because my twenty years were almost up and we were gonna move down here." He lit one cigarette from the end of another. He'd smoked when we first started going out, but he'd quit after Robert was born. He put the dead butt out on the floor and ground it out with the front of his foot. He was wearing the soft black leather loafers he always got at the Italian leather-goods place on Avenue X. They were so shiny, in the dark. Bobby always shined his own shoes. "I don't know why the hell anybody comes down here," he added. "I wouldn't retire here on a bet." Two hearts that beat as one: Fran and Bobby, Bobby and Fran. Our wedding song had been "I've Got You Under My Skin." That was one way of putting it.

I was shivering in my thin nightgown and I wondered if he could see through it in the light from the streetlamps that oozed through the half-open blinds. He said something but his voice was so low that I couldn't make it out, his head down, the cigarette in his mouth. Then he looked up and his eyes were shining, black, like the shoes, and I could tell he was repeating what he'd just said.

"You took my son. My son. My child. You took my son away from me. What, were you nuts? Were you crazy, you didn't think I'd come after you? With my boy with you, filling him full of garbage? And for what? Because I made a mistake and came at you a little bit. Jesus, I should have broken both your legs, you bitch, so you couldn't've run.

"You had every fucking thing you could want. 'Why are you letting her work, Bob?' the other guys would say, but I let it go, figured if it made you happy, so be it. You had your house. My mother took care of your kid when you were at work, when you were late. All you had to do was pick up the phone. She'd say, how come she doesn't invite me over. Bob? I'd say, Ma, you got to give her a little space. Always standing up for you. Being the nice guy. Taking the kid to the park. Telling my friends to mind their own business. She's not too friendly, Bob, they'd say, and I'd tell them, well, she's just quiet. Knowing it was a lie, because you could be plenty nice when you wanted to. But you didn't want to be.

"You think it was such a goddamn picnic living with you, Fran, you always out of the house bandaging people up or whatever, give me your tired, your poor, but God forbid my husband needs a break. Sitting at the kitchen table pretending to listen to me, your skinny little Irish lips getting tighter and tighter when I talk, like you got something sour in your mouth. My mother's a bitch, my friends are crude. You tell my boy I'm a bigot,

Fran? You're telling my son things when you don't know shit.

"You want to hear something fucking sad? I loved you. I really fucking loved you, Frances. But nothing was ever right, nothing was ever good enough. You wanted to do what you wanted to do, go off with your sister, go off to the hospital, go off with your dyke girlfriends, just go off, go off, instead of being home, where you belonged. And even when you stayed home you looked at me and you looked scared all the time, like something bad's gonna happen. What the hell do you think that's like, to look at your wife and see that she's always looking back at you, sideways, sneaky, like you're a grenade that's gonna go off in her hand. Half the time I only came at you to wipe that goddamned look off your face."

It was the first time in a long time it had been like this, the two of us really alone, without Robert a wall or a floor or a room away, so that I didn't have to think about protecting him, about keeping my voice down. I don't know why I didn't scream then. Maybe I was making the same mistake I'd always made, that sooner or later he'd see sense, that I'd see behind his eyes the Bobby who used to kiss my knuckles, one at a time, when my hands were chapped from washing them with Lubriderm at the hospital. "You had no right to hurt me, Bobby," I said.

"Hurt you? Hurt you? What the hell do you think you did to me? I used to come home, the house is all dark, I'm beating off in bed right next to my wife because she's sound asleep. My boy won't look me in the eye because she's been telling him shit—"

"I never said anything—"

"DON'T YOU FUCKING INTERRUPT ME!" My back was against the wall at the foot of the stairs, and I kept hoping that the walls were thin enough that somebody would hear. But they always did hear, other people, always had heard and did nothing, left us alone.

"I come home one night and my wife and my son are gone, but everything's still there so they couldn't have gone too far, and I go to see your sister, and your mother, and that big dyke you worked with at the hospital. And she has the nerve to say to me, you been beating on her all this time, haven't you? And I say, you been diddling her all this time, too. She shut the fucking door in my face and called the cops. The cops!" Bobby threw back his head and laughed. I could see that his hair was going silver at the temples. He looked good. Handsome. I couldn't stop shivering.

"It took me a while, I gotta give you that. Your sister, now, she is one tough bitch. No matter what I tried on her she wouldn't give you up. I had her so she wouldn't even pick up the phone, but she wouldn't give you up no matter what I did. That woman, what's-her-name, the one who's always on television with the snotty voice, you can't get near her, but some of her people are pussies, pure and simple. Jesus, talk about folding. The one who drove you down here, with the dogs, she was easy to shake up. And the guy in New York, when I threatened to have the New York City Police Department all over him like a cheap suit. That scared them, you could tell. They would have given you up sooner or later."

He took a drag on his cigarette and smiled. What a smile Bobby had always had. It changed his whole face. This one made him look so scary I almost looked away. "I didn't even need to wait," he said. "I got this little box on the phone, caller ID. All these scared little cunts in the city buy 'em, like it's somehow gonna help them when the bad man calls. You can scramble the numbers up so they don't come through, but my good luck is, I know a guy in the department, he can unscramble them. That little box sat there for a long time, Frannie, but I didn't take the damn thing off, and look what happened. Here I am. Because my son is loyal. A loyal boy. He calls his father and I write down the number and"—he waved his cigarette around the dark living room—"here I am. In Shitsville. Home of a woman who had everything a woman could want and left it all in a mess. In a big fucking mess for me to clean up."

"Bobby—"

"Ah, shit, Frances, don't bother. I don't want to hear your bullshit. Even when I was good you looked at me like I was gonna be bad any minute. You looked at me like you were just waiting." He laughed again. "I didn't want to keep you waiting, Fran. Not like you kept me waiting, a whole year, to see my boy."

"He's not here," I said.

"You don't think I know that? You don't think I know exactly where he is, and where he goes to school? That's why I waited, Fran. I could have been here two days after he called me. But I waited another week, and you know why? Because I'm a good father. I'm a god-damned good father. I waited so I wouldn't fuck up the school year. So he could finish at that piece-of-shit public school where you put him. Don't they all hate you, Fran, that you're getting special treatment for your kid because you're fucking the teacher?"

"I—"

"Never mind the lying. I'm so fucking tired of your lying. Lie, lie, lie." He sighed heavily. "Frannie, Frannie, Fran. I know where you been working, Fran, and for who. I even know how much money you make. I know your phone number here. You got a loose window in the back. The screen flips right out, and the pane is so flimsy it takes maybe a minute to get it out with a glass cutter. If I told you once, I told you a hundred times you're bad with security, Fran. Any animal could get in here. Anyone. My boy isn't safe here."

"We're not going back, Bobby."

"I wouldn't have you back on a bet, you bitch." He stubbed out his cigarette. "You know what the worst part about this whole thing is? I loved you so much, Frances Ann. Sometimes I used to fall asleep, after I had a couple of drinks, and I'd have dreams, but they weren't made-up dreams, crazy shit. They were like movies of real stuff, like home movies. Like that time we went to the beach when Robert was a baby and we put up that big umbrella so he wouldn't get burned, and I took all those pictures with the Instamatic, you sitting there next to that little box you kept him in. I was holding him, jumping the waves, and I looked back at you and you had that little smile you had sometimes, real sweet, real nice. I woke up and the burning in my gut was so bad I thought I was dying.

"I loved the shit out of you, and look what you did to me."

"I loved you, too, Bobby."

How come I had so lost the ability to read him, to understand what went on beneath the black holes of his eyes? Or maybe I'd never had it at all. A dozen times, as he'd talked and talked, I'd felt myself pressing into the wall behind me, so that my heels ached where the molding hit them. Maybe it was the words, or the sudden wash of feeling, the sadness that came over me like a kind of faintness, that made me yearn forward as I said those last words, and meant them with all my heart even as I felt the metal of that crowbar in my hand: I loved you, too, Bobby. They were barely out of my mouth when he came out of the chair, like a cat, so quick I scarcely knew it until he was holding me against the wall, pressing against me with his body, his forearm against my throat, the way the older cops had taught him when he was a rookie. He'd showed me once as a joke, so many years ago, my head buzzing, the floor coming up to meet my face. This time was no joke. He brought his knee hard against my wrist, and the crowbar fell to the carpet with a thump and rolled onto my foot, mocking me.

In the past it had always been like I'd been waiting for it, almost grateful, like he'd said, that the waiting was over. Maybe he was right, that I'd spent years with a look in my eyes that told him a scream was always hiding in my throat. But somehow it had always been Bobby, so that even when he was pushing me around, yelling right in my face, I could smell the smell of him, feel the feel of him that I knew so well. This time it was like a stranger coming at me. The hard hands no longer felt familiar, the breath tarred with cigarettes and some kind of booze was noxious; the feel of him through his pants, up against my groin, felt like something strange and criminal. Even the voice was no longer as hypnotic as it had once been, somehow different, diminished, tinny. Or maybe it was that I was somebody different, that Beth Crenshaw wasn't going to let this man bloody and beat her. I used all of me to fight back against it, my hands, my knees, my feet, everything but my voice, held captive in my throat by the iron of his arm. I let my eyes close, went limp, and started to slide down the wall, and I felt him relax, a noise in his throat like crooning, like purring, and as he let down his guard for just a moment I came up hard against him, surprised him, almost knocked him over.

"That's it," he said, reaching for me, grabbing me around the throat. And then I saw points of color against black, like the fireworks we watched every year on the Fourth from the Coney Island boardwalk. That's it. That's the last thing I remember.

My daughter has red hair and the sort of disposition associated with it, willful, a little wild. Since she learned to speak she has appended a question mark to almost every sentence she has spoken: Mommy, what this thing? Mommy, water hot? Mommy, have that? How come? Why not? Probably most people cannot understand her. Her words are like soup, the smooth broth of the vowels, the chunky consonants, and she swirls them around in her little mouth until they sound more like mush than anything else. Sometimes I even have to translate for her father, the beloved, the adored Daddy. But I know everything she says. Everything.

Sometimes people see us all together in the supermarket and they remark on the tangle of orange curls, like a flag above the wire cart. The two of us so blond, they cannot quite figure out where this rogue gene comes from. Loving Care No. 27, California Blonde, makes me look a little less like my daughter's mother, but I have a sentimental attachment to it. Besides, it makes me look a little more like Mike's wife, an attachment much more tenuous than the attachment between me and Grace Ann. "Gwacen," she calls herself, all one word. "Let's say grace," we say before holiday dinners, and she screams with laughter, two years old and full, as my father might have said, of piss and vinegar.

My name is Beth Crenshaw. I did not change it to Riordan, nor back to Flynn. I left Frances behind. Beth Crenshaw is the name of the me I am today, Grace Ann's mother. And Robert's mother, too. No matter what.

It was Mike who found me, half a day after I'd found Bobby smoking in my living room. There was a pile of dead butts on the floor and my nightgown was up around my sternum, as though he'd looked me over one more time. He didn't rape me; I checked. He'd contemptuously left the front door unlocked, Bobby, as though there was nothing worth safeguarding in the apartment anymore. I had an onyx and lapis lazuli necklace of bruises from ear to ear. I don't know whether that was what Bobby wanted, or whether he meant to kill me and miscalculated. Or perhaps at the last minute he saw in me what I'd always seen in him, someone hated, feared, and yet beloved, and could not give that final squeeze. Perhaps at the last minute the death grip was a hug instead, or his twisted version of one.

Or maybe this is exactly what he intended. "Frannie, Frannie, Fran," I can hear him say in his rich deep voice. "Killing's too good for you. I want you to suffer." And I do, every day.

"He went home," Mrs. Castro said when Mike and I ran to the apartment at the end of the row, Bennie's puzzled, troubled face peering from the kitchen doorway as he read our expressions. "He is home a long time."

I like to think his father met Robert outside, at the front door, and not in the living room. I like to think that if Robert had seen me on the floor, he would have made so much noise that someone would have heard him. That he would have flown to the Castros, screaming, crying. That he would have taken my side over Bobby's. I like to think that Bobby told him some story, some irresistible fairy tale about redemption, forgiveness, the happy family come back to life like Snow White awakened from her long sleep in the glass casket by her handsome prince. I like to think he did not know that he was leaving me until he was already going sixty miles an hour down some highway somewhere.

All I know is that my boy is gone, and I don't know where to find him. Mike made me go to the police, and they took pictures of my throat, and took down the address and telephone number of my husband, and duly noted the fact that he was a New York City police detective, and that I had no legal papers granting me custody of my own child. They listened carefully, and they took a few notes, and nodded their heads, but I could see in their eyes that the budget of a small-town police force, four men strong, didn't extend to flying to Brooklyn to look for a man who'd done to his wife what so many men had done. And I knew that even if it had, Bobby would not be there, just as I had not been there that day a year before when he'd come home from work. After all, what could I say Bobby had done that I had not done myself?

Mike found a private investigator, and together we went and I told him my story. He seemed like a nice man, a former Texas sheriff with a big stuffed sailfish over his desk and a hunk of Red Man tobacco puffing out his upper lip. He pushed the check back across the desk. "You seem like good people," he said, "so I'm not gonna bullshit you. Your boy is gone, and he's gonna be hard to find. Your ex is a cop, which means he knows things about making himself scarce. Look how easy it was for you. But let's say you go looking for him and maybe you find him. What then? You got no case, is what. You took this guy's kid and absconded with him. He took him back. It's maybe you who could get in trouble for this. Assault charges, you might try against him, but it won't necessarily help you get the child. He goes to court and says you disappeared with his boy for a year, you are gonna get your head handed to you."

"We won't give up on this boy," Mike said.

"I appreciate your sentiments, mister. I got two boys of my own. But what I'm saying to you is, you may not have a choice. You could grab him back, if you could find him. And then maybe your husband could grab him again. And so on, and so forth. You get the idea. Ping-Pong, only the kid's the ball." He turned to me, shaking his head. "If you were divorced and you had custody, I might be able to find him and you could get him back. You don't even have a custodial snatch here. I don't even know what to call the situation you got."

I knew what to call it. It was like death, except I had to go on living with it. I couldn't look at Mike Riordan when he stopped by with cardboard bakery boxes of cookies and stacks of magazines because I knew he had spent his day with kids at the local day camp, breathing in the sweet fragrance of their skin and hair, listening to the staccato sound of their light feet, hearing their high voices calling to one another across the ball field, teaching them how to kick a soccer ball into the goal the way my own boy had once done and, maybe, a thousand miles away, was doing again. I slept in my clothes and canceled out on Cindy whenever she asked me to dinner. And then one July day, three weeks after Bobby found me, almost a year to the day from the day Robert and I had disappeared, the bell rang in the still apartment, the air so thick with dust motes that it looked like a blizzard when I moved, and I lunged for the door like a crazy woman.

"Frannie," she said, in a voice so thick with sorrow I almost didn't hear the word. And Grace was in my arms and I in hers. She cleaned and cooked as though I was an invalid. She cried with me and read to me. Once I heard her on the phone. "She's not ready to talk yet," she said. Once she handed me an envelope. It was full of documents: my birth certificate. My nursing license. Robert's baptismal certificate. I ran my fingers over the notary's seals.

I hadn't even thought about that, right away, that I was free now, that I didn't have to hide because what I'd had worth hiding was already gone. But Mike had thought of it, and he'd found Grace through the college, and told her everything, and picked her up at the airport. And when Mrs. Levitt called and told me that she needed me to come, she was having fainting spells and heart palpitations, it was Mike who had put her up to it, though she didn't admit it until months later, when she was demanding I be nicer to him.

"You must make a life for your son to come back to, Mrs. Nurse," she said to me one day, eating a Happy Meal, handing me the toy, Donald Duck on a motorcycle. "Don't waste your time crying. Crying is nothing. It does nothing."

Cindy came by one night in August with a bottle of wine, and I drank most of it and finally cried, slurring my words, mucus dripping onto her shoulder as I told her all of it, all the blood and all the beatings, everything, both of Bobby's babies, the one he'd taken from me and the one I'd taken from myself. She put me in the bathtub with some sort of sweet-smelling oil, trimmed my hair and gave me a manicure, big as she was with child, with children. The day that Grace flew in and the day that Cindy pushed her way past me into the stale air of the apartment: those were the days when I started to come back to life.

I bought an answering machine so that if Robert called when I was out I would get his message; I bought one of those caller ID machines Bobby had boasted about so that if Robert called when I was home I would know where the call was coming from. I kept Robert's enrollment current at school. "Tell them he'll be back soon," I told Mike on the phone, though I told him not to stop by, no, there was nothing he could bring over, nothing I needed. Except the one thing I did not have.

No one came for the rent, and the home-care agency got me a new patient, whose wife had Alzheimer's. I relieved Mr. Dean while he went out bowling or to the movies with friends; I sat with his wife while she picked at her skirt and said, "I don't know. I don't know anymore." We were two crazy ladies, sitting in the living room of a little brick ranch house watching tabloid shows on television. We sat with tray tables in front of us; Mrs. Dean played some sort of solitaire that seemed to have no real rules, and I sent out flyers to schools and police departments. "Have you seen this boy?" the flyer said. Grace printed them on her computer. The photograph of Robert came out grainy, flat, anyboy in black and white.

Two schools called, and one police department, but the boys were too young, too old, too small, too light, too not mine. One night, after Mrs. Dean and I watched a miniseries about a beautiful woman who owned the best boutique in Beverly Hills, I came home to see a red light glowing in the darkness of the kitchen. For just a moment I thought it was the glowing tip of a cigarette, and thought that Bobby had come back to finish me off. But my heart leapt, too, because if Bobby was there, Robert would be with him. I was happy at the thought of Bobby's hands on my throat, as long as I could put my arms around Robert one last time.

It was only the light on the answering machine. There was no voice on the message for a few moments, only noise: traffic, big trucks, horns, a faint shouted conversation between two men in the background. Then a deep breath. "Mom," he said, and I bent over the machine and hugged it to my chest so that the sound was muffled for a moment.

"I'm all right. Daddy is all right, too. He's being really nice. He really missed me when I was gone." There's a silence there, on the tape, a long one. A car honks. The background noise sounds like highway traffic, a gas station, maybe, or a pay phone on a shopping strip. "Are you all right? Mom?" More silence. "We had lunch at McDonald's. Tell Bennie I said 'hi.' Tell him I saw *Batman* on TV." Another silence, another breath. "I miss you a lot. I have to go. I love you. Don't worry, I'm good. We move around a lot." Tears then. "I hope you're not hurt. I hope you're all right. I'm sorry. I have to go."

I listened to that tape all night, that first night. I felt as if I was there, could see the trucks whizz by, feel the breeze around the booth, see the boy feeding the phone with spare change, culled from the top of strange bureaus and the slots of vending machines. By morning I knew every word, every nuance, every shift in timbre and tone. He was afraid, my little boy. Maybe afraid Bobby was going to find him talking on the phone, the way I had that night in the kitchen. Maybe afraid of something more. I wasn't imagining it, the way his voice broke when he said he hoped I was all right. Mike heard it, too. "That son of a bitch told him you were dead," he said. "I just know it. I feel it."

A week later on the machine there was the recording of an operator. "You have a collect call. Caller, at the tone state your name." The operator cut it off there, while I sat and cried and played over and over again the snippet of dead air where the name should be. I changed the message on my machine, changed it to begin: This machine accepts collect calls. There were none, not after that one attempt.

In October, after school began again, I took $300 and flew to New York City. Grace thought I was coming in on Tuesday evening, but my flight landed just after dawn, and instead of taking a cab to her apartment I went to Brooklyn, to the narrow house Bobby and I had bought thirteen years before, where our words and our actions lived on in the walls, which we haunted. I rang the bell and a pretty girl, twenty-five, maybe thirty, opened it with a dishtowel in her hands. Her hair and eyes were dark; if she was not Italian, she could pass. She was the sort of woman Bobby Benedetto should have married, who would never have complained, soft and yielding as a feather pillow.

"He's not here," she said. "My husband and me, we rent the house from his mother. She lives over on Ocean Avenue. Maybe she can tell you where he's living now. I think maybe Florida someplace." My mirror still hung in the foyer, the one that Ann Benedetto had given us, and in it I could see my reflection, my hair brushing my shoulders now, brushing the collar of a dress I'd gotten on sale with Cindy, too flimsy, really, for an autumn day in the Northeast. I'd have to borrow a sweater from Grace. No, I said, I didn't need directions. I knew the way to Mrs. Benedetto's house. The other Mrs. Benedetto. The only Mrs. Benedetto.

I could hear the bell ringing inside, the gold chimes in the white hallway; I could tell by the faint sound of her footsteps from inside that she'd come from the kitchen to the front door. I remembered the day, maybe seven or eight years before, when we had stood there together looking out the window that gave onto the yard, both of us staring at Bobby out back with a beer, watching Robert weave in and out of the rows of tomato plants. I felt that day like loneliness was more than a feeling, that it was a state of being, like zero gravity or the bends, and we were in the place where you learned to feel it in your marrow, the bathysphere in which you felt it all around you, pressing in on you, on the dishwasher, the pot holders, the spice rack, the forks and spoons, the emptiness inside.

"I want to ask you something," I had said that day to Ann Benedetto. "What was your husband like?"

"What kind of question is that?"

I didn't know what kind of question it was. It was maybe the first direct one I'd asked Bobby's mother, but I was emboldened by the tenderness in my elbow where

I'd hit one of the dining-room chairs after he shoved me, after I said I wanted to stay home Sundays, not go to Ocean Avenue.

"Was he good to you?"

"He was my husband."

"Did he ever hit you?"

She'd narrowed her eyes to look at me, and her dislike was an atmosphere, too, as thick as the isolation of the two of us in that clean, clean room, our distance from each other and from the man outside, calling to his son.

"My son is a good man," she said. "Nobody can tell me different."

Her face was hard then, and it was hard when she opened the door to find me standing on her concrete steps, clean the way steps are when someone sweeps them every day. Her hair had just been done, the sculptured waves of iridescent black, the sheen of hair dye and hair spray. She gave me a long look, and I her, and then she began to close the door again. I held it open with the flat of my hand. "I want my son back home," I said.

"So do I," she said. "And we're both out of luck."

Grace told Mike about that, the two of them doing their dance around me, and he traveled to New York on his own, and hired a detective there. Mike made friends with some people who ran a group for missing children, and he mailed more flyers to more schools with Robert's picture, the one he had taken in Lake Plata during fifth grade, his smile big, his face thin, his eyes bright, a false tableau of trees and clouds and endless fields behind him. He's never given up, Mike, and neither have I. Four years it's been, and still I have the tape in my drawer, that I listen to from time to time when Grace Ann is napping. And that photograph, on my bedside table. "That's your brother," I tell my little girl. "You'll see him soon. When he comes home."

"Bruvver," Grace Ann says.

I imagine him, my Robert, his voice just beginning to break when he gets excited, the down on the curve of his jaw thickening until he can't help but see it when he looks in the mirror, turns his head on an angle, and feel it with the flat of his hand as though he's caressing and measuring himself. Maybe his father is with another woman now, just as I am with another man, and maybe when he's had too much to drink he smacks her, hard, knocks her down, even, and Robert tries to shut his eyes and his ears and maybe sometimes he has a few drinks himself, sneaks a can from the refrigerator, so that the hard sounds are softer, the cotton padding of beer wrapped around the sharp edges.

I see Robert in my mind's eye, and he's tall now, and he's handsome, and he feels things as deeply as he always did, but doesn't speak of them much. And maybe he has found a girl of his own and she tests him, taunts him, innocently, because sometimes it's fun to test and taunt, at least for most of us, and he grabs her, hard, and scares her a little bit. But it feels like love to her, the grip on her forearms, and she thinks it's because he loves her so much, and maybe in the beginning that is it. And by the time it turns to something else—well, it's too late.

I think of my Robert and I think of that maybe girl, and you know what? I don't give a damn about her, about her bruises and even her broken bones. I should. But I don't. I love my boy. I always have. I always will. Somewhere between my head, where I know so much, and my gut, where I can almost feel her pain, is my Robert. My heart.

In six months Robert will be sixteen, old enough to get on a plane, to pick up the phone, to make his own way. It's been four years since I lost him, but he knows where to find me. My phone number has never changed. When I left the apartment to move in with Mike, and later, when we bought this house, with its three bedrooms and its trellis of clematis by the garage, I gave our new address to the woman who had taken my place there. And maybe he'll knock at the apartment door and the woman will say, oh, your mother wanted you to know exactly where to find her. And he'll drive to the house and I'll open the door and he'll say, Mommy, it's all right. I've taken the best of both of you and left the rest behind. The part of the river that runs with blood stops with you. It does not flow on through me. I pray every day that that is true. I wonder sometimes why Captain McMichael said that day in the precinct house that Robert was no Benedetto. Was he teasing him? Or wishing him a happy life?

I would have a happy life now, if only he were here. Mike was telling the truth, when he said he was a patient man. He wasn't a fool; twice I told him to go away, and he went. For a while he dated a student teacher at the middle school, a little girl with a squeaky voice and long, long brown hair. I saw them once, going into a diner hand in hand, when I was on my way to the Deans' house. She made him look so big, in the way I made Bobby look so dark, so many years ago. Mike told me she broke up with him because she said he wasn't ready to make a commitment. But he was. Just not to her.

He took care of me, sometimes near, sometimes at a distance, for a long time before I bothered to take any care of him. I suppose I love him now, although it's not what I once thought of as love. I know that I love what he is, and what he has given me, a life that feels ordinary, uneventful, and full. It's hard to make ends meet, what with the retainers for the detectives and the trips Mike makes from time to time, when we get a lead that seems promising. He was promoted to principal; I work part-time and Cindy takes care of Grace Ann along with the twins. Chad bosses all three of them around. We run together every morning, Mike and I, with the baby in a special running stroller Cindy gave us for a gift when she threw me a shower. There's a bedroom in our house done in green and yellow where Mike's mother and my sister Grace sleep when they come to visit. But there's a bulletin board over the desk with a picture of the soccer team and a Yankees game schedule pinned to it. In the drawer of the desk there's a letter from Bennie, that I promised him I'd send to Robert if I ever had an address to send it to. It's Robert's room, that room. It's waiting for him, just as I am.

I think of myself as Beth Crenshaw most of the time now, because if I think of myself as Fran Benedetto there is a piece of me missing so big that the pain doubles me over, clawing at my gut, and Bobby gets me again, and I can't let that happen. Because I am Grace Ann Riordan's mother, too, a little girl who has nothing to fear except that she will be denied a second helping of crackers at snack time. She hears nothing through the walls except, perhaps, the occasional sound of her father saying her mother's name in a kind of groan: Beth, Beth. Her father loves her pure, and loves her mother the same. And her mother loves her father a little more each day. I trust him, deep down, which is more important than I once understood. "The luckiest day of my life was the day I met you," Mike said the day we were married at the municipal building. I don't know if it's legal, don't know if I'm divorced, don't even care. I don't give a damn for the law. What did the law ever do for me? Mike wanted to be my husband; that was good enough. The rest is all Frannie's life. That's not me. This is the me I made. The past? Like Mrs. Levitt said, "It's only a story."

Three or four times a year I let myself go back. The men take the children somewhere, bowling or to the movies, and Cindy and I have the night alone, just the two of us, and I drink a couple of glasses of wine, and I sob and I scream and she holds me and cries into my hair. "He loves you, honey," she says. "I know he does. He'll be back. He'll be back." The last time she said to me, "I want you to know that if I ever meet that man, I'm going to slip a serrated knife between his ribs." Then she put cucumber slices over my eyes to bring the swelling down. I don't know what made me say it, lying there, seeing a wash of green light through my lids. But I reached out my hand for her, and said, so low she had to lean toward me to hear, "When are you going to tell me about your sister?"

I don't know what her face looked like while she talked. I kept those cucumber slices where they were, so that she didn't have to face me if she didn't want to. She didn't cry; it was almost like she was talking about somebody else, talking about a little girl curled up in a chair in a dark corner of the living room, reading a book, reading *Mother West Wind's Children*. Listening to her mother call for her: Cindy. Cindy, come here. Cynthia Lee, I need you. Smiling to herself when her mother gave up, opened the screen door, went around to the side of the house, paused right beneath the living-room window, at the edge of the flower beds. "Cathy," she said, "go call your father for supper."

What could I say, as I held her close? That it wasn't her fault? That she should let the guilt go? Words, words. They mean nothing, less than nothing. I know.

Cindy thinks it's arbitrary, the nights I invite her over, something that happens now and then for no particular reason. That's not true. What happens, every once in a while, is that the phone rings. And on the other end I hear nothing but breathing. This happens to everyone, I tell myself, but I don't believe it. I stay on and listen to the sound of what I think of as love, until whoever is at the other end hangs up. I don't know whether I'm hearing Robert or Bobby, or some stranger. Maybe I'll never know. But I believe it's Robert, and I believe he knows I know, and I hang on. Six months ago the phone rang again, and I heard the breathing, and as I listened, Grace Ann looked up at me from her high chair and cried, in her demanding fashion, "Mama!" Whoever was on the phone hung up suddenly, a sound like a book banging shut. "Robert," I cried, but there was only the echoing emptiness of the severed connection. "Ober!" Grace Ann replied happily.

Those are the nights, after the phone calls, when Cindy and I sit together, alone, and I grieve with the sound of sweet breathing still in my ears.

Cindy stood up for Mike and me at the municipal building, holding Charlie. So did Craig, holding Cathy. And Grace. Chelsea has decided that Aunt Grace is Wonder Woman, with her easy polysyllabic vocabulary and her knotty biceps. Afterward we had a party by the Roerbackers' pool. "To our new daughter," said Mike's mother, and she gave me a cameo her husband had given her for her birthday years before, and hugged me tight. That was the only time I cried, that and afterward, when Mike said, "Can we have a baby right away?" I had a second glass of champagne, and when I went to the bathroom I looked at myself in the mirror for a long time, looked at myself in the silk suit, my hair curling around my face, Shhhhhell pink on my lips, I looked to make sure I knew who I was, that I was really real. I put my fingers to my mouth and shaped the word but did not say it, held it inside in deference to the day. Robert. Robert. I got pregnant that very night, in the four-poster in the bedroom of a guest house in Key West.

Robert, Robert. Where is he now? What does he feel or think? Maybe he's in Italy or Brazil, Canada or Mexico. I don't think he believes I'm dead, and I know he knows I love him. I know how persuasive Bobby can be, how he can hold you in thrall, make you wonder about things you're sure about, tolerate things you never thought you'd allow. I was only twenty-one when he started in on me. Maybe Bobby told Robert that I knew exactly where they'd gone, that I'd given him away to his father. Could Robert have believed that for even a moment? Did he wonder about it now, if he'd been the person at the other end of the phone when another child called my name, the name that once only he was entitled to? Perhaps none of the lies Bobby had to tell him, to woo him, to win him, had the simple power of that sound, the sound of someone else calling me *Mama*.

Cindy said, when I told her the truth, or most of it, "Just tell me one thing. Is Beth Crenshaw more or less the same person as—what's the other, now? I don't know why I have such a mental block about that name."

"Frances Benedetto."

"Is Beth more or less the same as Frances?"

"Only the names were changed," I said.

And I suppose in a way that's true. When I was Fran, Frannie, Frannie, Fran, I felt like two people at once, the woman who seemed so in control and content, and the one with the black eyes and broken bones, the one who loved her husband and feared and hated him, all at the same time. Beth Crenshaw is two people, too. There's the one who pulls weeds in the yard with her daughter's head glowing in the sunshine beside her, who smiles across the supper table at Mike and stacks his shirts neatly in the second drawer, who comes down the street in her little compact car and, for just a moment, forgetting, loves her lovely little life. And there's the one with the hole inside her, bigger than anything. There's not a day when I haven't wondered whether I did the right thing, leaving Bobby. But of course if I hadn't, there would have been no Mike. And therefore no Grace Ann. Your children make it impossible to regret your past. They're its finest fruits. Sometimes its only ones.

"Oh, honey," Cindy likes to say, "you had no choice."

Everyone says that, that I did the right thing, that I shouldn't look back, that I had no choice. Maybe they're right. I still don't know.